ABOUT THE AUTHOR

After many years as an actor in film and television Phil moved into writing and producing feature films, series and single dramas for TV and radio, documentary and animation.

In 2017 he published his first novel and has just completed his third – all standalone crime thrillers.

Through his company, Funky Medics, he produced and wrote animations and books for the UK, Europe and US on health education.

Originally from Haverfordwest in Pembrokeshire, he now lives near Cardiff.

Visit: philrowlandswriter.com

Published in Great Britain in 2021
By Diamond Crime

ISBN 978-1-8384026-2-4

Copyright © 2017/2021 Phil Rowlands

Diamond Crime is an imprint of Diamond Books Ltd.

Thanks to Greg, Jeff, Steve and Jen

Book cover design: jacksonbone.co.uk
Cover photograph: Christian Holzinger – Unsplash

Also by Phil Rowlands
Single Cell

And coming soon to Diamond Crime
Time Slip

For information about Diamond Crime authors
and their books, visit:
www.diamondbooks.co.uk

To my wonderful family
and
the memory of Walter, Elsie, Thelma and Leslie

SIENA

PHIL ROWLANDS

PROLOGUE

At Paddington Railway Station, six-year-old Ben Jenkins watched the train as it curved around the track and slowly approached the end of the platform. He had his new camera pressed tightly against his eye. His finger was ready to press the button. His dad had told him that if he was going to take a picture of the train, it was better to wait until it stopped before doing it. If it was moving the photo might be all blurry and he wanted his mum and friends to be able to see it properly. The train was still quite a long way from the big red buffer stops. Ben was tall enough to see them on the other side of the ticket barrier. He thought about the story his dad had told him this morning on the train up from Wales, about Paddington Bear coming from his home a long way away in a country called Peru and being all on his own until a family found him. Ben wished it had been his family. Playing with Paddington would be fun. Ben thought he would have time to look around to see if he was still here before the train stopped and he could take his photo.

There was no sign of a little bear in a blue coat and red hat, but he did see lots of people of all ages, colours, and sizes as he turned his head, still holding the camera in position. Another thing his dad had said was keep still and try not to wobble the camera. When he turned back to the platform the train had stopped and he waited for a moment, making sure he had the front of the engine in the small frame before pressing the button.

Suddenly a dark figure with a gun came out of the crowd and moved quickly towards a middle-aged man standing behind Ben. The man seemed to realise the danger and as the gun was raised, he frantically looked around then grabbed the small boy in front of him. Ben dropped his camera as he was snatched up and held tightly against the man's body. He struggled and screamed 'Daddy!'

Ceri Jenkins, only a couple of metres away but in a crush of people looking at the departures board, heard Ben's frantic cry. He searched for his son and saw him struggling in the man's arms, roared his name, shoving people out of his way as he hurtled towards him.

The first bullet hit Ben, exited his small body, and punched into the man holding him. The second slammed into the man's head as Ben fell from his arms, and the third and fourth hit Ceri as he threw himself at the dark figure with the gun. He was dead before he hit the ground. Then as quickly as he had appeared, the angel of death was gone. It had happened so fast that at first only a young man, now catatonic with shock and covered in blood and bits of brain, was aware that something terrible had happened. Soon others saw and the cacophony of panic began.

* * *

Sara Jenkins was walking fast on her way back to where she'd parked the Land Rover. She went into 'recent calls' on her mobile, clicked on 'Ceri', and waited for him to answer. Ceri's message kicked in.

'Hi, it's Ceri, leave a short one and I'll get back to you.'

'Hi, sweetheart, sorry, me again, running a bit late. I should be there before the train gets in but, if not, I won't be long. Love you both, gorgeous ones.' She mouthed two kisses.

She couldn't wait to see her two boys. She'd had the best of days and couldn't wait to tell them her news. Her meeting with an art dealer, Jon Trench, had been fantastic. He had loved her paintings and not only bought all five of them without haggling over prices, but had also commissioned eight more large works, for delivery over the next two years, for his corporate clients. It was a fantastic bit of good luck but after all the struggling to keep their heads above water, they deserved it. The money would take away the pressure and they could finally finish the last of the work on the converted barn they lived in. The boost to her depleted confidence as an artist was great too, and it made up for missing the family trip to London. Anyway, they could afford to go again now, and stay over for a couple of nights in a posh hotel. It would be a surprise treat for Ceri and Ben.

The money was already in their bank, so on her way to meet the train, Sara had rushed to the shops. She hadn't kept an eye on the time and was probably going to be late getting to the station. They wouldn't mind though. She had bought a Harry Potter dressing gown and pyjamas for Ben, blue suede pointy brogues that she knew Ceri would love, and a ridiculously expensive dark green duffel coat that she would try and get him to wear instead of his old worn leather one. She had a warm feeling as she imagined their faces, so alike, soft grey eyes shining with excitement: Ben giggling, and bubbling with words, trying to tell her about his day and get into the dressing-gown at the same time, and then Ceri kissing her gently, his financial worries eased, for now, by her success. That night, after Ben was in bed, they would talk over a bottle of red wine and then make love in front of the open fire. It would be the perfect end to a perfect day. Excitement and anticipation fluttered inside her stomach.

She ran the last bit to the ticket machine in the car park and got there just before another two hours kicked in. As she came out onto the road she felt a wave of tiredness. It had been a hectic couple of days.

At the station, Sara could see that the train hadn't arrived. It had been due in at five forty. Great they'd never know she was late. Pips for the six o'clock news on the radio broke into her thoughts. Reports were coming in of a fatal shooting at Paddington Station in London, earlier that afternoon. It was possible, although unconfirmed, that there had been three fatalities and that one was a child. It was too early to say if it was a terrorist attack. The warm, safe, familiar voice then said that train services to and from Paddington were likely to be disrupted for at least four hours. There was a number to ring if anyone was concerned about relatives or friends.

Fear hit Sara. A violent, thumping terror that made her breathless and dizzy. Her mind spun.

No, this was crazy. It couldn't have anything to do with Ceri or Ben. They would have been on the way home. But their train was at three fifteen. What time did it happen? Perhaps Ben had been worn out and they'd got the quarter to three instead and had gone for an ice cream in the little coffee place around the corner from the station. She tried to call Ceri but the phone went into answer mode again. As she thought about turning and going to find them, she

4

stopped, knowing they wouldn't have got the train before the one they booked. Their tickets were reserved and he wouldn't want to buy another two, and anyway they'd had a tight schedule with Buckingham Palace and the Natural History Museum. But she was certain that if Ceri said they were getting a particular train then they would. He was always exact, sticking to timetables and promises as though his life depended on it. She thought he might have OCD but he'd refused to take that seriously.

Her head was spinning and she had to force breath into her lungs and sense into her thoughts. She stopped the car across two spaces and tried to still the panic. It would be all right. They would just have to get a later train. Ceri would apologise for not answering his phone. He had probably not charged the battery before leaving home and it would have run out. Ben would hug her as tight as he could, butterfly-kissing her cheek with his eyelashes and giggling uncontrollably. It would all be an adventure for him and that would help take the pressure off Ceri. It would be all right. They would be all right.

Then she was pierced by an ice-cold reality and, deep in the pit of her stomach, she knew.

Sara threw herself out of the car and, fighting the weakness in her legs and the fear pounding in her chest, ran towards the station. As she went in through the entrance a police car, lights flashing, pulled up outside and two female officers got out and hurried onto the station concourse.

Sara was trying to control herself and not grab hold of the man at the gate and scream into his face. She took a deep breath to stop her body shaking and take the desperation out of her voice. 'Is there anyone I can talk to who might know more about what happened at Paddington? My husband and son should have been on the train that gets here at twenty to six but it still hasn't come in.'

'All I know is that it's been cancelled because of an incident and that we don't know yet when or what trains will be running.'

Sara knew that a number had been given out on the news but she couldn't remember it.

'They said on the news that there was a number to ring. What is it?'

'I don't know. You'll have to ask the station manager.'

Sara grabbed him and he tried to pull away.

Behind her the police officers saw the struggle and ran towards them as the man broke away from Sara and moved to a safe distance.

Part One

SOUTH WALES

CHAPTER ONE

Sara was standing in a small room with the older of the police officers close to her. She was showing her a photograph of Ceri and Ben she'd taken on her phone yesterday. She wanted her to send it to the police at Paddington. It would help to find them more quickly and she would know for sure if they were caught up in it. After a moment the officer said she had a number for the incident team leader at Paddington. They had already sent Sara's details and those of her son and husband and they were being checked. She took Sara's phone and sent the photos with a short explanatory message.

For a moment there was a silence then a radio crackled. The other officer, by the door, switched it off as it crackled again into a clearer call sign. She glanced at her partner then went out. Sara was trying hard to not let the panic and fear explode out of her.

'Mrs Jenkins…'

Sara looked up at the woman.

'Sara, call me Sara.'

She didn't want any formality. It would make it all the more real and frightening.

The officer smiled gently, her eyes giving nothing away.

'All right, and I'm Julie. We weren't given many details, Sara, just that there had been an incident involving three people including a child and that there were six tickets from this station that had been booked on a train leaving from Paddington near the time of the incident. We're here to help anyone waiting for people who were on trains out of Paddington in the last four hours. There are other police at all the stations on the different lines. Your husband and son…'

'Use their names. Ceri and Ben.' Sara fought to get the words out.

'Of course, I'm sorry…'

Just then the other officer opened the door.

'Julie, Control wants a word with you.'

Sara saw the shocked look she gave them and the quick movement of her head as she turned away.

'Sorry, Sara, I won't be long.'

Sara hardly dared to breathe.

'What is it? Have they found them?'

Julie moved towards the door. 'Cath will stay with you.'

She went out. Cath stayed by the door. She looked very young and uncomfortable.

Sara froze, her eyes fixed on the door.

Cath moved towards her as the door opened and Julie closed it quietly and came to Sara. Sara didn't, couldn't, move. She knew what Julie was going to say but she didn't want to listen. She closed her eyes, covered her ears.

Julie touched Sara's arm.

'Sara.'

It was a long moment before Sara looked at her and started to cry.

'No, don't say it, please.' It was almost a whisper but filled with desperation.

Julie held Sara's gaze.

'Sara, Ben and Ceri have been found. I am so sorry but there was nothing the medical teams could do. They were already dead by the time they arrived at the scene.'

Sara cried out and her body twisted violently. For a moment Julie and Cath managed to hold her, but then she threw herself backwards and hit her head on the corner of a large heavy metal set of drawers. She was out cold.

Cath called an ambulance and Julie checked Sara's breathing. It was shallow. She made her as comfortable as she could where she'd fallen, covering her with her tunic jacket.

* * *

The day before

Ceri put the pancakes and strawberries onto a tray with chocolate fudge ice cream, coffee, and a *Captain America* cup of orange juice. He'd have to come back for his Daddy's mug of tea and four rounds of toast covered in honey. He might even stuff down the toast before he went back again so the gannets wouldn't steal any. All of them were honey pigs. They'd said they didn't want any but he knew as soon as they saw his they would, and there was no more bread. He'd been going to take some of his home-made out of the freezer, but one of his two potential clients had called and then he got caught up on Facebook when he was poked by an old school friend he hadn't seen in twenty years.

Ceri was a boyish forty with an unruly mass of black curly hair, a gentle face, and smoky grey eyes that could never hide his real feelings. He was a graphic designer and he and Sara worked from the old barn they had bought just before Ben was born. It had been a wreck when they started and six years later still a work very much in progress. It was slowly getting there though, and when it was finished it would be just as they had planned and dreamed over the endless hours of weighing up design, quality, and cost. How long it would take to get there depended on a cash flow that rose and fell on how much work he had coming in and the sale of Sara's paintings. He thought they were brilliant and had said she should charge more, but she would accept whatever was offered, within reason. She had given in to his suggestions on price a couple of times and lost the sales, so, he didn't interfere now. She had sold plenty at her prices, but not enough to really make any difference to the money drain of the barn. In the garden he could see Sara and Ben rolling and giggling together on the grass and felt a pang that he wasn't part of it. He never quite managed the level of helpless hysteria that Sara could invoke in Ben. She was like that too, and many times Ceri had almost expired with embarrassment when she became uncontrollable, tears bouncing across her cheeks, screeching at something that sometimes only she had seen or sensed. Nowhere was safe, theatres, weddings, funerals, and once, at an exhibition of her work, a short man with a wig and terrible stutter had suggested meeting her later to talk about buying the most expensive painting she had for sale. She had spluttered and become helpless with laughter and Ceri had to take her outside and then go back in and apologise to him. In the end he had bought the painting, but for less than he would have paid before Sara's fit.

Ceri picked up the tray and went out into the garden.

'What's so funny?'

Ben was lying on top of Sara and looked up, hardly able to get the words out.

'Mummy made a smell.'

He gurgled with laughter again.

Sara tried to look shocked.

'No I didn't, you did!'

Sara rolled him off her and started tickling him and he snorted. Ceri put the tray on the slatted table.

'Come on, before the ice cream melts.'

Sara stopped the tickling, grabbed Ben's hand and pulled him up. The lure of food took over from laughter and he ran to the table and started to fill a pancake with strawberries and ice cream.

Ben was a real mix of the two of them. The eyes, nose, and mouth were Ceri and the slim, strong body, twinkly eyes, and quick smile, all Sara's.

Sara kissed Ceri. 'Come out and play with us.'

'Just get my toast and tea.'

Sara giggled as she watched Ben happily stuffing the loosely rolled pancake into his mouth. The ice cream and strawberries were dripping onto his Spiderman T-shirt.

In the kitchen, Ceri ate his toast and watched Ben throwing a strawberry and Sara, mouth open, trying to catch it.

He didn't really do food games but was happy with piggybacks, footie, and making up stories. It was just that he couldn't do silly very well, or strict, come to that: that was down to Sara too. Ben just laughed at him when he tried and then cried when Ceri panicked and resorted to shouting.

They were generally a good balance though, they knew their strengths, and so far were doing all right, making up the being-a-parent rules as they went along, and Ben was a happy, bright, independent but cuddly boy, although, of course, there were moments when the little angel turned.

Sara's mobile buzzed on the wooden table.

It was Jon Trench, a dealer who bought for rich corporate clients and who was coming to look at Sara's work.

'Just wanted to check that it's still on for tomorrow.' Trench was posh, Northern, and direct.

Ceri walked towards the door. 'Yes, it is. Did you want to speak to Sara?'

'No, just tell her I might be a little later than 10.30. I had to fit in another meeting in Swansea.'

'Sure. I won't be here, but…'

'Sorry, another call.'

Not a chatty man, Mr Trench, and probably not interested in whether Ceri was there or not.

He put the phone down as Sara came into the kitchen.

'Who was that?'

'Jon Trench, checking you were still OK for tomorrow and that he'd be a bit late.' Sara's face was covered in ice cream. 'Isn't in the mouth better?'

Sara smiled. 'That's a bit mucky for you.'

'I can be mucky.' He wrapped his arms around her and went for a big kiss but Sara wiped her face over his cheek and pulled away, grabbing a cloth from the sink, holding it under the tap, flicking water at him, and then running out of the door.

13

* * *

It was almost eleven p.m. when Sara and Ceri carried the last canvas downstairs and into the living room. It was a huge space with floor-to-ceiling windows, two large and drooping sofas, a wooden floor (that had taken five days of fights and tears as they'd stripped, sanded, and varnished it to perfection), rugs, TV, and a couple of designer chairs that friends with more money than taste had given them. Sara's paintings covered the walls. It was a timeline of her creative steps and stumbles. Two Gwen John copies and the rest a variety of originals, mostly abstract, portraits and landscapes.

Propped up around the room were four of the five large paintings that Trench had chosen from the photos she had sent him of her colourful abstracts.

Ceri and Sara carefully placed the fifth canvas onto a large easel in the centre of the room. It was Ceri's favourite; an emotional whirlpool of deep purples and blues that changed with the light and, at times, was so powerful it took his breath away.

He stood looking at it, Sara behind him, her eyes screwed up in the light. She was searching for flaws in the artistry. It would never be finished for her. There would always be another level to which she could take it.

'I love it.' Ceri touched it gently.

'It doesn't have to go.' Sara put her arms around his waist and fitted herself into his shape.

Ceri turned into her and kissed her.

'Yes it does, but if he doesn't pay whatever you want for this, his heart is full of darkness and he has no soul.' He kissed her again. 'We need the money, gorgeous.'

'What about the others?' A shadow of doubt edged the words.

'He'll love them.'

'You're biased.'

'So? Doesn't mean I can't be honest.'

'You sure about that?'

'Look, sweetheart, Trench knows what his clients want. He wouldn't waste time coming down here if he didn't rate your work. He'll be knocked out when he sees them in the flesh. Promise.'

'I hope so.' Sara looked around at the canvases then moved to the one against the sofa and, squatted down and studied it. 'I just need…'

Ceri pulled her up. 'Come to bed.'

'It won't take long. You go, you'll need to be up for Ben, he's so excited about going on the train and seeing the dinosaurs. I'll only be half an hour.'

Ceri kissed her. 'OK, but I want sex when I get back… if that's OK with you.'

Sara cuddled into him. 'It is.'

'And red wine…'

'That too.'

'In front of the fire… with no clothes on.'

Sara laughed. 'Go to bed.'

It took her longer than she thought and it was nearly one a.m. when she kissed Ben and pulled the duvet over him, cleaned her teeth, and then climbed into bed, snuggling up to a toasty-warm, gently snoring Ceri.

Next day they were late waking up and it was a mad panic to get Ben washed and fed. But Sara managed to stuff food down both her boys and, although she was unwashed, spiky-eyed, and hungry, she loaded them into the old Land Rover, that, to her surprise, started straight away.

'Did that start first time?' said Ceri. 'Old Trenchy won't stand a chance, he'll throw money at you.'

'Why?' said Ben. 'It'll hurt Mummy if it hits her…' He thought for a moment. 'Unless it's paper.'

Ceri turned in his seat. 'It better had be. Hundreds of notes.'

'Millions!' shouted Ben.

'Trillions!' shouted Sara.

'Squillions!'

'Zillions!'

'Onions!' screamed Ben.

Sara exploded with laughter as they pulled onto the main road and turned right…

.

CHAPTER TWO

In the hospital, where she had been put into a small private room after examination and a scan, Sara, on the edge of consciousness, the fractured images of a laughing Ben and Ceri too hard to hold onto, was lost, drowning in a deep and continuous pain.

It was too much to expect her to be able to understand that her boys had gone. That she would never see them again. Never feel Ben's breath against her face or Ceri's arms around her.

All she knew and wanted was for time to stop and go back.

She would persuade Ben and Ceri to leave it until the next day so they could all go together, either to celebrate the sale of her paintings, or make up for the disappointment when they were too big, too colourful, too fucking emotional.

Please, please.

But it was too late.

Darkness, raw and ugly, wrapped around her.

Suddenly a harsh sound entered her world and rose from the very bottom of her soul, sliced through her heart, and howled out of her.

The nurse jumped inches off the chair she had pulled close to the bed to hear the ragged moaning. She struggled to find the red alarm button.

Sara writhed and fought as the nurse tried to hold her down. She caught the nurse in the face with her head and blood spurted out of the woman's nose. She was thrown back against the chair and onto the floor. Sara threw herself on top of her as other nurses arrived with shouted commands and she felt a sharp sting as the needle smacked into her skin.

In moments she had stilled and slipped back into unconsciousness.

* * *

Later that night they moved Sara from the hospital to a small secure room at a private clinic.

She had been kept heavily sedated for the next two days and then slipped into a catatonic depression that lasted for another three. The consultant psychiatrist looking after her, Eve Mayberry, allowed Sara's father, Gary, to visit and he sat with her, often silently, for hours. He was the only one Sara would, in her lucid moments, agree to seeing.

Dr Mayberry, when she judged the time to be right, guided him. 'You have to talk to her about Ben and Ceri. It will be hard but she needs to see the reality of their deaths. At the moment she won't acknowledge it, it's too much for her to take in, but she must in order to begin the healing process.'

It was the toughest thing Gary had ever had to do, but he held Sara's hand and tried not to react to her denials, grief, and anger. Slowly, over the next week, she had seemed to begin to accept what had happened.

One morning as he was talking about his twin five-year-old daughters, at home with his young wife in Spain, she started to cry, silently. 'Oh, sweetheart, I'm sorry, I shouldn't have talked about the girls…'

'No, it's not that.' Her look of anguish and despair was heartbreaking but he couldn't make it better. 'I just don't want to be here anymore.'

She didn't expect him to understand, but then in a moment of clarity, realised that, of course, he did.

'You must have felt the same when Mum died.' Sara's mum had died suddenly when she was nineteen and in her first year at art school.

'I did.' He looked at her for a long moment then kissed her hand. 'I wanted to end all the pain. I was selfish, didn't think about you, but, in the end, I wasn't brave enough to do it…'

He paused and pushed back the emotion. He had to be strong for her. 'You told me that living was the act of courage and that together we would get through it. And we did, the bad nights and dark days.' He smiled. 'It's my turn now.'

Gary had loved Ben and Ceri but he would wait to give in to his own grief and try to help her find a way out of this absolute darkness. At times though the great emptiness in her exhausted him and he was unsure of how much good he was doing, but each day he came back and sat with her and she opened up a little more by the time he left. They sometimes didn't talk about Ben and Ceri, but memories of holidays when she was little, or strange things he had done to earn money when he left his journalism job to become a full-time writer. He was still doing it but now added to his meagre earnings with interpretation work.

Then one morning in the fourth week he went in to find her dressed and sitting on the bed. She wanted to go home to be where her boys were. Dr Mayberry had tried to dissuade her but Sara seemed to have found a strength. The psychiatrist was worried it wouldn't last and made Gary responsible for checking she took her medication. He was going to stay with her as long as she wanted, certainly until after the funeral. He had managed to persuade them to release the bodies and they were now in a funeral home until a burial was arranged. Sara knew she had to leave the clinic and find a silence from the care and words of those who meant well but had no fraction of understanding of what had taken place in her life.

Outside the clinic Sara stood looking at the Land Rover, then smiled at her dad. It was a reaction only and didn't reach her eyes. 'How did you get it?'

'Station. I realised that was where it would be and found it, as usual, unlocked with the spare key under the mat. I remembered from last time that was where you hid it.'

In truth, Gary had picked it up from the railway station but had almost hit the guy in charge of the parking when he refused to remove the clamp without him paying the £100 for not having a valid ticket. In the end he had just given in, there were more important things than money. The key though had still been in the ignition.

Sara opened the passenger door. 'Let's go.'

The Land Rover started first time. Gary smiled at her. 'I gave it a bit of a going over to make sure it lasted while I was driving it.'

Sara touched his arm. 'Can we go and see my boys?'

Gary glanced at her, saw the determination. 'Yes, of course.'

* * *

They sat in the car outside the funeral home. Sara had the strangest feeling that she would go in and find there had been a mistake and it wasn't Ben and Ceri. Lost for a moment in that safe corner of her mind, she almost smiled at the thought, then, without warning, reality crashed in with a violence that made her spasm and cry out. Lost, she looked across at her father, who reached over and managed awkwardly to pull her into his arms.

'Are you sure you want to do this, sweetheart?'

Sara moved away from him. 'I have to see them again.'

She struggled with opening her door then the catch gave and she got out and walked quickly towards the entrance.

Gary hurried after her.

She left him and the young trainee undertaker outside the door. In the cramped and gently lit chapel of rest the large and small coffins were on stands, side by side.

Sara stopped and wiped the tears away. She didn't want them to see her upset. Moving without thought she reached the stands. Her head was down and as though a great weight was on it, she struggled to lift it. She kept her eyes tightly shut then, using every bit of willpower she had, she opened them and looked into the coffins. Only Ben and Ceri's heads were showing. Soft white material covered the rest of them. The faces looked pale and calm, untroubled by the death that had surprised them. She gently kissed Ceri then touched her lips to Ben's mouth. His eyelashes, so long and silky, touched her cheek as she laid her head against his.

Slowly she lifted away from him and stood looking at her two beautiful boys, so alike, so still. If she breathed into their mouths, would they be able to take life from her?

'I should have been with you.'

She touched her face and then both of theirs. Hers was warm. She heard their voices and Ben's bubbling giggles… It was too much for her to take and she slowly crumpled to the floor.

Gary, from the doorway, saw and tried to reach her but wasn't quick enough to catch her. He picked her up and carried her out of the room.

He gently put her into the car and fastened the seat belt around her.

'There's a space at the Crem in four days. Cancellation, a family wanted earth not fire. Shall I book it?' The trainee undertaker wasn't experienced enough with life and death to respect the moment.

He saw Gary's face and moved back warily. 'Sorry, it's just there are others who would take it.'

Gary couldn't stop the laugh that burst out of him. 'No, you insensitive little prick, we're going to bury them. So all we need you to do is to provide a cardboard coffin for the two of them to be in together.'

Gary took Sara back to the barn and held her as the shock slowly slipped and the loss shook her. He gave her the medication, a strong anti-depressant, and a 'knock-out pill' that Dr Mayberry had told him would help to shut out reality for a time. She could take both together.

The next day when Sara woke feeling sick and spaced out, Gary was still there. He had slept beside her on the bed.

When they talked about the burial, as they had to, Sara knew that it was something she must steel herself to do, without allowing the self-destructive emotions to take control.

Neither she nor Ceri were religious, so she was going to bury them in a humanist plot on the top of a cliff overlooking a beach. It was near where Ceri had given Ben his first lesson on his old surfboard. Ben was a natural and loved the huge waves and even managed to stand up on the board for a few seconds. Ceri had caught him as he was thrown off but he tried again the next time they went and did it. It seemed a lifetime ago but it was only a few months.

* * *

The next day Sara and Gary organised the people and the plot. Ceri's parents had come as soon as they heard about Ceri and Ben's deaths, but Sara, still in the clinic, was too unwell to see them and they had said their goodbyes to their son and grandson. They would be coming to the burial, although it was at odds with their

Christian beliefs. Gary's wife and children weren't able to come and Sara's oldest friend, Jamie, had promised to stay with her after her dad had gone and she was on her own. A few other close friends said they understood that Sara didn't want them at the burial but promised they would be there to give her love and support when it was needed.

It was a wonderful warm and clear day on the clifftop overlooking the bay. Ceri's parents, Tom and Dilys, and his sister, Sian, fervent Welsh Baptists, kept their faith away from Sara but shared the reality of their grief. Gary, showing a strength that Sara never knew he had, held her hand as their small group walked across the field to the burial plots, led by the celebrant and those carrying the coffin.

The plot was not as near the edge as Sara had wanted it to be. The celebrant explained that erosion of the cliff was not a problem yet but it was always better to be on the safe side. She was a woman in her fifties, warm and understanding, who had been a humanist for twenty years and lived in a village ten miles from Sara. Gary had found her through a website. She had spent a day with Sara to talk about Ceri and Ben and explain that although there was a loose structure, the burial could be done in any way Sara wanted.

As the large green cardboard coffin was lowered into the grave, Sara closed her eyes and saw Ceri and Ben laughing hysterically. The memory came from their last holiday when they were staying at a farmhouse in Normandy. It was a weekend in November and she had warned them constantly about not touching the antique painted wood-burning stove then had done it herself burning her hand. Ben and Ceri had been uncontrollable with laughter.

Sara didn't want any words to be said about her boys, and they listened to 'Songbird' by Eva Cassidy played on her phone as the earth covered the coffin. It was a song that Ceri had loved and had sung to calm Ben when he was troubled and couldn't sleep.

Soon afterwards Tom, Dilys, and Sian hugged Sara and tried to persuade her to come and stay with them. They were kind, but full of Baptist guilt at the distance they'd kept when their son was alive. They left after Sara had refused, needing to touch the roots of their faith in their Christian home, and be in a community of belief that was known and safe.

The celebrant and her helpers went too. They had another burial near Cardiff at the end of the day.

Sara and her father sat looking down at the waves crashing onto the beach and the surfers, some standing, some flat on boards, some body surfing with arms and legs stretched out to let the waves take them towards the waters' edge.

'Ceri and Ben will love the sand and waves. It'll make me happy to think of them here.'

It was the first time she had spoken for three hours.

As they got up to leave, the setting sun threw shadows over the water and shafts of light touched the mound of earth. Sara asked her father to leave her alone and she knelt by the plot. He waited for her by the edge of the field so he could still keep her in sight.

Sara smiled as she saw her boys in her mind.

'I don't know if I will be able to live without you but I'll try. You will have to be my light.'

She blew two kisses and then without looking back walked slowly towards her father.

* * *

Somehow Sara held herself together so that Gary was able to leave and return to Alicante.

She sat at the table in the garden and held his hands. He kissed her fingers. 'I have to go back, Isabella and the girls need me there, but…'

He hesitated and looked closely at Sara. 'Isabella wants you to come and stay with us for as long as you want. Her father has offered to turn his workshop into a studio for you to paint. But really it's so I will be able to take care of you.'

Sara felt a surge of love for her often absent father. It was hard for him.

'It's sweet of her but it will tear me apart to live in a family like yours when mine is broken and empty.
Thank you, but I have to try and do this on my own. I want to be in a place where I can feel and touch them.'

CHAPTER THREE

After her father left Sara fell back into darkness. Time stood still. Nothing changed. There was little to give her hope and a vision of the future. The barn, once a place of warmth, noise, and love became a shell into which she could withdraw and become invisible. She wanted to be alone. To live within the shadows and tears and use her anger, guilt, and grief to create and make physical the torment that spread inside her. Her painting was obsessive and she would work until she had no more control over what she was doing. Without food and sleep and with only wine to sustain her, she tried to drive out the demons and make them less real in her illumination of their image. Before, she had drunk little alcohol but now it became a willing and overpowering accomplice.

The friends who had promised to be there for her came, trying to find a way to help but there was nothing that they could do. Sara knew how hard it must be for them to try to stay close to her. But her natural sense of balance for kindness and care was numb and too far away for her to reach. If only they had felt able to be straight with her: 'I don't and can't have any idea of the agony you're going through but have to feel that I at least tried.' That would have been honest, but none of them could bear to seem that uncaring in their truth. The old

Sara would have known and never have rejected them, but this new deadened and dark Sara didn't care. They couldn't do the one thing she wanted more than life itself. Make the worst thing that could ever happen not have happened. But no matter how caring and desperate to be of use those closest to her needed to be, they wanted to go without guilt when they had failed. It was too painful, too difficult, and too destructive. Even though they tried to handle her rage, the alcohol and abuse, it eventually wore them down and they stopped coming.

Only Jamie stayed. She had been Sara's constant friend since they were ten years old. She lived in Scotland now, with her husband, Davey. They couldn't have children and Jamie didn't want to adopt. But they had money, and knowing that Gary couldn't afford it, they had paid for the clinic.

Jamie couldn't understand what it meant to lose your child, your soul mate, your lover, your world, in a sharp snap of time. The thought of Davey disappearing from her life in the same way was hard enough. She didn't push Sara to talk or to take her medication and when she managed to persuade her to go to appointments with the therapist, Jamie went with her. She'd even dealt with the art dealer who had called for progress on the work he had commissioned and managed to persuade him to give Sara more time and agree that she should contact him when she was ready.

Some days Jamie hardly saw her as Sara stayed in her studio upstairs or in the large downstairs room, filling canvases with wild and tormented images. She was just there to soak up some of the desperation and anger and do what she could when Sara was incoherent and needed a human sponge. She'd cover her up and sit with her when she passed out or clean up the mess after she was sick. Jamie's sense of time had stopped too, locked in the pain of Sara's world. She escaped by walking the hills around the barn or talking to Davey, in long rambling calls, when it got too much. But mostly she managed to hold on to the right sort of reality and closed herself to the insults and angry words. But she knew the day would come when either Sara turned a corner and began to listen or she would have to leave.

And that day finally arrived.

It was a sunny but cold late summer's day. Jamie had been out early, walking, and had felt her energy renewed. She had gone into the village to get some food and collect paint and a roll of canvas that had been on order. When she got back Sara was in the kitchen. She was mixing paint in the sink that Jamie had scrubbed and bleached. They had agreed that Sara would use the other larger butler's sink next to it for all the work stuff.

Jamie felt the anger rise within her but tried to be calm.

'Why are you using that one? You promised we could keep it clean.'

Sara didn't stop what she was doing.

'It's my sink, I can do what I like in it.'

'Yes, but I cleaned it, like everything else, the kitchen, the bathroom.'

Sara stopped and tipped the mixed paint over the floor. She was unsteady and Jamie realised that she had been at the wine already.

'Are you going to clean that too?'

She came and stood in front of Jamie and put her face close to hers. Her breathing was sharp and hoarse, catching on the dryness in her mouth.

'Are you?'

Jamie moved away, trying to keep in control.

'Why are you still here? I don't want you. You're a fucking freak, following me round like a little dog, sniffing at my arse, wanting to be my friend. Go back to your nice, cosy, childless world and leave me alone.'

Jamie held her glare, trying not to react to Sara's words.

'That's not fair.'

Sara pushed her hard but Jamie, stronger and heavier, held her with one hand and just managed to stop her spontaneous slap before it reached Sara's face.

Sara laughed at her. 'Can't do it, can you. You dried-up little failure. Hit me, go on, hit me. It'll make you feel better. And me. I like the pain. It takes it away from here.'

She banged her fist against her head, hard, again and again. Jamie grabbed her hands, pulled them down. Sara struggled and eventually stopped. Jamie relaxed and Sara smashed her head into Jamie's. Although she saw it coming and managed to move, the blow stunned her. She leaned against the table. Sara exhausted, shocked and repulsed by what she had done, watched her. She tried to think of the words to make it right but she was too confused.

Jamie touched her head and when she spoke there was a coldness that burned Sara like ice.

'I have tried to understand and give you space and just be here to help make your life more normal, take away things that you don't need to do, so you can try and find a way through all this.'

'I didn't ask you to be here.'

'No, but I thought I could help. I know now I can't, not until you want to help yourself. You keep hurting me but I was willing to take it because I knew that for you to release the pain it needed someone to receive and absorb it. I thought I could be stronger but I'm afraid that you might break me too. I know how you feel and how dark your life is, but…'

Sara barked a laugh, stopping Jamie. It was harsh and jagged. 'Do you? You know what it is to lose the child that you conceived, nurtured and grew inside you, do you? You know what it is to have the choice taken away from you?' She was struggling, fighting the fear and panic that were rushing inside her making it hard to speak. 'To want to die so your child could live, and not be able to do it? And you know what it is to lose the man that made your child with you? So that you will never fucking ever be able to hold them, touch them, feel their love, again. Do you know, Jamie? Do you fucking know?'

Jamie felt tears stinging her eyes.

'How could I know? All I can do is to be here to love you and hope that will help in some way.'

The words tore out of Sara, bitter and violent. 'I don't want your fucking love! And I don't want you!'

Jamie knew at that moment she would have to go, before their friendship was destroyed for ever.

Sara sat on the floor and watched as Jamie went out of the kitchen, knowing that she should stop her but she couldn't move or speak.

She was still there as Jamie drove away. Another part of her that she thought was dead now felt pain too. But it was too late.

CHAPTER FOUR

Sara just wanted to be on her own. She stopped going to the therapist and she stopped regularly taking the variety of drugs that Eve Mayberry prescribed and sent to the chemist in the village. Sometimes Sara picked them up and sometimes she didn't. Unknown to Sara, Jamie was still picking up all the bills and talking to Dr Mayberry. She knew that her care would have to be at a distance. Perhaps when she was stronger she might go back but, for now, Davey was determined that she stayed at home and allowed herself to heal. Her heart was breaking for Sara.

But Sara didn't want anyone.

She just wanted to be left alone.

She didn't need the mantra of therapy. The constant insistence that *it really helps to talk, to let out what is inside, to make it real outside of your inner world*. It was confusing and wrong and jumbled her thoughts.

Even in those times when she could think clearly, she found that the idea that talking about 'the tragedy' would somehow make her accept her alien broken state, was an anathema. Nothing could take away that vacuum of loss. No words, no understanding, no comforting touches, no real or mystic vehicle of faith, and certainly no amount of 'healing' would give her what they wanted. A way into the light for her and satisfaction for them that they had made her well.

Some of the drugs she took when it was too hard did help her to get to sleep, but then her dreams tore and shook her awake and her heart was broken again. Others calmed and stunned her mind but that wasn't healing. It only opened up another wave of attack, violent and destructive, when the numbness went.

The only way she could be saved was to treat the cause not the effect. Bring back Ceri and Ben. But she couldn't do that.

Some days, like today, she had lost sense of time and place; knew, somewhere deep inside, that there was something she should remember but the second bottle of wine had blocked it out. She vaguely knew it had been light and now it was dark.

She hadn't moved from the corner of Ben's room, his clothes covering her, her fist bloody and swollen from hitting the wall until the pain got through. It was a good pain, physical, not in her mind where it couldn't be controlled.

And then, suddenly, there was a noise, different, alien, to the world she inhabited where she knew every cry, sigh, creak, and click. But this was something else. Not the presence she longed to hear, had tried to force back, but an unwelcome and unwanted thing.

Slowly her mind cleared and focused. She had to protect the spirit of life still here.

Even though the darkness in the house was deep she knew her space and, even pissed like this, did not need sight or light to move around in it.

Against the bedroom door there was Ceri's old school cricket bat that had waited for Ben to grow old enough to use. She grabbed the handle and held it against her leg and moved slowly to the stairs.

A shadowy figure, safe in the darkness, came over the top stair, a red light on a camera blinking in front of it.

The man saw Sara as she lifted the bat. For a moment his instinct was still on shooting fast, and he raised his arm too late to protect himself and the bat smacked hard across his face, smashing into the camera. He was knocked down the stairs. It had happened so quickly there hadn't been time to shout but now Sara heard herself howl, 'Get out of my house or I'll fucking kill you,' as she rushed down towards him. The man scrabbled out of the never locked door leaving bits of his camera on the floor.

He was a deluded would-be paparazzo from Swansea who, by chance, found out the widow and mother of the father and son shot at Paddington was living thirty miles away from him. He needed a boost to his non-existent career and was hoping to sell the mad-with-grief shots to his picture editor acquaintance on a Sunday tabloid. He'd paid to hear from someone who lived in the same village as Sara that she was 'not doing well' and rarely wore clothes as she took out bottles and cried into the night. The gossip was that the door was never locked and she wouldn't answer if anyone knocked, so it wouldn't be breaking in.

Nothing happened, no one reported being attacked and no photo of her ever appeared in any newspaper.

She was left alone and soon the vague memory of what had happened, disappeared.

Over the next months, very little on the shooting was discovered. The descriptions of the gunman were too diverse to be of any use in tracing him. The middle-aged man who had held Ben had been from Siena. His name was Vittorio Rietti. As for the deaths of Ceri and Ben. They were just in the wrong place at the wrong time. A sad but simple tragedy of fate.

CHAPTER FIVE

Six months later

Ben's face was blurred as she tried to see his eyelashes butterfly kiss her cheek. His bubbling laugh tumbled his breath, sweet and fresh, across her lips. She surged with love for this perfect little boy. Then a sudden screaming shot ripped his head away, his eyelash stuck to her, his mouth open, terrible, silent, the blood cascading, blinding her.

'Ben!'

The tortured cry woke her as it always did, sweating and breathless. She lay there, panting, the wet sheet and duvet quickly turning cold. It was always this bad. Waking with relief but knowing instantly that nightmare and reality were the same. But this time it was just Ben. Why wasn't Ceri always part of her dreams? Did she blame him for the horror, destroying the memory of their love? It hurt too much. She couldn't bear the guilt. If she had been with them, it might have been different. They wouldn't have rushed back, perhaps even stayed the night, come back the next day. Then came the rage. He should have protected Ben. He was bigger, stronger. When Ben was born Ceri had said that he wouldn't let anything hurt him, ever. But he did. Why did he do that? He promised.

The screech of the phone made her jump. She scrabbled and found it on the floor.

'Yes?' Her voice was rough, harsh.

'Is that Sara Jenkins?' There was something familiar about the voice but a name or a face was too distant.

'Yes.'

It was a male voice. Panic hit her. Had she been too pissed to know that she'd given her number to someone? She couldn't even remember where she had been to meet anyone. She hardly went out, preferring the feral world she inhabited. Not warm or friendly but it was at least safe, known. The paintings that filled her days and nights, some finished, some only started and then discarded, were stacked against the walls of her studio. Soon she'd have to move some, to have room to work. Thoughts crisscrossed, jumbled.

'It's Farsons, your paint's in.' Relief brought her to the edge of the bed, nausea and pain filling her at the too quick movement.

'I'll come in later.' Phlegm filled her throat and a cough grated and exploded against the phone.

'Are you all right?' She could hear the concern that he wouldn't see his money and the specialist paint would have to be found another home. Not easy in a small village.

Sara tried a laugh that almost worked then died. 'Too much to drink.' The 'again' was silent but both heard it.

'You'll be in before one thirty? We're closed this afternoon.' He had learned you had to be sure with this one that she remembered what she'd said. Of course he knew the reason why and it was terrible, but life had to go on. He was running a business, not a therapy group.

A flash of anger bit at her head but she pushed it away. 'Yes.'

'Good.'

'Bye.' She put the phone down. What a little turd. He was forty, fat, frustrated and, she was sure, flaccid. But he saved her a sixty-mile round trip to the supplier in Swansea, so she kept her distance and tried not to upset him. She could have ordered online and had it delivered. But she didn't want anyone coming to the barn and it was easier to have someone to deal with the details she couldn't get her head around.

She almost felt as though she could move now, the fear of her night slipping away as the cold and hungover day took its place. Jesus, what time was it? She looked at her wrist. Why? She hadn't worn a watch for months, not since the inquest and the 'death by person unknown' verdict. The same thought always followed. Did it matter who had done it? Would it turn her loss into a nice, neat package that she could fold away and slip into a lavender-smelling drawer in her heart? Would it take away the constant longing to smell, touch, and take back into the womb her baby so she could start again, do things differently? Keep him safe.

The phone rang again. Shit, what was this? Nobody rang her anymore.

She picked it up, waited.

Another male voice, hurried, whispered. 'Trish, it's me, can you talk? Mags is in the garden, I have to see you…'

Sara hung up. Still, for a moment she wondered why he had to see Trish. Did Mags know? Were they having an affair? Despite what had happened to her, life, messy, sneaky, uncontrollable, went on, leading the journey from beginning to end, calling the shots. What would happen to Trish, Mags, and the unknown man?

'Shit!' Sara closed her eyes tight then opened them. Why did she have no control over all this crap that came into her head? Was it to interrupt the madness that would sit, arrogant and strong, if she had to replay again and again the images of her mutilated boys? Without the dross of everyday life that filled the corners, closed the gaps, kept away the truth when it got too much, would she have killed herself by now? She hadn't, she was still here, fighting, sure that one day she would give up. Not today. Perhaps if it had been raining harder, the pounding in her head worse, it might have been. But she would push through this one and see what came about another day.

Through the gap in the thick, too-long drapes, the early April sun was distorting, trying to edge its way in. Her mind forced itself to focus. Time? She had to get to the shop by one thirty. Her eyes found the clock on the littered table by the bed. It was twelve. She had to move. Standing seemed to work, then her stomach heaved and she felt sick, suddenly, unstoppably. She managed to get to the lavatory in the large bathroom before throwing up. There were no doors to open on the way. She never shut doors. Always wanted to hear the footsteps, the laughter and the cries that would never come.

Finally she stopped retching. She felt weak but it was not something that disturbed her anymore. It was an old friend, cleansing, clearing her for the battle of the day. At the back of her mind she knew it had to be damaging, not good for her. But if the drinking dulled the pain she could cope with this bit of daily discomfort. It never went on for long, she didn't eat enough for that. But for some strange metabolic reason her body never changed shape. Perhaps it was her gift from nature to make up for its desecration of all that was good in her life.

She turned on the shower next to the big old bath, waited for it to warm up, and stood under the flow, her face turned up to the water.

* * *

She parked the Land Rover in the small car park at the side of the Spar. There were only a couple of other shops on the road that ran through the village. A delicatessen and off-licence to cater for the rich middle class who wanted the rural peace but not the paucity of choice, a chemist, and, opposite where she'd parked, Farsons, an ironmonger's that sold household and DIY equipment and did picture framing on the side. They'd also get canvas, stretchers, and paints for Sara, but business wasn't good anymore and they'd talked of closing down.

Her barn was about two miles outside the village, a home that until the 'worst day' was a rambling, cluttered space that was filled with love, hopes, and plans and dreams for the future. The shell was still there but its heart had gone. Still, it was paid for after an exhausting fight for Ceri's insurance and she didn't want to be anywhere else. There was enough money left after paying off the mortgage to keep her going for a couple of years, or until she gave up and joined her boys.

There was a man being served as Sara came into the shop. She didn't take notice until fat, forty and flaccid

Jem Stokes raised his voice. 'Mrs Jenkins, I was just telling Mr Brodsky that you might let him have some canvas.'

'What?' Sara tried to work out what he'd said. Brodsky turned round.

'Hello, I'm Peter Brodsky.'

Brodsky was in his forties, tall, fit, with thick grey-blond hair, and twinkling blue eyes that held her look. 'I'd brought some canvas with me but it got lost at Heathrow. I'm a bit of a hobby painter, landscapes. Not very good but it passes the time. This gentleman was telling me that you're an artist, were coming in, and might be persuaded to loan me some until I get an order in.' He smiled easily. It was infectious. Sara found herself smiling back.

'Yes, of course. Where are you from?'

Why did she say that? It had come out before she could stop it.

'Montreal, I teach at the university there, but my great-grandfather was from around here somewhere. I've taken a six-month sabbatical to find my roots.' He laughed, warm and friendly. 'Middle age, I guess, trying to make sense of life. I've got a small cottage on Home Farm.'

Sara was disturbed by him, embarrassed by the way his eyes kept contact. She wondered if Stokes had told him about her. It was a good story. Driven to madness and drink by tragedy.

Stokes coughed nervously as if he'd read her mind. 'I'll get your paints.'

Brodsky picked up a package from the counter. 'Perhaps I could come round tomorrow?'

'Yes, in the afternoon. I live a couple of miles past Home Farm. It's a converted barn. You can see it from the road.'

'Thanks, I'll see you then.' He smiled and went out.

Sara watched as the door shut. What the hell was she doing inviting him to her house? She'd hardly talked to anyone for months, except Stokes and she didn't count him, and almost no one had been to the barn since it had happened. Her choice. She was in control. Then a sudden panic hit. She didn't want him to come to her home. It was her security. She couldn't trust it with a stranger. It might betray her. As with all these attacks, logic flashed, keeping her on the edge. She could always drop the canvas off. Yes, she'd do that.

'Here you go.' Stokes was putting the paints into a box. 'Hell of a long way to come, just to find your roots.'

She didn't want to talk to him. He was looking at her breasts. She smiled coldly and he turned away, embarrassed he'd been caught. She picked up the bill he'd put on the counter, paid, and went out.

Jem Stokes watched her through the glass of the door as she crossed the road and put the paint in the back of the Land Rover. His tongue touched his dry lips then he locked the door and hung the closed sign.

CHAPTER SIX

Sara sat in the Land Rover, disturbed by Peter Brodsky and angry that she had let him seduce her into momentary normality. They had only met for a few minutes. Too little time to do any harm.

Was it?

It had taken less time to take away the two lives she had cherished above all others. With that reality, anything was possible. And now, uncomprehendingly, this man had found a way into her head. But that was unfair, unwelcome, filled with danger. She didn't want change. She was safe in her insanity. She didn't want reason. There was no place there that wasn't filled with pain. No room for social smiles and warm words. It was her chosen hell. Her cold cell of atonement for not being there to save them, or not dying with them. That would have been preferable to the constant agony of being alive.

She shut her eyes tightly and tried to control the jumbling, razor-edged thoughts. She bit her lip until she tasted blood. It was a controlled and well-known pain. For a moment it worked and she watched as a woman pulled a small screaming child out of the chemist's and tried to placate it. But the child battled on and finally the woman gave in, picked it up… and the tears stopped.

Suddenly, without warning, Sara saw Ben, her beautiful Ben, laughing, uncontrollable. Then, as if it were too much for her soul to bear, the snapshot disappeared.

'Shit!' Why did she say he could come? She had allowed no one else into her space. But she'd had no control. It was instinctive. Something deeply buried had for a moment searched for light and been touched by a beam of new life and could not deny it or return to the moment before.

Then sanity came, quickly, starkly and she started the engine and moved into the road. It had seemed hours since she had got into the Land Rover, but the woman and child had not moved and the closed sign was still swinging inside the glass door of the shop.

It had happened like this since the murders. Time was inexplicable and transient. Nothing stayed very long except the pain. One thought quickly overtaken by the next. One plan conceived then dismissed with another. Her reality ebbing and flowing in opposites. Laughter with tears. Numbness with longing. Harmony with discord. Life with death.

That evening she drank too much wine, again, and with grief overcoming her, was curled up on the floor of her studio. Stacked around the room, a storyboard of her mind in the ramshackle paintings, some leaning against a wall, others thrown into a corner.

One was a self-portrait, drawn and strained, the lines deeply etched into the pale mask of her skin, blood red tears falling into a whirlpool of Ben's face, tearing with jagged edges out of her shaven and swollen vagina. Her innocence had gone and she craved the visceral. It just bled out of her. This was her art now.

She felt dizzy, unreal, the colours began to merge and swim. She was so tired. Sick and tired. Tired of life and the death that haunted her. Perhaps tomorrow she would find the strength to go to her boys. Yes. She had waited too long. This time she would do it. But at the back of her mind there was a doubt. Not a doubt that she would be able to do it. She could, should, and would. It was the how. How? That was her problem. Each time the thought of nothingness warmed and excited her but somehow it never happened. Then with a clear almost intense shock she realized the absurd truth. It was because she had never had a clear idea of the way to kill herself. Jesus! How pathetic. To be restrained and defeated by ignorance. The realisation was a turning point. Now she could do it. Nothing would stop her.

Not this time. This time she would find the way. The light would be there to guide her. Think hard. Concentrate. Don't let that sneaky little speck of fear of the unknown cloud the moment. But it was already too late. She tried to form a plan but her mind was too confused by the wine. Her eyes gave up trying to focus and slowly closed. Then, head on floor, she was asleep.

It was the same every night, but by morning, she was in her bed, the memory was gone, and the torture began again.

* * *

There was what looked like blood as she bent over the lavatory. She retched again. This time nothing came. It was over. She knew it wasn't blood but red wine. She sat back against the wall and a searing stab of pain in her head made her cry out. She crawled up and scrambled for the foil packet of pills she kept on the shelf by the loo. She stuck her mouth under the tap, filled it, and pushed the pills in, the water dribbling down her chin. She swallowed, held her breath and fought to keep them down.

Her head was thudding. It was consuming her, outside as well as in. Twin hammers in harmony, one driven by the pounding blood swelling against her veins, the other clearer, more definite. Like metal on wood, a banging on a door. The huge front door of the barn, with its heavy double horseshoe knocker. Shit. It was clearer now. There was someone at the door.

Nobody came here.

Don't answer it.

They'll go away.

Peter Brodsky stood back from the door and looked at the huge eighteenth-century barn, the stonework worn and patched, the windows and roof new and stark. Around it the garden was wild. Brambles, weeds, knee-high grass, once-cared-for flowers all fought for light and space. He liked this uncontrolled spread of nature. It was a living, changing landscape. Not clinical, neat, and formalised for praise but a rough and determined show of strength. A sign from the gods that they were in control, their rooted armies ready to take over the land.

Brodsky shook his head. Jesus Christ, where did that shit come from?

He moved back to the door and knocked again loudly. A shadow and a coldness crossed his thoughts.

There was darkness here as though the world in which house and garden sat had been touched by evil.

Sara pulled on a T-shirt. It was the one Ben and Ceri had given her for her birthday with 'God is a Mummy' in faded red lettering almost hidden now with dark spatters of paint. Ben had giggled uncontrollably as she unwrapped the present they had found in a shop run by sixties hippies in St Ives. They'd gone there to visit the Tate, play on the beaches, and watch the dolphins. Ben was five. Five. Sara's breath caught in her throat, the spasm choking until tears released it. Her little boy was five, safe and protected. He only had another year to live. Her eyes dried, filling with rage. God wasn't a mummy. He was cruel, angry and uncaring. No mummy would allow what happened to her Ben to happen. She dragged the shirt over her head, struggling when it pulled against her hair, and threw it into a corner and tried to hold herself together as the grief shook her.

Brodsky turned the large knob on the door. He expected it to be locked. It wasn't. That gave him a problem. If it had been locked he would have just walked away, come back another time, got the number from Farsons. Phoned first. But this had taken the choice away. He had to go in. He shut the door behind him, listened.

'Mrs Jenkins?'

He tried again, louder this time.

'Mrs Jenkins?'

There was no answer but he suddenly became aware of a moaning. No, not moaning. What the hell was it called? The Irish had a word. Years ago, he'd been to an

Irish funeral in Canada, of a fifty-year-old IRA man whose past had caught up with him. Brodsky had been one of a group of ice hockey buddies who drank at the bar he ran. There'd been a wake: a drunken celebration of a wasted life; a mist of tears, song, recriminations, and shadows, and somewhere in the lost hours towards dawn he had heard it as the man's daughters and wife gave in to the weight of lost lives. It was the same sound he heard now. Keening, the pissed old bastard priest had called it. Grieving their fecking hearts out, he had said. Those words from a man of God had shocked Brodsky's Canadian Catholic soul. The memory amused him.

He listened again. The sound was coming from the top of the house.

He was in a large hall, empty, uncared for, cobwebs laced across the corners, its walls stacked with canvases and boxes. Near the front door on hooks at child level were brightly coloured coats, hats, and scarves, and underneath, red, yellow, and blue Wellington boots. A small bike, cars, and other toys were scattered around the floor. It was a sad and heartless space. Brodsky moved quickly towards the stairs.

'Mrs Jenkins'?

Still the keening, louder now, as he reached the top and moved along a corridor towards a room at the end. He passed an open door and glanced in. It was a child's room with a Spiderman mural on the wall.

Sara was standing, naked, fixed on a painting of a young boy, happy, smiling, his grey eyes piercing and hypnotic. Brodsky moved towards her and expected shock and screams as she realised he was there. He was

49

close to her when she turned to him. There was no surprise, no fear, just agony. He wanted to reach out, touch her, ease the torment he saw in her face. The power of her pain was intense. He tried to speak but he had nothing to say.

Her eyes were pleading, her voice small and broken. 'Hold me.'

Instinctively he put his arms around her and she collapsed against him, wrapping herself into him. He felt the warmth of her body and tried to pull away as he felt arousal but she pulled him into her, pressing against him, her hand reaching to hold him. He felt powerless to stop her.

'Hurt me.'

It was enough. Broke the spell. Gently he tried to push her away but she fought him.

'No.'

They struggled around the room until he freed her hands and twisting away, moved out of her reach. It was clumsy, awkward and she fell against the painting of the boy. She stopped as the stretchers broke and covered the canvas, protecting it with her body.

Brodsky sat on the floor watching her.

Suddenly she got up. 'I'm sorry.' She walked out of the room.

Brodsky watched her go. 'Jesus.'

CHAPTER SEVEN

For a moment Brodsky didn't know what to do. Stunned and rooted by the violence and passion of her grief. Shocked by his reaction to the touch of her naked body. He had wanted to help, reach out, hold her, ease her pain. Unbelievably, he had wanted her too. In that one moment he had lost humanity. Only her need for him to inflict pain on her had stopped him.

Jesus Christ!

It was a long time since he had been surprised or affected by the heat of a damaged and burning life, but there was something of her that had seeped into him. Mocked him. Led him. He had just been strong enough to reject the urge but he felt weakened by it.

Shit!

Focus.

Assess.

A woman he'd only met once, a woman drowning in grief, whose husband and son had been killed because they got in the way. Life doesn't get any shittier than that. Not a calm platform for normality. He had come uninvited into her home. Her grief was private, desperate, raw, naked, not neat and packaged. Not your everyday introduction to other lives. What the fuck did he expect except the unbelievable?

'She's a drunk,' the guy in the shop had said, 'pushed everyone away from her, driven off those that had tried to help. She's a stain on the community.' But he had seen in his eyes that the guy was no different from what he had become just now. He had wanted her too. He felt a sudden rage against that fat little bastard with the dry lips. They shared a darkness and it made him feel unclean.

Should he go to her? Talk to her. Try to help.

It would be safer to go then come back another time, expected, pick up the canvas and leave, only seeing her again when he repaid his debt.

Perhaps some days were better for her than others.

How would he know?

Watch and wait.

Wait for the sound of keening to stop.

Knock at the door and then run away if she was naked and wanted to be hurt.

Look at all sides.

Was it safe to leave her? She wasn't exactly balanced. Would he go and then hear that she had killed herself? He would have saved her if he had stayed. Was it safe to stay? What could he do?

He tried to calm the thoughts but they tumbled without sense. Then he had a moment of hot panic. What if she said he attacked her and that he had tried to rape her? Is she phoning the police? Now.

It seemed an age had passed since the explosion of stillness when she had left the room but it was only, he knew, moments, his transient thoughts layered in the same frame of time.

Get a grip, man, and just get out.

He stood up, looked around the room. It was an untidy shrine to the boy in the painting.

Then his breath caught as he saw the disgust and agony of the birth and death all around him.

The work was too painful to judge its worth.

It screamed.

And then he almost did as he turned.

Sara was in the doorway. She was wearing a too-big man's duffle coat, fastened but hanging off her. It was dark green and looked as though it was new. She was holding a roll of canvas.

'Jesus, you gave me a fright,' he said.

'I'm sorry.' Sara's face was puffy, her eyes raw and red but calm.

'No need. Are you all right?

She held his look.

'No.'

There was nothing to say to that. It hung in the air. A reflection of the stupidity of his words. He'd just experienced how not all right she was. Fuck!

'Sometimes, it's too much.'

He nodded so she would know he understood.

She held out the canvas. 'You need to stretch and prime it.'

'Thanks. I'll replace it as soon as mine comes.' He felt awkward.

She almost smiled. 'I have things to do.'

'Sure, I'll go.'

She moved away from the door.

'I don't want anyone here.'

Brodsky hesitated then made for the stairs. 'I shouldn't have come.'

'No.'

CHAPTER EIGHT

Sara felt a part of the raw, angry, wild garden. It was what it was. Nothing more. No hidden beauty. No pretence at soft and gentle. It had no feelings, gave no warmth, had no harsh words, no kindness, and wanted nothing in return for her being there. It closed around her. Wrapping her in its welcome. Not comforting. Not threatening. It was a reality. Uncared for, uncultivated, left to be its darkest self. Nobody cared. They left it alone. It knew nothing of their world. Didn't want any part of their world.

But it had once.

Once it had enjoyed laughter and beauty and innocence.

But that was another life in another time.

She felt numbed and cold. Even in the coat that had never been worn until now. The early spring weather was unusually cool with frequent storms.

After her madness she had scrabbled under the bed until she had found the coat. There were other clothes around the room but she didn't want them. It was only this coat that would give her strength. And reason. A calm understanding of what she needed to do to sink back into her world.

A world that had no place for the living.

She had found the canvas, and the man, the Canadian, had gone.

He had accepted what had happened.

He did not seem to judge.

The shadows of shock were still there, deep inside his eyes. But with an instinctive understanding she knew it was for himself too, not her alone. She accepted that but a small part of her wondered, which edge of his darkness had been touched by her pain?

In that moment, when she felt the shreds of torment, he had reached out to her.

And then the fear had wrapped itself around her and it was too late.

When he had gone she picked up the pieces of the broken frame, gently freed the canvas, and smoothed it into her body.

Time meant nothing as it came and went.

Later she re-stretched the painting on a frame, took it into her bedroom, and leaned it against the wall.

The tears had come again.

She must have used up the eighty per cent or so of her body that was water. It had been months of never-ending tears. A torrent of tears.

If all the tears had come at once it would have been enough. She would have shrivelled and died. But her body had betrayed her and kept finding pools to feed the pain, giving her the almost comic task of finding a right way of doing the job so she could be with her boys.

Suddenly she had felt a need to lose herself in the touch and smell of creation.

There was a painting that she was working on. A storm of colour pouring out of a gaping mouth, but now, in this moment, it disturbed her and she couldn't work on it.

So she had come into the garden.

To find what?

Nothingness.

Here in the turmoil of nature she was nothing. When she was gone, it would still be here, exactly as it was now. Perhaps, briefly, it would be eased into somebody else's shape but in the end it would return. It was in control.

CHAPTER NINE

Peter Brodsky, sitting at the table in the cottage kitchen, checked the time again. He had Skype open and was waiting for his son, Marcus, to call. The email asking if Peter had time to talk to him had arrived sometime during the night. He was surprised Marcus had asked for a video call. It hadn't happened in the three years since he had gone to university in the US. They hadn't spoken properly for over a year. Mostly it was just calls and texts from Marcus about practicalities, not chatty information about daily life, friends, academic success or failure, the confusion that was the loving norm for close families. His allowance hadn't come through, he needed some cash to buy course books or go on trips, or just to show he was grateful and that he was fine. But the messages were always too short, with too much that wasn't said because of the past and its hidden agendas. Peter promised himself that he would make more effort, even visit, but that hadn't happened yet.

His relationship with Marcus had really changed since the divorce from Fran, eight years ago. The marriage had been hanging on by its fingertips for years and it had been obvious that a complete break would do far less damage than the constant destructive rows that seemed to fill the rare times he and his wife were in the same place at the same time. She had blamed Peter, his work at McGill University and the travelling to meetings and conferences. He had felt that she had no interest in trying to understand his situation... but the truth was they had just stopped loving each other and, trying to divert the blame for the upset and pain it caused their son, had made it bitter. Once or twice, Marcus had become an emotional weapon in their struggle for the moral edge. That had been unforgivable. In a rare moment of agreement, they had decided that Marcus should stay with Fran at their home but could be with Peter any time that he wanted. But it hadn't happened. The visits to Peter, fifty miles away, at the lakeside summerhouse, contained to weekends or holidays; the finite time strained, with both trying too hard. Also, Peter had been out of the country more with the new job he had taken on with a Foundation in Toronto. He still taught at the university but only six times a year. Then Marcus had gone to study in Boston, where his mother had been born but left when she was ten. A broken home was not a happy place for him.

Waiting was getting difficult. Peter was apprehensive, not sure that he would be able to be what his son might want him to be for whatever he needed to talk about. He checked the time again. Four minutes late. Perhaps he had decided that it wasn't going to be worth it and wasn't going to call.

Then he almost jumped as the call tone came through, hesitated briefly then pressed accept. His video was working but the dots were still moving, trying to open the stream on Marcus. Then he appeared. He had long thick fair hair, tied in a bun on top of his head. His face was almost handsome, but coloured by a small scar across his cheek to under his right eye. It was from falling off a swing, a badly stitched cut when he was eleven. He had his mother's deep brown eyes and since the last time Peter had seen a photograph, sent to him by Fran, he had grown a hipster beard. Peter could see the frown he'd always had since he was little when he was worried or anxious and he felt a surge of love for him.

'Marcus, you look great.'

'Hi, Dad, how are you?'

'Good, and you?'

'OK, I guess.'

'What is it?'

With Marcus he was always direct, leaving no time for chat to ease the words that might be hiding the real story. Find the problem and solve it. Open the secret straight away and sort it. He taught psychology and the slow gentle manipulation, insight, and understanding that it needed. Why couldn't he ever take the same pathway now with his son?

'Debbie's going to have a baby.'

Marcus and Debbie had been together since his first year at university. They'd met at the Starbucks on the campus where both were part-time baristas. She was six years older than him and for the last two years had had a job as a paralegal at a prestigious Boston law firm, which paid her enough to support both of them and cover the rent on their apartment. Fran had told him about her during one of their tricky chats about their son and his future. She had spoken to Debbie, liked her, and thought she was good for Marcus. Peter thought she was too old and would tie him down. Fran suggested that with Peter's history on relationships, he had no right to judge her. If Marcus was happy that was all that mattered. He didn't agree but neither did he want to prolong the conversation so he'd said nothing more and she hung up on him. Not for the first time.

'Is that good?'

Marcus looked confused for a moment.

'Yes, Dad, it's great, but the timing's not so good. I'm going to leave college.'

'No!'

It was said before Peter could stop it. Marcus ignored him.

'To get a job. Debs will have to stop work in a couple of months or so. We've got enough savings for me to take my finals but the master's will have to go on hold until she goes back to work. I'll be able to do it and look after the baby then.'

'Why didn't you tell me before?'

Marcus laughed. There was no humour in it.

'Would you have been interested? And I'm telling you now.'

'That's not fair.'

'Isn't it? When have you ever put yourself out to listen to me?'

For a moment he held Peter's look then glanced down.

'I know it wasn't good between us after your mom and I split up and I've let things get more difficult since you went to the US, but I've made sure that you've always had enough money to keep going and some spare for a few extras too, and...'

Marcus's look of disappointment stopped him.

'It's not about money, it's about support, advice, just being there on the end of a phone, asking me how it's all going. Just doing stuff that shows you care. Oh, Jesus! This was a mistake. Goodbye, Dad, I'll let you know if it's a boy or girl and then you can decide what you want to do with us. Perhaps set up a trust fund for your grandchild. Then you won't have to see them.'

The rush of fear and guilt almost made Peter cry out. But Marcus was right. That had been the biggest problem all along. He had missed so much of his son's life. The realisation of his selfishness and guilt for not being there had made him overcompensate by giving him money and things he thought he would want. It wasn't right and he knew it, but it was easy. He had let his responsibility to a world larger than family take precedence, destroy his marriage, and leave a brittle and edgy relationship with his son.

'No, wait, Marcus, please give me a minute.'

Marcus shook his head, looked hard at Peter, then gave in.

'All right, I'm listening.'

Peter hesitated for a moment then realised Marcus wasn't going to wait for him to get his thoughts in order.

'I'm sorry. I haven't been, and still am not, the dad I should be. I haven't got any excuses. I was, am, selfish and find it hard to open up about what I feel inside and do what I know I should do. I make mistakes all the time with you. I thought if I made sure you didn't have to worry about material things it would show that I loved you. I know, now, it wasn't the way. I am so proud of who you are, Marcus. Despite me, you have become a great and able young man, caring, hard-working, and with the responsibility and determination to face...'

Marcus looked close to tears and cut Peter off.

'It's too late. It was never enough. I never wanted things.'

Peter's phone rang. For a moment he thought it might be Sara. Why? She didn't have his number. He paused then ignored it and didn't check the number ID.

'Oh, shit, Dad, don't bother.' It had only been a second's distraction, but it was too long and Marcus ended the call.

Peter tried to Skype him back but there was no answer.

It was five p.m. They had only talked for fifteen minutes.

* * *

It had been a disturbing day before the call with Marcus. He had slept badly, Sara Jenkins burned into his thoughts, bringing waves of disgust at how he had nearly lost control and responded to her body as she pressed it against him.

She had touched him deeply and it stopped him being able to close down as he normally did before going to sleep. He had half-dozed all through the darkest part of the night.

Then, as soon as it was light, he'd realised that he was not going to get to sleep. So he had tried to progress on the small landscape he had started yesterday before it had got too dark. It was a thick and brooding wood on the edges of the farmland that he had found interesting and matched the way he was feeling.

But nothing worked. It was just a mess of shape and colour and he had finally given up and gone for a long walk. When he got back he checked his mail and found the one from Marcus. It was a half an hour before the call was due.

Now, trying to put the call from Marcus into perspective and find a way to try and make it right, he opened a bottle of wine that he'd brought with him from the airport. It was a rich Rioja and when he went to drink the large glass he'd poured, realised that it was corked. He angrily poured it down the sink. Taking his mood out on something that couldn't be hurt, was a step forward at least. It wouldn't fight back either. It was a childish and pathetic reasoning and made him smile.

He wouldn't be able to go back to the painting now and, anyway, he wanted a different energy to try and deal with what he was feeling. So he wrapped himself up and went outside and walking quickly to the edges of the small wood, paused for a moment then carried on into the trees. It was only half an acre of woodland that led to a small range of hills and he was soon free of the trees and moving quickly up the first gentle slope.

Twenty minutes and two hills later he stopped. He was not as fit as he would have liked and breathing heavily, but it felt good, the physical exertion driving out his guilt over Marcus. He looked around at the scattered buildings, their lights beginning to twinkle in the dusk.

In the distance was one large shape creeping into the darkness. He strained his eyes towards it and saw Sara

Jenkins' barn. The wild and straggled overgrowth seemed to fit it perfectly, protecting and threatening it at the same time.

Suddenly he saw something moving there, and then it was gone. It slipped into the dark shadows near the wall. It might have been a distortion of the light but it might not. There was a sudden flash of concern for her. It was as though he cared for this tragic woman that he had met only a couple of times but had held naked against him. She knew what he had felt and wanted at that moment but it didn't touch her.

He decided that he would check it out. If it was her, he would apologise and leave, but if it wasn't, then she wouldn't be alone. He started running towards the barn.

He hadn't moved this fast for years, and just as he thought he was doing all right, he slipped and went crashing to the ground. For a moment he lay there and thoughts flashed in and out. Was he being stupid? Did he imagine whatever it was he thought he saw? What would he do if he found someone there? Would she want to be saved? Fuck it. There didn't have to be a logical reason. It was instinct. He got up and started running again. It was getting closer now and he slowed so that neither the noise of him crashing around or his breathing would be heard.

He felt a sharp sting as he caught his face on something as he pushed through the high broken hedging but ignored it and stopped, listening. He could hear something. It sounded like laughter that stopped quickly at a hiss. Shit, there could be two of them. He paused for a moment and looked around for a weapon.

There was nothing but an old rusty bucket. It would have to do. Slowly, carefully now, he moved towards the sound coming from around the side of the building. There were no lights on and it had got really dark. He glanced at his watch. It was three quarters of an hour since he had left the house.

He edged around the side of the building.

'If she's pissed, she might let you fuck her or give you a blow job.'

The voice was young and as he turned the corner he saw two boys who were probably twelve or thirteen.

He slammed the bucket hard against the stone side of the barn and the two boys jumped, screamed, and ran.

Peter leaned back against the wall and laughed. Shit, he was relieved.

He could leave, go now, there was no reason to stay. He had checked it out and it was just a couple of local kids living out a fantasy, and he'd scared them off. But she was still vulnerable and on her own. He might as well check if she was all right. If she didn't answer he wouldn't go in. What if something had happened? What if his visit had been the final straw? His erection pushed against her the final insult. Would that have driven her over the edge? Enough to kill herself? He realized he couldn't go away without making sure that nothing had happened to her.

He stood for a moment, still, listening to the night, the shadows changing as the clouds moved and shut out the pale light of the moon. The garden was scary like this and he imagined himself at twelve years old, creeping in, braving the dark with its hidden dangers, to experience the thrill of anticipation of a first sexual opportunity. He also knew that if it had been him at twelve years old and someone like Sara had appeared naked and offered herself, he would have run a mile. What would those boys have done if he hadn't arrived? Would they have gone further and assaulted her? It was a different world now to the one he grew up in, and kids less easy to control.

He looked towards the first floor of the barn.

Had she heard the noise of the bucket slamming against the wall and the scream? Would it have bothered her? Was she so drunk that it became part of her own cacophony?

He walked towards the door, praying that this time it would be locked and the decision would be made. He could just leave quietly and she would never know he'd been there.

But the door was open; not wide, just as though it hadn't been shut properly.

Shit, shit!

He would have to go in. Was there any point in calling her name? If she hadn't reacted to the bucket and screams, she wouldn't hear him. But he couldn't just walk into the house. Could he? Did he want to? Not if it was going to be a repeat of the last time. But there was no keening. No sound at all. No lights seeping through the door from the hallway.

Slowly he pushed the heavy door wide open and looked around. What if something had happened to her? He had to go in.

Jesus!

'Mrs Jenkins?'

Nothing, he tried again, his voice louder. Where the hell was she? The door was closing. He ignored it, moved across the tiled floor trying to adjust to the blackness, darker and denser than outside where the clouds had thinned again and let through a wash of lightness. What if she was sitting there naked? Waiting? Then he remembered the heavy doorknocker he'd used the first time he came. He'd slam that hard. She'd be bound to hear that in the stillness.

He turned and she was standing there, holding a cricket bat.

'Jesus Christ!' His heart almost stopped and he fought to keep his legs from giving way. 'Will you stop doing that?'

She almost smiled. 'I saw you scare those two little bastards away. They were lucky it was you. I was going to beat the shit out of them. Usually I'm too out of it to care but tonight I wasn't. Why did you come here?'

His breath was short but he tried to sound calm and hoped his heart was not as loud as it sounded to him.

'I was out walking, took a different route through the woods behind the farm, climbed a couple of hills and must have gone further than I thought. I stopped to get my bearings, watched the lights come on, realized I was lost, then recognized your garden and saw something move. So I thought I'd check it out. Where were you?'

She watched him. It was a long moment, uncomfortable, awkward.

'Watching.'

He was relieved. He could go now. She was fully clothed, dressed in the duffle coat and obviously more a threat than in danger. But there was something that stopped him and he held her look.

Suddenly she pushed past him and disappeared into the house.

What the fuck did he do now? He stood in the hallway, seeing the bike, boots, and toys, a shadow of the past.

This woman, this house even, had unsettled, disturbed, and unbalanced him. He had, in the past, felt threatened, uncomfortable, even scared at times, at the ache of a human spirit but this was different. The cause was understandable but the palpable agony was something he couldn't touch and that shook him deeply.

'Jesus.' He looked around.

She had disappeared. The house was still and unwelcoming.

He decided it was a mistake to stay but, as he turned, Sara was in a doorway he hadn't seen, a huge church candle flickering across her face.

For a moment she held his look then turned and walked away.

She moved into the darkness, the light flickering in front of her.

Perhaps it would be safe. At least she had clothes on. And didn't seem too pissed. As long as he could keep away from her it would be fine.

He followed her along a narrow hallway that opened out into a large and cluttered kitchen lit by candles. There was an old Aga with flames that glowed behind dirty glass but didn't seem to throw out much heat, a large wooden table filled with paper and paints, and, like all the other rooms he had seen, there were canvases piled on the floor and leaning against the walls. Near a door that probably led into the garden was an untidy pile of logs.

There were two sinks, one covered in paint, the other spotless; the only thing in the kitchen that was. There was an easel with a canvas. A black background with a starkly white child's head held in a woman's hands, its mouth open, blood trickling over the fingers. The eyes were shocking, alive, accusing but edged with love.

It was painful but drew him in.

'Wine is all I've got.'

He pulled himself away and watched as she unscrewed the cap on the bottle.

'That works for me.'

She rinsed a glass out in the sink and then filled it and gave it to him.

'Thanks.' She filled another glass then sat on the edge of the sink and just touched him with a look, her eyes flat and empty. Peter was uncomfortable. 'Those kids make a habit of this then?'

Her eyes went cold. 'I can handle it.'

He held her look for a minute.

'I guess you can at that.' He had some wine then glanced at the easel. 'That's a powerful piece. Do you mind showing me some more of your work?'

'Why?'

'I'm interested.'

'No.'

'OK.'

She turned away. He put his glass down.

'You want me to go?'

Now there was a deep hurt in her eyes and they started to fill with tears. She came towards him.

'Hold me.' Her voice was again brittle, broken. 'Please.'

Only for a moment did he hesitate then held her. She pulled him tightly to her but this time it was innocent. 'Thank you.'

Peter smiled. 'They were only kids.'

He felt her move closer.

'You didn't know that.'

'No.' He laughed.

She pulled away slightly and looked up at him.

'Why did you come here?'

'You were on your own. I wanted to be sure that you were all right. Are you?'

She laughed. 'No. I'm a drunk.' She pulled his head towards her and kissed him gently on the lips.

'No...' He tried to pull away but she held him and kissed him again and he felt her tongue and gave in to it.

She was naked under the coat and as he gently sucked on her nipple she moaned and put her hand against him and rubbed his hardness then undid his trousers and took him into his mouth. He moved her away from him and pulled her down on to the floor, on top of him. It was unstoppable for both of them, fast, hard, uncaring, and as he exploded violently inside her she came too, twisting her face away from him.

For a moment he couldn't move as his heart pounded and he floated in a strange half world where all sense of time and place was confused and unreal. Then a great tiredness seeped over him and he closed his eyes.

He didn't know how long it was before he became aware of her lying on top of him. She was totally still. He couldn't feel her breathing. Oh, Jesus, she'd died.

He felt her neck for a pulse.

'What are you doing?' Her voice was quiet.

'Are you all right?'

She looked at him. 'Are you?'

'Not really.'

She hesitated 'Will you stay with me tonight?'

'Yes.' There was no hesitation.

She got up quickly, grabbed the coat and wrapped it around her, then went out of the kitchen.

Peter didn't move as he slowly came back to consciousness and the realisation of what had happened washed over him. Jesus, what had he done? He was half naked and going numb on the cold hard slate tiles. He pulled up his pants and stood up. He wasn't sure he could walk. He hadn't had sex like that ever. It was brutal, without love. He had never done anything like that before. He felt ashamed. A classy move, taking advantage of a woman who was, at the least, disturbed, for a five-minute fuck on the kitchen floor. It was the last thing that should have happened. He had wanted to protect her. Oh, shit! What was he going to do now? He wanted to get out of there but he couldn't just leave, could he?

He poured some more wine and looked out at the darkness in the garden. Could he?

He shivered, Jesus, it should be warmer with that old stove.

He opened the Aga and threw in some logs. The plates on the top insulated under the covers were too hot to touch, as was a small oven. He closed the covers and the door and with the logs now burning started to feel some heat.

Sara was sitting on the floor up against the wall in Ben's room trying to understand what had just happened. She had suddenly needed to feel something that was not just a hopeless and desperate longing for time to go back. Why now? Was it because this man had cared in some way? Had not been driven away? She felt his strength and that a shadow of what consumed her was in him too. She had felt it that first time when he had broken away. As though in some way he understood the emptiness that filled her. Yet, now, something had changed in him. His desperation had matched hers. After, for a moment, there was warmth and she felt a need for him.

She heard the sound of the stairs and then he was at the door. He looked at her for a long moment and then smiled. 'Mind if I use what I can find to get us something to eat?'

'Why?'

'Because you asked me to stay and I'm hungry and don't want to play sex and run and I think you need a friend…' He stopped and smiled again. 'Will that do for now?'

He went out of the room.

Sara was confused at how she felt but knew that a small part of her had opened up. She was calmer. The sex had helped the physical, but it was her spirit that had let in a splinter of light. She wanted some peace of mind and body. Perhaps this day she would start to find a way that was not so painful. Why did this happen so quickly after one moment of giving in? Was she waiting for this last chance to find out if she had any more life in her? She tried to stop the thoughts bouncing around but it was too hard. Suddenly she tuned in to sounds from downstairs, a clatter of cooking and music. Normality.

For a moment she wanted to scream, drive out this shadow of a stranger that had entered her chaotic world and unbalanced it.

But not this time, this time she wanted to face it and not run away. Tomorrow she might but now, in this moment, she wanted it.

She got up quickly, took off the coat, went into the bathroom and stood under the shower.

* * *

Peter had found tins of chickpeas, dried tomatoes, red onions in peppered oil, various herbs and spices, risotto rice, olive oil, and other dried bits and pieces and thrown it all into a large frying pan. There seemed to be little fresh food, except for a couple of eggs, but there were a fair amount of things in one side of the freezer, fish, chicken, and what looked like homemade bread. It was difficult to see what else was there as the ice in the rest of it was thick and lumpy. He found some foil and put the bread in the oven. He was going to use the fish but decided in the end not to risk it. He suddenly realized he was having fun, which felt bizarre given the circumstances. It had been a while since he had been creative with cooking but when it was not just for him and he had the will, he could do it well enough. He had cleared a space on the table, washed a couple of plates from the back of a cupboard, and searched drawers until he came up with forks and discovered a box of wine.

When Sara came into the kitchen half an hour later everything was almost ready. The bread was hot and wrapped in the foil on the table. The large candle threw shadows around the canvas faces and cluttered kitchen, and the smaller candles he had used to see as he prepared the food were burned down and starting to flicker.

Sara was in jeans and a thick oversized jumper, and although she looked fragile and less tight he felt that mayhem could still be just a slip away. She replaced the candles with new ones and watched as he tasted the food. 'What is it?'

'Wait and see… sit down'. He expected argument but she sat without response. 'I found some bread in the freezer.'

Giving the food a last stir he heard her cry out and looked round.

She had torn away the foil and was touching the bread, tears rolling down her cheeks. It was not like the other times he had seen her cry. This was sadness, not rage, and bearable to both of them. He knelt by the side of her but stopped his instinctive move to touch her. She wouldn't want that. And, if he was honest, he was a little afraid she'd go for him with the fork. But she was more transfixed than threatening.

'What is it'?

'Ceri made the bread.' Her voice sounded like it came from another mouth, soft, caring, and not of the world in which she now lived.

'Ceri.' He repeated it without thinking and thought that it could have been made just before he was killed. Homemade bread, even stored in the freezer, never resisted temptation long. A couple of days at the most before it was heated up and gone. Jesus Christ. Why did these meaningless thoughts ricochet at the wrong moment?

'Ben loved it. We always had to stop him eating too much.'

'I'm sorry, I didn't think.' He went to move it but she stopped him.

'No! It's all right.' She removed the rest of the foil, broke off a piece, and gave him half. He took a bite then stopped.

'Not good?' She tried it. He was right. It tasted stale.

'OK, worth a try.' He wrapped the bread up in the foil and dropped it in the box he had found to put the empty tins in, then brought the pan of food over and placed it on the board and spooned it onto the plates. It smelled good.

'Eat.'

He expected her to react but not in the way she did, like an obedient child.

Peter couldn't take in the change in her. Perhaps this was a moment of calm before chaos.

'OK?'

He watched her closely as she tried the food. He needed her approval before he started on his own.

'Yes, it's really nice.'

The music stopped. She looked around, aware that something had changed but not what it was.

He started to get up.

'No… leave it.'

He relaxed and carried on eating. He was pleased with it. It was really good.

She finished before him, emptied her wine and poured more. Then she looked at him for a long moment.

'I don't cook any more. My boys wouldn't believe it. We all helped, made things up. We were a good team. Didn't use recipes much.' She smiled briefly. 'I did a courgette roulade from one once. It was beautiful to look at, just like the picture, but it tasted as though something had rotted inside it. Mum's icky, Ben called it. It was all free-fall food after that.'

She looked away. 'I don't understand what I feel now.'

She knew she had less turmoil, less pain from the scrapes in her heart. Was the physical release after all this time enough to do that? It felt as though for a moment the rage had gone and although she was still raw and hurting, now, at this moment she could bear it. And this man who had seen her cracked and screaming and had come to make sure she was all right, wasn't afraid and, for once, she didn't want to be alone, not tonight, not now. She felt there was something in him that would understand and not hurt her. And she needed for the first time to be held. Would it be safe to trust him? He was watching her.

'Do you want me to go?'

He poured himself more wine, filled her glass, and put the plates in the sink.

'Do you want to?'

'No.' He sat down again. 'Look, I can't begin to understand what is going on inside you and how you got through until now. I don't even know the details, just what the guy in the shop told me. I can be here if you want me to be… or not, but I have nothing clever to say, no tricks, no advice except that, as I said, I think you could do with a friend.' He moved his chair nearer but not too close. 'It seems to me that what happened earlier was a shock to both of us but I think it was OK too. It disturbed me at first but then I understood. We both took what we wanted, needed. I don't know why but perhaps being in the right place at the right time happens now and again. I've been here twice and each time I didn't know if you would have killed yourself when I found you. I know you wanted to… or thought you did. But I had to find out.'

There was a noise outside and he glanced towards the window. It was the wind rattling something hanging near the glass.

'How about we see what happens?'

Her eyes had closed and she was asleep.

He quietly moved around, putting the leftover food in the fridge and the glasses on the sink. She had started to snore.

He lifted her out of the chair and carried her upstairs and into the bedroom. He laid her gently on the bed and covered her with the duvet that was on the floor. He lay down by the side of her.

Sometime during the night she had woken him up and he had taken off his clothes and got into bed with her and for a moment had just held her... Then they kissed.

CHAPTER TEN

Peter woke up not knowing where he was. Slowly his head cleared and it started to make sense. It was grey outside, the rain beating on the glass. In here it was cold, freezing. He was on his own in the king-size bed. He pulled the duvet over him and looked around. The window side of the large room was not too cluttered and allowed a clear path to the door, but the rest was a ragged mass of things in piles and on hangers, canvases, overflowing boxes, and stacks of books and CDs that were covered in clothes. It was a feral place, somewhere to hide away from the world.

He thought about what had happened in the night. It had been less frantic the second time, more an act of comfort than the desperation and intensity of the first. Finally with Sara wrapped inside his arms they had fallen asleep, but he had woken in a panic when she had screamed for Ben. It was a cry of longing. He wasn't sure whether she had woken but he had held her until she had calmed and was breathing deeply. It had been a long time before he followed her into sleep.

He looked at his watch. It was nearly one p.m.

Where was Sara? He was exhausted but dragged himself up, scrabbled around the floor until he found his pants by the side of the bed and went out.

He showered, drying himself with the damp towel he found on the radiator. The bathroom was large and looked like it was moulded to suit the family that was once alive here. It was a spacious room with a large bathtub and separate shower. Near the toilet was a child seat and in a corner there was a pile of rubber toys. It was a cold and practical room now but he could almost hear the happy wisps of laughter at bath time.

He found Sara downstairs. Watched her from the doorway of the large room, greyness seeping through the huge windows with a single shaft of sunlight adding hope to the day. Sara had placed the easel so she had the best of it. She was dressed in a paint-spattered outsize denim shirt and was barefoot. She looked up at him and smiled then went back to the canvas.

'Can I see?' He moved towards her.

'No…' She swirled the brush in water in a chipped and paint-covered mug with 'Daddy's' on the side, wiped the brush on her shirt, and came over to him. 'It's the first time since Ceri. It was good that it was you.'

He didn't know what he had expected her to say but it wasn't that. Now, whatever words he used wouldn't mean anything. He knew that something had happened between them that neither had thought about and there was now a slight touch between them. He put his arms around her and she cuddled close for a moment then pulled away. 'I need to carry on.'

'I'll go, then.' He hesitated, not sure how to play it. 'Do you want to meet up later… or you could come over to me for a meal… you know where I am?'

She didn't seem to have heard him. He was nearly out of the room when a wet rag hit him on the head.

Surprised, he turned round. Sara smiled. 'Let's leave it until tomorrow night but come here. I'll see if I can remember how to throw a curry together.'

He chucked the rag back and she caught it.

'I'll come about eight?'

Sara smiled at him again then went back to the canvas.

As he walked back across the fields, Peter felt dizzy and stood waiting for it to pass. Too much of everything except sleep. His head cleared and he stood in the sunshine looking back at the barn. He started to think about Sara's body and the way it felt when he was inside her.

His mobile buzzed with an incoming text. He checked it and started walking quickly towards the trees on the hill that led to his cottage.

* * *

The light was going by the time Sara moved away from the canvas and studied the outline of the figures. There were two, hard-edged but without form, sexless, facing away from each other, and one, smaller, childlike, innocent, whose shadow touched the nearer of the other two. Even at this early stage it was a powerful image. Sara's face was wet with tears. There was no sound, no movement, just a heart leaking into an empty space. She knew this would happen again.

In the night she had woken in Peter's arms, their feet entwined, their faces close together. It was how she always slept with Ceri, like one body with two hearts.

Peter was watching her and as she tried to move he had kissed her and then they had made love, gently and slowly, and afterwards she had felt like she was floating, the weight that had held her down for so long was, for that moment in time, lifted. For now, she was in a safe place. She had slept then and when she had slipped out of bed without waking him had felt a need to paint with an energy that was positive and optimistic.

Now, hours after he had gone, she was alone in the house and the comfort of closeness and the spell of the creative leaked away.

The demons began to surface. How could she have betrayed her boys?

It was sudden and sharp and took her breath away but then her mind spun again and there was a new reality growing that shocked her. She was in a world that was still here, and now in this newly opened present there was no Ceri or Ben. Not gone, just out of time. Last night had begun the slow burn of healing, let in a light that she thought lost. The pain now was a different thing. It still consumed her but she knew it would not destroy her. It still tore at her soul but did not crush her as it had.

Suddenly there was a harsh jolt of memory. It hadn't been the first time since Ceri. Once before, she had tried to break the spell of grief with sex. She was helplessly drunk and had offered herself to a young man who had spent a week mending the roof of the barn. He had been surprised but happy at the rambling offer to fuck the weird widow. But she had frozen just as he pushed into her and he had only just managed to pull out, painfully… and leave her there on her own. Sara knew what was happening but couldn't speak or move. Her muscles had cramped and frozen. For a moment after he had gone, she thought she would die but slowly her body relaxed and she'd had no other effects except that she was sober. It would have been a relief to just slip away then and not have to face life again but she still existed, brittle, broken, alive.

That had been six months ago. She wouldn't let it happen again. But it had last night and this time she had wanted it and it had unlocked her, not shut her down.

Now, looking at the canvas, her tears stopped and an image flashed into her mind.

She was about seven years old and her family was moving from the only home she had known into a rented house the other side of the country. Everything was in storage except for the load they had packed into the old Volvo estate. It was time to leave and she had finally caught Frankie, her cat, after chasing her round the house for ages, and was trying to put the struggling animal into a basket. Suddenly Frankie's legs locked and she rolled onto her side, baring her teeth and was completely still. Sara had screamed to Daddy that she was dead. He had said to pick her up and hold her. She wasn't dead, probably just in shock. Frankie knew something was happening and she wanted none of it and had shut down. Of course Sara didn't really understand what it meant but had done what her dad said, and slowly the cat had relaxed. By the time they started the long journey Frankie was happily asleep on a roof-high pile of bedding next to Sara. She had reacted with the roofer in the same way, her mind shutting down the

83

body to stop what it was doing. It had worked except there was no one to cuddle her and make it all right for her to come back.

It was almost dark now and she thought about getting a drink but felt exhausted and lay down on the sofa thinking she would get something to eat soon. She couldn't remember wanting food before, she just ate sometimes to soak up the alcohol, but now she wanted poached eggs on toast. In the middle of working out whether she'd seen eggs in the kitchen she fell asleep.

She woke up freezing. It was still dark and the wind was rattling the shutters on the upstairs windows. They were never shut now and the ones outside her bedroom had one side hanging off and probably wouldn't last much longer. She had pulled a throw over her and she curled up, not wanting to make the dash upstairs. There was a sudden smack of rain against the windows and a distant rumble of thunder followed by a jagged slash of light in the darkness beyond the garden. Sara counted to six before the thunder came again – six miles. This time there was a huge crack that split the sky, hurling a flashlight beam into the room as the rain powered into a torrent. She had always loved storms and sometimes, before Ben was born, she and Ceri would sit, wrapped in a tarpaulin, as the maelstrom raged around them. They were scared at times but told each other that together they could endure anything nature could throw at them. They could and did, until it had enlisted fate and beaten them.

Sara felt the sense of peace that had touched her fading, and despair started, filled its space. She fought the panic knowing that, as always, she would be defeated if she gave in to it. It was easier to sink in the comfort of a cruel truth than try and find a way through the guilt.

But this time, as if a change had already begun, it would be different. Instead of lying there, the emptiness inside her filled with an ice-cold reality. She knew that she would, at least, try to begin a journey to a space where she might be able to lessen the self-pity and shame. The suddenness of the thought gave her a small hope. This man Peter had unlocked something in her that would, perhaps, help her find a way to live. Or at least exist until it was time for her to join her boys.

She knew Ceri would have been relieved that she had found some comfort at last. He would have been frustrated with her taking so long to start to fight, letting herself sink into the mess she had become. He had been so proud of her strength and how she wouldn't give in when she believed she was in the right or something had threatened their world. What he didn't know was that she could only be that person with him in her life. He gave her the love, strength, determination, and courage that she had lacked before she met him. He had made her believe in herself as an artist, gave her the space and belief to throw it out to the world. Taught her that failure was a signpost to success. He was her axis and without him her world rocked and fell.

Then she heard his voice so strongly she struggled to breathe.

'Come on, gorgeous, you have to do it, for us as well as you. You'll never lose us, we'll always be here and nothing will change that. It's been long enough, sweetheart.'

Then as she stared into the darkness, she saw them by the window, Ben's arm around Ceri's neck, his other hand playing with his ear as he smiled at her.

'Love you, Mummy.'

She started to move but they slowly faded.

'I love you too, sweetheart.'

But it was too late, they were gone and she was alone.

Shit... what had happened there? She had never seen them before when she was awake. Would they come back? Please, please, come back! But they wouldn't. She knew that they had come for a reason and even if it was solely conjured up in her mind, to give her something to build on.

For the first time since they had died, she felt their warmth.

She remembered now that Ceri always thought poached eggs on toast made everything right; that's why it had come into her head. She got off the sofa, the throw still wrapped around her, and went into the kitchen. After a scrabble through the detritus she found the eggs and took the bread Peter had thrown away and unwrapped it. It would be OK toasted.

After eating Sara felt better and looked around the kitchen. It was a tip.

She hadn't touched it for months, only moving things if they were in her way, or if something was rotten and beginning to smell. It had never bothered her before. Now it did. Was it touching souls with Ceri and Ben? Had she really conjured them up or had they come to her from another world? It didn't matter whether they were real or not. She had felt their love and concern and knew that Ceri was right. They would never leave her. It was time to stop her descent and, perhaps, this man who had come into her life had touched her spirit enough for her to at least try.

She could begin by cleaning up the mess in here. It would be a first step.

But suddenly she felt exhausted.

It could wait until tomorrow.

* * *

The next day, she started just as it was getting light.

By the time she had finished there were ten large black bags outside the back door, the table was clear, and those canvases she had not thrown onto the fire in the garden were in her studio. Then she moved upstairs. She had been ruthless, seeing the work for what it was, keeping only that which had possibilities.

After it was done, she sat at the table in the kitchen and for the first time since the day before the boys died, she planned a meal; the curry she had told Peter she would make. She had no fresh vegetables but found some prawns buried in the ice at the bottom of the freezer, huge king-size ones that must have cost them a fortune. She had plenty of rice and there were tins of tomatoes, beans, mushrooms, and also, in the freezer, a large bag of sliced onions. With the spices and curry paste, there would be enough. At the back of a cupboard, she found a slow cooker they had bought when Ben was born to make life easier but had hardly used because they never thought of it in time. She prepared everything and threw it all in and left it to work its magic.

She spent what was left of the light on the painting in the big room. Then she put a pile of clothes into the washing machine and changed the sheets and duvet cover on her bed. That was something that she had tried to do each couple of weeks despite the drinking. If she ran out of things she would buy more and that, together with two cycles each of warm and cold weather clothes, was the sum of her normality. Then she scrubbed the bath, which hadn't been used for over a year, and ran the water deep and hot, finding some of Ben's bubbles to use. As she lowered herself in, she cried at the memory of the last bath with Ben, but it was a warm feeling and she felt he was near. Lying back, she could feel him in her arms, his laugh gurgling as he covered her face with the sweet-smelling bubbles.

CHAPTER ELEVEN

Peter walked along the road to the barn. There was something exhilarating about darkness and the fear it could generate when shadows became monsters and normal night-sounds would scream and moan. The road was deserted and once he had passed the last house at the edge of the village he was wrapped in complete darkness, the heavy clouds shutting out the stars.

Yesterday after he'd got back to the cottage, he was exhausted and had just wasted the rest of the day, then was asleep by ten but was woken in the early morning by a call from his boss in Canada that lasted for over two hours. Afterwards he had found it hard to get back to sleep and had lain there thinking about Sara. Around six a.m. he had drifted into a deep and troubled sleep and felt shattered again when he eventually came round about eleven. He had gone to the pub for lunch, picked up some wine and expensive chocolate and ginger biscuits from the deli, did a couple of hours on a paper he was writing on the research he had completed just before he left for his sabbatical, sent a long email to Marcus, and then left with enough time to get to Sara's by eight.

They were sitting at the table, opposite each other, the plates from the meal piled into the sink, and they had started on the second bottle of wine. The curry wasn't the best she'd ever made but not the worst either, and Sara was surprised that he'd had seconds. So had she.

They had talked about Canada and the university in which Peter taught and what he knew about his descendent and where he had lived. Words and stories that were safe and easy. When Sara went to the bathroom, Peter realised that he had done all the talking and that Sara had hardly spoken, just a nudge now and again. He was impressed because that was normally how he liked to play it, but she knew the black art of listening too. When she came back, she poured them more wine and sat down. Peter smiled at her then touched her hand.

'Sorry, I haven't stopped talking about me and you must be bored shitless by now.'

She laughed and moved her hand. 'No.' He thought she was going to say more but she didn't.

He looked at her for a long minute. She held his gaze.

'Can I see the painting you were working on?'

She moved towards him and kissed him. He was so surprised he almost jerked away. For a second there was a flicker of something in her eyes and then she kissed him again, and this time he responded. It was a long kiss, her hands around his face. Then she stood, pulled him up, and led him out of the room.

* * *

Sara was lying in Peter's arms, her head on his chest. She could hear his heartbeat. His eyes were closed.

'I don't know how to say this.' She tapped his chest with her finger.

He opened his eyes and turned to face her. He didn't speak, just touched her hair, moving it away from her face, his eyes holding hers.

'Let me finish before you say anything.'

She breathed deeply, let the air out slowly then smiled.

'I saw Ceri and Ben. They were in the room where I'm painting. I was sleeping on the sofa and the storm woke me up. It's never happened before except in my dreams but this time I was wide awake. They felt real and it was so good to see them.' Tears filled her eyes. 'I never thought I would again. I was feeling hungry, trying to remember if there were any eggs. Ceri's comfort food. Eggs on toast. Suddenly they were there, by the window. Ceri said I had to do it for them too and that it was time… He was saying that I had lived with this enough.' She smiled, 'I think he was telling me to stop being a slut too and clean the house. He hated it when it got too messy. Ben was playing with his ear. He said he loved me and then I wanted to hold them but they disappeared. I asked them to stay but knew they couldn't, except inside me. I hope they come again but I will always remember this time. I don't know if I will be able to make it but I know I have to try and I know that somehow they thought it was okay with you, and this is going to make you think I've really lost it, that they brought you to me.'

She looked for a reaction but he just smiled.

'Say something, even if it's "I'm going to have you sectioned as soon as I escape".'

Peter laughed. 'Later.'

Sara waited.

'Is that all?'

Peter smiled. 'I'm not sure how I found you. I would like to think it's coincidence but I believe that sometimes, to make that first step, we have to really know if we want to make the journey. Whether Ceri and Ben were really there is not important, but that you made a choice is. Us meeting like this could have made it harder but I think it helped. I am not a threat to you. I met someone who had a deep pain but that isn't why I stayed around. If you remember, you gave me a little insight into your emotional state the first time I came here and still I came back. We both needed to trust and somehow it happened. And, more to the point, I haven't felt this sexed-up since I was sixteen.'

Sara rolled him over and straddled him.

* * *

The next day Peter helped Sara to make a move on the rest of the house but by lunchtime they had both had enough.

Sara wanted to paint and Peter went back to meet the guy he had rented the cottage from, who needed to look at the boiler which had been playing up.

Before he left Peter watched her from the door, totally absorbed in what she was doing.

'Sure you want me to come back later?'

She stopped and turned around. 'Do you want to?'

He looked at her for a moment then smiled. 'Of course.'

'Yes, then.'

Peter felt uncomfortable. What the hell was wrong with him? Cross with himself he hurried out of the house.

Sara waited until she heard the front door shut, then stood back from the easel and studied what she had done.

Not good yet but getting there.

There was a sense of life in the figures and the hard lines she had started with had softened and given them a sense of movement and depth.

She heard the splatter of rain on the glass in the windows and looked out. It had clouded over as the wind had strengthened and the light was no longer good enough to work.

She watched the clouds darken. The rain became torrential. Shit, this was supposed to be spring.

She looked back at the figures and moved closer to the easel.

It was making sense again. The desperation that she had felt when she dragged images on to the canvas, that eviscerated her with their brutal and jagged truth, was gone. It was no longer an extension of the rage burning her. An instinctive connection to her work had found its way back and, since that first morning after Peter had stayed, she was able to see more clearly. Even in the short days since the last time she had been out of control, she had discovered a part of her that she thought she'd lost; a sense of who she was. It wasn't complete but she now had a shadow of direction. So much had changed so quickly in her. She felt she could now move slowly forward on her terms. Whatever had happened with Peter was not something to analyse. She wasn't going to fight against it but use it to build her strength. It was enough that it had happened and opened her mind to allow her boys in again, whole and unmarked, and they had, in their presence, given her the means to start to heal. She knew that she had one searing question but she needed to come from a place of calm to find the answer. She just wanted to know why it had happened. If it was a mistake, being in the wrong place at the wrong time, what had driven that man to hold her Ben in front of him? What sort of man was he? Did he have a family? His reality would help hers.

Suddenly she felt as if the breath had been driven out of her. She breathed deeply and waited until her heartbeat slowed. She had to control it now that she had started the journey. She had to think things through and find a way to handle this.

The shock to her was that she thought she could.

Sara had always had great drive and acted on her instinct without doubt. She felt that she could begin to harness that again. It would take time but she wouldn't let herself be distracted by her familiar and safe self-pity and guilt. It would slip in when she was weak but she wouldn't let it take hold any more.

Perhaps Peter would be able to help. It was unfair to put this load on someone she had only just met but she had a deep feeling that she could talk to him about anything and that he would not judge her. Was that why he was here? To support her? Why should he? Did he want to be used? But perhaps by using him she was in some way helping his journey too? There was a depth to him and a need. It was why it had happened between them.

She went into the kitchen, put the kettle on, and

smiled at the normality of making a cup of tea and a feeling of ease that she hadn't had since the nightmare started. It surprised her. Still, she knew there would always be a mist of loss that wrapped her spirit and squeezed her heart even though she would find a way to ride on the back of this new life. She owed it to her boys. She had a flash of concern that she did not feel guilty about sex with Peter. No sense of betrayal to her other life; a parallel life that would always now live alongside with its memories and sadness at what might have been. She forced herself to stop the spinning thoughts. They were too real now that she had opened her mind again to an outside world.

CHAPTER TWELVE

Over the next weeks Peter gradually stopped going back to the rented cottage and they had talked, eaten, drank, and made love… then talked again. He had an easy way with words and a sense of the ridiculous, and his warmth was magnetic. Their words were like a waterfall. A sharing of the history of why they were here now in this time and place. Their different worlds wound around them and Sara found herself laughing at the miserable comedy of his marriage and sharing moments of Ceri and Ben that brought laughter quickly followed by the tears of guilt and loss. But it was good to talk about them and Peter gave her a secure space to do it. He had an understanding of the depths in which she struggled to find a truth that would give her comfort and safety. And she understood his pain at separation from his son, although estrangement, unlike loss, had less chance of closure.

His life in academia was a rich source for his self-deprecating stories. And from his hedonistic adventures with his cohort of academics in the continuum of international keynotes and conferences, she knew that marriage to him then would not have been simple.

They were both amused in the way that their sense of normality with each other grew, and the comfort and naturalness, when they shared their bodies.

Sara felt as though for the first time since the killings she was able to open her heart to someone else about the feral animal she had become and the rage that made her bleed with the need for revenge; to destroy that which had mutilated her existence.

There was not always agreement between them. The way they seemed comfortable with argument and strong emotions led to an understanding and acceptance of the difference and strength of their opinions. Making their opposing thoughts engage created a balance and focus that suggested a positive direction for Sara: the possibility of a normal life, different from her old one, but one that could be just as real and fulfilling.

Sara was no longer hesitant about her beliefs and was regaining some of the confidence and authority that had dissipated with her grief.

They argued about the right of retribution over reconciliation. Whether the destruction of that which had destroyed you would bring peace or yet more pain. Certainly killing the killer would not bring back those who were the victims. Did the biblical excuse, 'an eye for an eye', make it moral and right to take a life, however evil you felt it to be?

One time, while waiting for the kettle to boil, Peter was looking out of the kitchen window into the overgrown garden. The tangle of nature felt fierce and untamed but although it could be reshaped with care and attention, at its heart it remained unpredictable, and without control would revert back to its raw state. It was the same with grief, despondency, and psychological healing. The kettle switched itself off and Peter poured the water over the tea bags. Sara, sitting at the table, was drawing on a large sketchpad.

'If I had the chance to kill the killer, would I be able to do it?'

He held her look.

'If you mean, emotionally and not morally, right or wrong not being a part of the equation, then yes, I think you would. But the harder question is, why would you do it?'

'Why should they have a life when I don't.' She glanced at Peter. 'I know it won't change anything.'

Peter sat at the table and looked at the sketch. It was of him, asleep, his form abstract, but his essence was there. He smiled at her.

'Would it stop you blaming yourself?'

'No.'

'That was quick.'

'Easy question.'

'Was it?'

'You don't think so?'

'On the surface, yes, but, if you still carried the blame despite you having no responsibility for what happened, then what good would it do? Ultimately the only way to make that work would be to kill yourself and that would defeat the objective.'

'That's too clever for me.'

'No, it's not. Think about it? Do you blame Ceri or Ben or the Italian for being there, or you, for not being there?'

'No, but I blame the Italian for Ben. Did he think the risk of killing a child would stop the gunman?' Instantly she had to push back tears. Peter waited as she closed her eyes.

'You want me to stop?'

Sara looked at him for a long moment.

'I don't know.'

'We could save it for another time?'

Sara thought about it.

'No. It wouldn't get any easier.' She paused. 'I think I need to understand the difference between what is real and what I am making real.'

'What happened is real, you feeling responsible for it, is not. It's good to pin the blame but if it's not where it is deserved, then that resolve is false and won't give you the answer.

'So what do I do?'

'Don't scatter the responsibility for what happened. Find where it should lie, not where it might be easiest to place, and then work out what to do.'

'Kill them.' She almost laughed then touched Peter's hand. 'Can we stop for now?'

'Sure. Let's go for a walk.' He stood up.

She came over and put her arms around him.

'Thank you for listening.'

'There'll be a payback.'

'Will there?'

'After the walk.'

'Why not before?'

'Now, that's a thought.'

He put his arms around her and pulled her up to him.

* * *

They talked more every day, opening and closing doors, throwing random possibilities around, but always came back to the same main points, blame and retribution. At first Peter argued for and Sara against, then he accepted that would only lead into a deeper and darker void especially if she, the victim, became the perpetrator. The breaker was always not who or how but why it happened? If that was answered then reason could find a way out of the vacuum and into a different life. It would never be the same again once you had accepted that you might be able to move forward.

Another time she talked through the day it happened and he held her as the strength seeped from her. He listened and waited and comforted and shared the anger at fate. She told him about Jamie, her best friend, and how she had wanted to hurt her for caring too much and had driven her away. She was the last friend to endure with her and after she had gone Sara was completely alone. It was… what she'd wanted.

Even the calls with her dad had stopped, but both she and he knew that if the time ever came and there was something more he was able to do then he would help her. Now she didn't need to face his perfect family. Soon perhaps it would be easier, but not yet.

Peter listened and when there was something to say he only suggested, never directed, and so she had found ways through her thoughts that gave a clarity and positive reason. It wasn't always a forward step but sometimes sideways and sometimes no steps at all. Don't waste energy on things you can't change, adapt to others and be open to the new and untried.

* * *

One night after making love, they talked about how Sara was really finding strength again but still fought and struggled with her guilt. Peter turned on his side to face her.

'What about Vittorio Rietti?'

For a moment Sara was puzzled.

'What do I feel about him now?'

'No. About why he died?'

'What do you mean?'

Peter held her hands.

'Was he, like Ceri and Ben, in the wrong place at the wrong time or, I don't know, had he done something terrible that made someone want to kill him? Was he an innocent victim or complicit in his own death?

'Why is that important?'

'It mightn't be. But it might find a reason for what happened to him.'

'And that would help me in some way?'

'It could change the perspective of what happened.'

'I don't understand.'

Peter thought for a moment.

'Say I need to find a way through an argument with someone. So that I can be objective, I have to look at both sides before finding a solution. When that happens, it might change my perspective of what I think is right and then I'd have to concede to the other person. Was the reason Rietti used Ben a belief that because he was a small child it would stop the killer? If that was true, then he must have known it was random and not a professional targeting him for anything that he'd done. So, accepting that, if the blame for what happened to Ben and Ceri is taken away from

Rietti, even though what he did was to try and protect himself, is that going to help you, or make it harder for you to start to move on?

Sara tried to shut out the emotional response to what Peter was saying and focus with some objectivity. He had helped her find a way to do that during the long hours they had talked. She made sense of it now.

'But then wouldn't I have to find whether it was his fault. And if it wasn't, wouldn't that make it harder because I would have nothing then. I would have to either give up looking for someone to blame and accept what had happened, or try and discover why Rietti was killed and who had done it. And that would be impossible for me to do without knowing about him and his life.'

Peter let that settle for a moment.

'Of course, but what I meant was that without the agitation of trying to focus all the blame on Rietti, your memories of Ceri and Ben would not be coloured by blaming him. Does that make sense?'

'I'm not sure. I need to run it through again.'

'I'll give you a bit of space and go and get us some wine.'

'That I understand.'

He leaned over, gave her an awkward hug, and went out of the bedroom.

Sara listened to his footsteps as he went along the landing and down the stairs. Then she started picking through the seams of what he had said, trying to keep the logic and sense in. He didn't take long and was soon back in the room with the wine. He filled her glass.

'Any thoughts?'

She kissed him 'Not yet. I don't have your clear sight. I still see the bits of glue that get in the way.'

He took her glass, lifted the duvet, and got into bed. 'Let's think of something else to do then.'

In the middle of that night Peter was woken by a noise. It sounded like a screech owl. Then he realised that Sara wasn't there and that the screeching was not an owl. It was Sara. He didn't look out of the window but scrambled downstairs naked. The front door was wide open and as he rushed through it he saw her standing, naked too, frozen and screaming. He wrapped his arms around her. He realised she was asleep and her body had locked. He carried her into the house. It would have looked comic as he struggled with her in front of him, stiff as a board, but at that moment he didn't see the funny side.

He got into the house, wrapped a coat around her, and spoke softly. What he said probably didn't make sense; it didn't have to, it was the humanity that would touch her, not the meaning. She stopped screaming and he felt her relax, and almost dropped her as she became a dead weight but managed to lift her again and carry her upstairs. He got into bed with her and held her tightly. He could feel warmth start to come back into her and after a while she started to snore gently. Only then did Peter react to what had happened.

He cried.

* * *

The next day he hadn't told her about the night's adventure but had persuaded her to not to paint and to go for a walk. It was one of those bitterly cold, silver sky days with slashes of sunshine that promised warmth but then disappeared.

They had walked and talked for miles but they had been quiet as they sat on the dropped trunk of an old tree and drank coffee with brandy that Peter had insisted on bringing.

Sara looked towards the trees. 'I want to go to Siena.'

'What?'

'I want to go to Siena and find his family.'

'Why?' Peter was surprised.

'I think it was because of what we talked about yesterday. It makes sense to see if I can find a reason to blame or not blame Rietti. I can't do that from here.'

She turned to face him.

'You're sure that you think it'll help?'

Sara shrugged. 'Sure. Now that's a word that's been missing from my life, but yes, I am.'

Peter came and squatted in front of her.

'Is there a point to it? What will you do if you find out? How will it help even if you find his family? Don't you think they want to know why he died too, especially if he is as innocent a victim as he seems?'

'We have a shared history. If I can find a reason, it will help.' She smiled. 'And if not, what artist wouldn't want to spend time in Siena?' She kissed him. 'I've thought it through and I am going. You got me there with all that about perspective, so don't think there's any point in trying to stop me. You should know what a stubborn cow I am by now.'

She smiled innocently and he laughed. 'Then I'll come with you, I could do...'

'No, I want to do this on my own.'

'Do you know what you are doing?'

'Yes, don't be so bloody condescending, I am really up for it and that's all down to you. You are a wonderful man and I want you to understand that you have helped me find my life again.'

She made a face, stuck her finger in her mouth, and pretended to vomit.

'Sorry, that didn't mean to sound as shit as it did.'

Peter laughed. 'I understand. Mind if I stay and look after your home? I've sort of grown out of the cottage. I can keep the locals at bay and do a few jobs around the place. If you need me to come to you just shout and if you decide not to come back for the next six months let me know and I'll move on. When will you go?'

'As soon as I can.' She pushed him over and kissed him. 'What about an al fresco fuck to celebrate?'

'In this weather?'

'Is that a no?'

'No, but if it breaks off, it's down to you.'

* * *

Peter sat in the Land Rover. A feeling of sadness swept over him then he pushed it away and took out his phone and pressed speed dial.

As he waited, he thought about the sense of loss he'd felt as they said goodbye at the small airport. It had surprised him. But Sara had a new brightness in her eyes and he was pleased for her.

She'd hugged him. 'I'll call when I get to the hotel.'

'Text me when you land?'

She'd laughed. 'I will.'

They kissed again. She'd pulled away then joined the line waiting to go through security. She'd turned and blown a kiss. He'd done the same. 'Safe travels.' He said it loudly and an old couple had smiled at him as they passed. Sara had waved again then gone through and he'd watched until she was out of sight.

As the phone number continued to ring, he held his breath and decided that if it wasn't answered by the time he had to let go then he'd hang up, his version of *Sliding Doors*.

It was picked up.

Peter held the phone away from him, let out his breath gently, then brought it close again. 'It's Dupard. Siena is on her way.'

The woman's voice was soft. 'Good. Well done, Simon. Let me know when you get there.'

'Sure.' He dropped the phone onto the passenger seat, turned on the ignition, pressed the starter, and was surprised it fired first time. Whenever he had been in it before it had always taken patience and calm before it would start. Sara had told him not to swear at it. If he did, it wouldn't move. The Land Rover was old and loved and needed care and understanding.

CHAPTER THIRTEEN

THE INTERNATIONAL INVESTIGATION FORCE is based in Toronto Canada. A joint venture funded by Europe, Canada, and the US. The budget is agreed and distributed from a private fund that doesn't appear on any government or law enforcement budget. The money comes from a variety of sources: individuals, black money confiscated from major drugs and fraud cases, and hidden government slush funds to fight serial crime, terrorism, and cyber-crime. The head of the organisation is Julien Laboule from Quebec, once head of NATO forces in Afghanistan. The IIF is called into action when serious crime is linked across different countries and the individual enforcement agencies have had little or no success in finding the perpetrators. It works mainly on high profile cases and is autonomous. IIF involvement is not officially recognised, nor made public. This is useful on two levels. Firstly, because the force can move without publicly accepted boundaries getting in the way, and secondly because blame for failure does not touch the official law enforcement bodies while success is apportioned to them. The IIF occupies the eighteenth to twentieth floors of an office block in the financial sector of Toronto. Officially it is a private foundation which works on the global monetary balance.

'Shadow' was the codename for an IIF search for a killer.

Victims had been targeted in Toronto, Paris, Madrid, and most recently London.

They were:

Toronto – a high-profile politician,

Paris – the design head of a fashion house,

Madrid – a global opera star,

London – an Italian wine grower and exporter.

What made this a case for the IIF was that, once terrorism had been taken out of the equation, there was a huge public outcry in each of the countries. Juliette Tankerry, the politician, was about to stand for leader of the governing Liberal Party and was massively popular. Charlie Foucet, the head of the fashion house, had just donated 250 million euros to provide education hubs around France focussing on the creative arts. Manuela Contrerra, the opera singer, had an international following and was due to sing at the Pope's visit to Spain the day after she was killed. Vittorio Rietti, the Italian, was the anomaly. Although he was extremely wealthy and a local celebrity in Tuscany, he hadn't the profile of the others. The only commonality was, that apart from Rietti who had inherited his business from his father, all had come from under-privileged backgrounds and had found success through hard work, tenacity and astounding ability.

The involvement of the IIF was requested by a crisis group of senior police and politicians from Canada, Spain, France, and the UK. Italy was not involved. There was a huge amount of public and political pressure to find the killer. There was unease, particularly from those who lived in the same worlds as the other victims and the rich and famous. IIF was a last resort. Its maverick and creative evaluations might just find what others had missed.

Success would also ensure the organisation's continuance, despite the increasing grumblings from the visible law enforcement hierarchy that would welcome a share of its funding were it to be closed down. But as long as it did the dirty work successfully the IIF was safe. So there was a further incentive for getting the job done quickly.

All of the killings had the same MO. A figure appearing, always among crowds of people, and disappearing before anyone but those closest realised what had taken place. The killer, almost a silhouette, used a Beretta 92FS with a silencer. Two shots were fired – one to the head and one to the heart. The only deviation was in London, where, after the first shot had gone through the little boy and the second had hit Rietti as he dropped him, an extra two shots were fired at the father as he came at the killer. Those were also head and heart shots.

There was never any positive description of the killer from those few who saw anything but the aftermath and the picture was always identical; a figure, average size, dressed in something dark, who used a gun at close range, and was hardly seen before disappearing again.

One thing everyone found puzzling was that all hits seemed professional, both in the number and placing of the shots and the speed and efficiency with which they all happened. They had been highly risky attacks, planned to a point where risk was at a minimum. Yet even in London, the assassin got clean away, which showed cool and deliberate expertise.

Yet London had broken the pattern in two ways. The other victims had been killed in their home countries. But the man who died at Paddington station was from Siena, visiting London on business, and the two others had been collateral damage. There was a great deal of supposition that it had been a copycat killing. But it was too exact, and for those who wanted the feather of success to land on them, not really a viable option.

None of the victims had seemed to have any connections or history which could have led to what happened; apart from perhaps the politician who had held very liberal views on immigration and abortion.

A huge amount of public money across the four countries had been wasted trying to find 'the Shadow,' the name a UK tabloid had hung on the killer after the London attack, and now adopted by the IIF.

Simon Dupard was running the IIF ground team on Shadow. Before he joined the IIF in 2009 as a psychological profile lead, he was a senior lecturer in Criminal Psychology at Montreal's McGill University. His book, the *Psychology of the Unstable Mind,* was into its fifteenth reprint and a classic on criminal behaviour and psychological profiling. He had advised on profiling with various crime agencies in Canada and was recommended to the IIF, who were looking to recruit. It was not an easy transition for him, entering into a world of which he had little experience, but he needed a challenge and a change of life. And he was very good at it, eventually moving into the investigation side as well as the profiling. His real name was Peter Brodsky but at the IIF, all senior field investigators and profilers had a work name, life and history. If anyone had checked on Brodsky all they would have found was that after leaving McGill, he returned six times each year as a part-time lecturer, wrote books, worked with a private Foundation and lived a quiet life at his lakeside home. He and his wife had divorced in 2012 and he had one son who lived in the US. Brodsky was currently and officially on a short sabbatical from his work at McGill.

It was Dupard who came up with Operation Siena. It had been almost twelve months since the London murders and they still had nothing. None of the victims had led lives that could suggest a reason for the killings other than the imbalance and distress caused by their loss. The killer was confident, intelligent, and ruthless. Dupard knew that if it had been an organised crime hit, they would by now, have had at least some leads from their networks around the world. That meant that this person was below the radar. Who were they working for? And why was there this seeming randomness amongst the victims?

Of all the people connected with those who died, it was only in London that there was someone outside of the close circle of the victims. Sara Jenkins, the woman whose husband and son had been killed.

She was the only one who might not have been known to the killer. Little had been in the media about her and her photograph had not appeared anywhere.

The professionals had failed. Perhaps an amateur could be the unwitting bait to draw out the killer.

It would be tricky, impossible if her mental state was irreparable, but as of now Dupard felt Sara Jenkins was the best shot they had. He had to fight hard to get the operation authorized and the amount of money involved would be tightly controlled. It had eventually come down to him laying his job on the line and taking responsibility for getting her on board. How he would do it was not part of the executive collusion. He was on his own. If it went wrong and the shit hit, then he would be the only one covered. But he relished the challenge.

He had no real plan apart from trying to get to know Sara and then see where his instinct took him. He had doubts about using her, but he was good at shutting out anything that wasn't part of the mindset needed to make a project evolve. He had tenacity and determination and his expertise was in psychological structuring and cognisance.

He left Toronto for Wales in March. The UK police had not been informed, only his direct boss knew where he was, and it was only she who would have contact with him.

Part Two

SIENA

CHAPTER FOURTEEN

Sara stayed in the Hotel Copella, a small, family-run boutique hotel she had found on the internet. Expensive because it was Siena and tourist time but she booked for a couple of days, hoping to find something cheaper once she was there.

The people were very friendly and, understanding she was on a tight budget, they suggested where she might try but warned that most places would be booked by now because of the festival of the Palio. However, one of the owner's two daughters, Maria, suggested she try Signora Valeria, the mother of her best friend, Julia.

The large house was in a small street not far from the city centre. It was a beautiful old townhouse, in the middle of a terrace and had balconies on the top two floors. There was a small park opposite. She stood for a moment letting the distant sounds of the city wash over her then rang the bell.

The signora was in her late forties, attractive and friendly.

'Signora Valeria?'

'You must be the lady Maria told me about.'

Her English was good but a heavy accent obscured some of the words.

'Yes, Sara Jenkins. Maria said you might have a room free.'

'My daughter's room. I am going to rent it out whilst she is in college. It needs a bit of a lift with new paint and some repairs before I put it on the list. It is still a nice room but the cost will be less for now.'

'That sounds just right.'

'Let me show you, then you can decide.'

'Thank you.'

Signora Valeria led the way upstairs. Sara had already decided to take the room if it was half decent. She liked the house, which was cool after the heat and had the warmth and comfort of a proper home.

The room was a large loft space that stretched the width and depth of the house. It had a shower near the bed area, a sofa and one deep armchair, a desk, and stripped and painted floorboards. There was a cello in the corner and a balcony, overlooking the small park that gave a clear view over the city roofs to the Duomo. It did need a cosmetic touch but it was fine.

'It's lovely. How much?'

'Twenty-five euros a night with breakfast and thirty if you want an evening meal.'

'Just breakfast, and that's fine.'

'When would you like to move in?'

'Now?'

Signora Valeria hesitated for a moment then smiled.

'Yes… and I insist you eat with me tonight and tell me why you are in Siena. My daughter is studying English in Florence. I need to speak more so I can help her when she comes home.'

'Thank you. That would be lovely.'

They ate in a small, elegant, minimalist dining room off her living room. The other people staying at the moment usually had food earlier in another larger room next to the kitchen but tonight Sara was Signora Valeria's private guest and had been told to call her Elena. The homemade pasta and spicy garlic and tomato sauce was a speciality of Siena and delicious. She chatted, sometimes searching for words, about her daughter and her divorce. She told Sara she was lucky to be in Siena at such a special time, although it meant that the streets were crowded and some people behaved badly. But it was all a part of the madness that was the Palio, the horse race that would take place in the Piazza del Campo and was now less than two weeks away. She talked enough that Sara didn't have to say why she was in Siena, which was a relief, although she had her story ready. At ten o'clock, Sara excused herself, saying she needed to make a call. If she was honest, she had found it exhausting concentrating on what Elena was saying, but the woman had made her feel very welcome and, after the bottle of wine they had shared, Sara felt relaxed and sleepy.

Up in her room she called Peter.

'Elena seems really nice and the room's great. And from here I can see the Duomo all lit up.'

Peter laughed.

'Sounds wonderful, wish I was there with you. You should have let me come. I know, sorry, I miss you. I've been to Rome but always wanted to see Siena.'

Sara stood on the balcony looking over the lights of the city and the large dome of the Duomo.

'Next time.'

'I can't wait.' He paused briefly. 'Everything's fine here. I've fixed a couple of the doors that didn't shut properly and had a go at the garden but gave up because I couldn't see any difference.'

'Too impatient.'

'Guess I am good at that. But it's nice being here although I miss not waking up with you.'

'Cheesy.'

'Yes, but I'm not used to this. It's been a long time since I felt this way. Tell me what you're going to do tomorrow?'

'Just explore, get to know the city a bit, look at some paintings and start to make a plan.'

'Busy day.'

Sara laughed. 'I suppose I might have to spread it over a couple of days.' She tried to stop a yawn but failed. 'Sorry, I'm exhausted.'

'I'll let you go then. Have a good day… And if you decide you want me there, just shout and I'll get on the first flight.' He hesitated for a moment. 'When you sort out a plan, talk to me before you set off. Just helps sometime to say it out loud.

'Yes, I will. Night, Peter.'

'Night, sweetheart, sleep tight.'

She threw the phone on the bed and smiled at his 'sweetheart'. It was nice and made her feel wanted.

She had spoken to Peter every night, sometimes just to say hello. They were easy and relaxed calls. But she realised she missed his closeness, irreverence, no bullshit sense and, of course, the sex. But there wasn't really space for him now and she didn't want to take away from what she wanted to do. Perhaps when she had talked to Rietti's family and had some sort of closure she would let herself think more than a day ahead. If and when that happened, there would be time for them both to decide if it could work between them. She didn't really know him but he had broken through the spell of grief and darkness, eased her pain, and made her see some possibility of hope for the future. Knowing he was around was comforting and gave her an added strength to do what she needed.

Then early the next morning he phoned and told her there had been a change of plan.

'I talked to Marcus this morning and he was really shaky. Said he'd had a huge fight with Debbie and stormed out. He's in more debt than he can manage and will have to drop out of college and get a job. I'm worried about him, so I need to go and talk things through with him. Show him I care…'

'Of course, he has to come first. You have to go.'

'I'm leaving straight away so I won't be able to sort someone out to look after the barn. I'll call if I can but don't worry if you don't hear from me soon. I need to put all my energies into him.'

She was disappointed but tried to sound positive. 'You must. I'll be here if you need me.'

'Thank you, sweetheart, I'll make it up to you. My flight from London is at four. I should just make it.'

'Yes, go, go… and safe travels.'

'Be careful, and don't put yourself in any danger. Promise me!'

'I won't.'

'Good.'

And he was gone.

Sara was sad that she wouldn't talk to him, she'd got used to their calls, but she'd have enough to do to keep her occupied. She arranged for a farmer who owned the land behind her barn to keep an eye on the place. He had been a friend before the killings and had tried to help her but she had called him a cunt once too often. Surprisingly, he was pleased to hear from her. Spending time in Siena would be healing, he said. That night her demons exploded back into her dreams and she woke early, exhausted and afraid she wouldn't be able to go on. But she forced herself to walk around the city and by the end of the day her resolve had returned. She had used some of the 'shit-removing' positives that Peter had taught her about the 'control or be controlled' power of reality. Never use denial when the truth is there and never close your eyes to what you see. There will always be a hook on which to hang your sanity. You only have to believe you will find it. Her hook was exploring the life of Vittorio Rietti.

The next few days she walked around the streets getting to know more of the city. She stayed in the old part with its beautiful buildings, narrow lanes, and the breathtaking frescoes which seemed to be around every corner in the most unexpected of places – in alleys, on the sides of buildings, above doorways, and once, on a wide expanse of wall, the old and contemporary joined together as graffiti, adding a cheeky touch to the fading figures of six Madonnas.

At night she ate and drank a couple of glasses of wine at small cafés and restaurants away from the busy core of the city, but she could feel its beating heart.

Then she began the search. She explored Siena newspaper archives online and found the reports on the killing of Vittorio Rietti. He had been in the UK to attend the Cheltenham Festival and to promote his wines at Fortnum and Mason. He owned six racehorses and bought regularly from yearling sales in both the UK and Ireland. His obituary had been glowing. He had seemed universally popular and appeared often on the society pages of magazines and newspapers with his second wife, Francesca. He had been in his late fifties, handsome and tanned, his eyes engaging. In most of the pictures he had an easy and natural smile and looked a happy and contented man. But he had been a man someone wanted to kill.

In the Piccolomino Library, Sara was looking at a Pinturicchio fresco. She was on her way to the address she had found in the electoral register for the Rietti family but had been drawn in as she passed the Duomo. It was ten in the morning and immersing herself in beauty and peace for a couple of hours would relax her.

Four hours in the place seemed to pass in minutes and she knew that with so much to hold her there, if she didn't move now she would get lost again. She pulled herself away and left the library. As she walked away from the Duomo the doubts and fears tumbled back in. What would she say to whoever answered the door? They would, as Peter had said, be in a confusion of disbelief and loss. Time wouldn't take that away. But she had a right to ask.

It took her a while to find the street where the large townhouse sat in a centuries-old terrace of crumbling elegance and style. It had four floors and there was a balcony covered with large plants and cascading flowers. It overlooked an exquisite park and gardens and a small church with an ornate bell tower. Did Rietti look out at this lovely garden and wonder at the beauty and innocence of nature? Was he at peace, or were there dark secrets in his heart that would soon destroy the world of someone he didn't know existed? Had he known it was inevitable that fate would find him when he thought he was safe? Or did arrogance and privilege make him feel he was untouchable? Sara felt the sharp pain and tasted blood from her bitten lip.

She licked it away and pushed the button on the videophone, breathing deeply to calm the panic that twisted and bounced inside her.

The screen lit up. 'Uno Minute, Signora Rodrigo.'

The voice was young and husky. Rietti's daughter?

'Do you speak English?'

There was a pause. 'Yes, a little.'

'Signorina Rietti?'

The response was slow but clear.

'No, my name is Teresa Foria. Signora Rietti and her family have gone. I am doing some work on the wall paintings. The architect of the renovation for the new owners, Signora Rodrigo, is meeting me here.'

Sara thought she wanted her to know that someone knew she was in the house and would soon be there. Perhaps she had seen traces of blood on Sara's lip. She had to fight hard for words. She had known what she would say to Rietti's wife or daughter but now struggled to make sense.

'Where did they go?'

'I don't know. I am sorry.'

'Thank you.' What could she do now? Where would she look?

As she reached the bottom step, the voice came again. 'Hello.'

Sara stopped. 'Yes?'

'Ask Father Antonio at Santa Maria, across the Giardini... the Gardens... he will know. He was their priest. I did some work for him in the church and he told me about them and their tragedy. He speaks English good.'

Their tragedy!

Sara wanted to scream at this faceless, careless voice but tried to put a smile in her reply. 'Thank you.'

For a moment she didn't know what to do. Could she face talking to anyone else? But she had no choice. She opened the gate into the Gardens.

Father Antonio had thick greying hair, a long skinny body, and the face of a dissolute angel. He was on his knees by the church door. Sara watched him for a moment as he poured water into a bucket from a jug, then she went over to him.

'Father Antonio?'

'Yes.'

'My name is Sara Jenkins. I'm a journalist working on a story for the *Guardian* newspaper in the UK. Signorina Foria, who is working on Signora Rietti's old house, suggested you might know how I could get in touch with her.'

'Ah yes, Teresa, a pretty girl, very clever painter, she did some beautiful work in my church. She still comes here sometimes to sit and eat lunch in the peace of the churchyard. Why do you want to talk to Signora Rietti?'

His look was direct but there was gentleness there too. A good mix for a priest

'I want to give a platform to women who were broken and left without closure after the unsolved murders of those closest to them. Wives, mothers, lovers, and daughters. They're so often the forgotten ones. My sister's husband was killed in a knife attack five years ago and she is still suffering. She is the reason I'm doing the story. The paper was interested because Signor Rietti was killed in London.'

'That was a terrible thing to happen. I read the *Guardian* when I lived in the UK and still enjoy the weekend paper online.'

His voice was warm and there was a slight hint of a Birmingham accent to his fluent English.

'Your English is very good.'

'Thank you. I taught for ten years in a school in Birmingham where the students were so culturally diverse that I realised clarity and correct vowels were the only way they would understand a little of what I was trying to teach them. I still have many friends there, so keep up with my English.'

He looked up at her and for a moment Sara thought he was going to ask what her last feature had been about but he held her eyes for only a moment then carried on mixing up in his bucket and telling her about life in his Birmingham school.

As he talked, he used a small trowel to point between the thick and uneven floor slabs around the entrance to the church. After the last corner was finished, he put the trowel in the bucket. 'Then I was a teacher and now I am a priest and in these difficult times, repairman too.' He laughed and stood up. 'I'll make us some tea. There is a seat outside in the sunshine. I'll clean up and bring it out there.'

She found the bench at the edge of the small graveyard. Across the gardens she could just see the corner of Rietti's balcony, a beautiful crimson bougainvillea billowing downwards. Sitting in the sunshine, waiting for the priest, she closed her eyes to enjoy the warmth on her face.

Father Antonio brought two mugs of tea, handed her one and sat next to her. Sara smiled and thanked him.

'Signora Rietti decided to sell and move to a house that she has in Florence. Maria, her youngest stepdaughter, is doing her Masters at the university there and the other, Rosa, a beautiful girl, is a model in Rome. The girl's mother died in a riding accident when Maria was a few months old. Francesca married Vittorio when Rosa was seven and Maria was two. A year later, their son, Franco, was born. He's a musician and lives in Genoa. I've known them since I was given this church fifteen years ago. It was a great tragedy when Vittorio was murdered. The heart of the family is broken.'

Sara somehow kept the horror she felt from showing in her face and the words raging out of her. But the priest was distracted by an old couple slowly walking towards them. He waved to them and smiled at Sara. 'Forgive me, I will have to leave you, but if you give me your number I will talk to a dear friend of Vittorio and see if he will talk to you and perhaps introduce you to Signora Rietti.'

Sara handed him one of the freelance journalist cards she had printed at the airport.

At the gateway she looked back towards the church. The couple and the priest were close together. The old man had tears on his cheeks and the priest, holding his hands was looking into his eyes, his lips moving with silent words, the world shut out. The old woman gently wiped the old man's eyes with her scarf. It was a touching and moving image and Sara wanted to remember it. She took out her phone but hesitated; it was too private a moment for the intrusion of a photograph, so she searched and found an old envelope and a pen in her bag and outlined the shapes. She felt moved by the sadness in the old man's face and the care in the others', but she had to leave them there. It was their moment in time that she couldn't share but wouldn't forget.

She had started drawing again since she had come to Siena, observational stuff, landscapes, buildings, people. Her pad and pencils were always with her in the large tapestry bag Ceri had bought for her to help contain the mess of many. It was a chance to look into other people's lives and worlds. It helped with her new reality to use the simple instinctive form and style that she had once loved but moved away from as a love for the abstract had taken over.

* * *

Dupard had been in Siena for three days, keeping Sara under a tight surveillance. He and his team would be close enough to help if she stumbled into something she couldn't handle and would 'pull her' if they felt she was in real danger. He was under the radar as an academic who wanted to study the beauty that was Siena. The IIF upset law agencies around the world with their insistence on autonomy but they were tolerated. They were considered arrogant, ruthless, and self-serving, but the bottom line was that they could go outside the boundaries that normal law enforcement agencies had to observe and even in these 'tight belt' times had a larger pot to spend than most. More importantly there was less chance of information slipping into the wrong ears and ruining an operation. The fewer people who knew what was going on, the more containable it was.

Later, Dupard would use IIF official partners in Italy to connect to the local police. But for now, the team would be made up of the people he had brought with him from Rome and the lead investigators, ex-police who spoke English, now working in the private sector, that he had recruited in Siena and Florence when he was planning the operation. They shared shifts around the clock.

He had listened to Sara's conversation with the priest. He didn't know how the system worked that caught and fed him the audio through her phone. It was enough that it did. Sara had done well to get the priest on her side and perhaps when she met with this friend of Rietti's he would give her direction. She was very bright and if she found a way, would go all out to search for a connection.

Not for one moment did he doubt the necessity of his manipulation of Sara. She had touched him and for a moment had opened his heart to the tragedy of her life. But there was no remorse or regret for what might have been. It was a wasted energy that dissipated instinct and got in the way. Dupard had to find a killer and Sara had to find a reason for Ceri and Ben's death. Equal gain for both.

Father Antonio called Sara the next day saying that he had talked to Rietti's friend, Carlo Braggio, and that he would be happy to talk to her. He gave her Braggio's mobile number.

She rang him. His voice was deep, rich and friendly. He said he would meet her but it would have to be in Florence and he gave her the name and address of a café. They arranged a time for the following day.

Sara decided to drive, and rented a car from a friend of Signora Valeria, who had a small garage near the guesthouse and sometimes hired out to tourists.

CHAPTER FIVETEEN

Early the next morning Sara was on the road. The journey took an hour and a half and the countryside around her passed without her really noticing. Her mind was full of waterfall memories of her boys and thoughts of Father Antonio, Signora Rietti, and what she would say to Braggio. Father Antonio had told her that he was an internationally known and loved painter so, with her joy in the art she had seen in Siena, they would have something to share to help them relax with each other. But she didn't think that would make it any easier to ask this man why someone had wanted to kill his friend.

Dupard was close to Florence and ahead of Sara. His team was already there as backup around the Square where the café was situated. He hadn't slept well. His mind had raced with possibilities and before he left he talked to his office in Toronto and organised another detailed search through the lives and movements of all the victims. Perhaps something would come to light that had been missed by the teams across Europe who had been working the killings. Not fucking likely after all this time and the thousands of hours put in. But, shit! There had to be something. A connection, however tenuous, not just that they were all rich and well known.

As he reached the outskirts of Florence, his phone rang. For a moment he thought it was Sara. Why? She didn't have this number. Was his subconscious making a point? Was this a first nudge of guilt at using her? He shut his mind off and answered the phone.

'Hi, boss, it's Selma. I'm here. '

'Good. Giorgio?'

'He's keeping up but she's a bit of a sprinter. They'll be here in about thirty minutes.'

'Good.'

He hung up and started looking for somewhere to park near the Square.

Sara had found a place to leave the car and was looking for Café Bella Rosa. Was she ready for this? Suddenly she was unsure of what she was doing? Could she handle it? Would this man talk to her? Tell her the truth about Rietti? Suddenly she wanted to talk to Peter, wanted him to reassure her that she was doing the right thing. She had tried last night but his phone was unreachable. He had told her that it would be but there was always the chance that he was some place where it worked. She scrambled through her thoughts for his wisdom. Nothing would come. She gave up. She was on her own but could do this.

Dupard was sitting inside a bar watching Sara as she approached Bella Rosa. He was cold, focused, and out of her sightline.

As she reached the café, a man sitting at a table watched her for a moment and then stood up. 'Signora Jenkins?' She recognised the voice. Braggio, in his seventies, was a bear of a man with an intelligent, strong face, a mane of shoulder-length white hair, a thick beard, and piercing blue eyes that now held hers and seemed to look deep inside her. She felt dwarfed by him but he took her hand gently and smiled. 'It is a pleasure to meet you. Father Antonio is a good man and I trust his instinct for the good in others.'

He pulled a chair out for her. 'What can I get you?'

'Espresso, please.'

He went into the café.

Instinctively Sara felt no fear of this man but worried that he would know she was not being truthful with him.

He came back with her coffee.

'I thought you might need this. It will relax you.' He smiled, sat down opposite her, and leaned back.

'You want to talk to me about Vittorio.'

His English was lightly accented and fluent.

Sara went through her story of writing a feature for the *Guardian* and that she wanted to speak to Signor Rietti's wife. She knew that being left alone with no reason for her husband's death would be torture for her and, from the response of other women she had interviewed, it sometimes helped to talk it through with someone outside close friends and family. It might even release something that might give understanding, or at least a focus for the unthinkable thing that had happened.

Braggio looked at her, then got up from his chair and took her hand. 'Come with me, there is something I want you to see.'

For a moment Sara hesitated then stood.

Dupard watched them walk away from the café. They disappeared into the park.

Selma said, 'They're going into that small church on the other side of the Square. I'll give it five minutes then follow them in.'

Dupard spoke quietly. 'Wait for them to come out. She'll be safe with the painter.'

He had sent a photo of Braggio to Rome and had got back enough on the man to think he was no threat to Sara.

They would pick her up again when she came out. He had lost contact with her phone inside the thick walls of the church so would know nothing of what was said. He wasn't particularly concerned. It would have been nice to know, but he wasn't going to sweat about it.

Inside, the church was tiny. No more than thirty people could be seated. But it was beautiful, with richly coloured frescoes on the walls, marble tiles, small bronzes, and a tiny but ornate altar.

Braggio and Sara were looking at a painting that filled a small alcove and was lit by a gentle light. It was a simple portrait of a woman and a little girl, their faces together, their focus on each other, unaware they were being watched. The relationship between them was deep and intense. You knew that this woman would kill for her child and that their understanding and bond was complete and unbreakable. The skill of the artist in creating the depth and beauty, the vivid sense of life and story in the painting, was shocking. The work was untitled and the artist unknown but dated from the early 1600s. Sara had never seen anything like it before ,or felt anything connect with her in the same visceral way.

Braggio was speaking quietly. 'My grandfather had a house here in the piazza and I must have been twelve years old when he brought me to the church and showed me this masterpiece. It was what first warmed the lifeblood of art in my soul and to me it was perfection. Even at that young age I could feel the power of love that was as desperate as it was all-consuming. I have tried since then to reach this breath of life.' He glanced around the church. 'I have a deep faith but it is only here that I can touch it. It refreshes me and gives me strength to try and be a good and compassionate man.' He smiled 'I have told you my secrets.' He paused for a long moment, his eyes on hers, then touched her gently on the cheek. 'Now, you tell me, Sara, what has caused such a darkness in your heart?'

For a moment Sara was stunned. Then she felt a great surge of release and as he held her tightly, the tears and words came.

They were in a pew in front of the altar. They were sitting, her hands in his, surrounded by the peace that filled this place. Sara told him everything. He was silent for a moment after she had finished, exhausted. When he spoke his voice was soothing, safe.

'I do not claim to know everything of Vittorio's world, but I would never have thought that he had done anything to cause what happened to him. He was a gentle but complicated man, strong-minded, particularly if he believed he was in the right. He was a lion in business but always fair and, as far as I know, honest. Our worlds were different but I loved him. He was my friend. It was an unbelievable thing that happened.'

Sara trusted this man she had only just met but his words were like salt in an open wound.

'I will talk to Francesca,' he said. 'Tell her what you have told me, and ask if she will meet with you. I cannot promise she will. Give me your number and I will call you this evening. Are you driving back now to Siena?'

Sara nodded. 'If I can remember where I left the car.'

He stood and pulled her gently up and for a moment held her. Sara felt his strength and the warmth in him calmed her. She kissed his cheek. 'Thank you.'

'I will walk with you and somehow we will find your car.' He laughed. 'I hope to meet some friends on the way. If we do you must call me Carlo and smile warmly at me. It is a long time since I had a beautiful woman on my arm and they will see that I am not yet finished with life. That will be all the thanks I need.'

* * *

On the drive back to Siena, Sara thought about Carlo Braggio and what he had said about Rietti. Perhaps he was as innocent as Ben and Ceri were. Just in the wrong place at the wrong time. If that was true then what would she do next? If Rietti's wife had no insight then she would have to start again. Find other friends, people that came into his life, in business and socially.

She was in the outside lane, overtaking a lorry. A car suddenly appeared in the rear-view mirror, lights flashing, horn blaring. It must have braked just before hitting her. For a moment she slowed to annoy the driver, a woman, then thought, 'Fuck you,' and accelerated, pushing the car up to one hundred and fifty, the other one chasing.

Dupard, keeping his distance, saw and pulled out after the other car, narrowly missing someone coming up fast behind. 'Jesus!' He then had to brake sharply as Sara pulled into the slower lane and the other car screamed past. 'Fuck!' He let a couple of cars and trucks go then pulled in behind a bus. His phone rang. 'Yes?'

'That was fun… just going to get ahead of her,' Selma said. 'Sharp for a man of your age, boss.'

'Just make sure we don't lose her.' Dupard smiled: they were a good team.

Sara needed to pee. She stopped in a small village and had a coffee. She was feeling good, the adrenalin rush of speed and danger had been distracting and she enjoyed sitting outside the small café, sketching the people and the houses. She realised she was looking forward to meeting Signora Rietti, and as she got back on the road she thought about what she would say to her.

She was in Siena about five, dropped off the car. Realising she hadn't eaten much since early morning, she had a meal before going back to the guesthouse.

Carlo called her about nine. 'I have an exhibition opening in Siena tomorrow night, at the Biale Curriti. Francesca will be there and will talk to you. I will text you the address.'

'Thank you, Carlo.'

'Good night, Sara, I hope you sleep well. It is always good to have unlocked demons and shown them light. It is not a state they enjoy. It steals their power.'

Sara went out on to the small balcony took in the lights and sounds from the city centre, fuzzy, and comforting, in the distance. Her phone buzzed. The address from Carlo. She finished off the wine she had started before the call. She was exhausted and quickly undressed and got into bed. She had been going to have a shower but it might have refreshed her. For now she wanted to sleep. She turned off the light and, as she had done as a child, pulled the duvet over her head, closed her eyes, and waited for the yawn that would slide her into sleep. For a moment she thought it would never come and tried to force it, but that didn't ever work.

Then it came and within five minutes she was asleep.

* * *

Dupard was eating alone, his iPad in front of him, listening to voice messages through headphones and reading others. There was nothing new on the search he had put in place. His mobile rang. He checked the number, dropped the headphones around his neck, and accepted the call but didn't say anything. A quiet male voice spoke in slow Italian. Dupard was reasonably fluent but at normal speed it was hard for him to catch everything, so those that knew him took their time.

'The Paliano and Francesca families had nothing to do with it. Rietti wasn't one of their tame civilians. They're fucked off that I asked but will put out the word to see if they can find anything. He lived on their patch and they're pissed, they should have been told if someone had put a hit out. I'm not sure they believed my bullshit about the debt. Don't ask again, we're all paid up.'

Dupard hung up. 'Not until the next time, Adolfo.' He stopped a waiter passing by the table. 'Another glass of the Classico, please.'

'Si, signor.'

Dupard pulled the headphones up, looked down, and tapped the screen as a mail pinged in.

CHAPTER SIXTEEN

It was midday in the Piazza del Duomo. Sara had been sitting at a table outside Bar Sergio for the last couple of hours. One of the waiters, tall, good-looking, with long hair in a ponytail, had seen her sketching the faces around the Piazza. After an hour he said she could stay there as long as she bought lunch before going. He had flirted with her and asked her to come to a concert with him that night. Sara had surprised herself by playing the game. She hadn't done that for years. The waiter kept bringing her little biscuits and more coffee. She had made him stop after three. As always, when she drew, her interior took over and time disappeared. She had started with the Duomo then moved on to faces and was now intent on an old woman dancing on the steps of the Duomo to the music inside her head. It was hot and she must have been boiling but she kept on going. She was tiny, thin, with hair tied in a bun, a creased face, and one of the most beautiful smiles Sara had ever seen. Around the Piazza were other street entertainers, jugglers, human statues, and a clown with an old trombone who was entrancing a group of children, young and not so young, with ageless simple and silly fun.

'She is my grandmother.' It was Giulio, the waiter, his English slow and heavy with accent. 'It is embarrassing but makes her happy.' He put a pizza on the table.

Sara smiled at him. She looked at the old woman as she spun twice, stopped, and just managed to keep her balance. 'She's not, is she?'

Giulio smiled. 'No, but I thought you might pity me and let me take you out tonight.'

'Sorry, I already have a date.'

He turned at an angry shout from inside, blew her a kiss, and hurried away.

* * *

Sara arrived at the Biale Curriti at eight o'clock. She had decided to wear an old but expensive black dress and the red silk jacket she hadn't worn for years but had thrown into her case when packing. Red suede boots and a silver necklace that could be bent into different shapes completed the look. She had glanced in the mirror before leaving and, considering she was out of practice, thought she'd do.

Strangely, now that she was close to asking the questions, she was calm. Not relaxed and easy, but calm.

As she walked into the gallery entrance she saw that people were showing invitations. Already there was a crowd there. For a moment she thought about what she would do if they wouldn't let her in. But as she started to explain, she saw Carlo move away from a group he was greeting and come towards her. He kissed her on both cheeks.

'Sara, let me get you a drink then I will leave you to look around and find Francesca. We will talk later.'

Sara moved around the exhibition. It was a wonderful mix of abstract landscape paintings as well as portraits, made with graphite and charcoal, acrylics and oils. All had a painful truth and beauty, tearing through the fragile surface into the soul beneath, the colours, vibrant and rich, bleeding life into the world they inhabited. There was a portrait of an old man, his face like crumpled parchment, his eyes fierce, proud, angry, intelligent, and knowing but challenging that his journey was almost over. It took Sara's breath away.

'There is much of Carlo in that.'

Sara turned to see a beautiful woman in her late forties. 'I'm Francesca Rietti. Irina has allowed us to use her office to talk. It is too noisy here.'

She had a stillness and elegance and her simple dress was Versace, the sort of simple that would have cost thousands.

From the other side of the gallery, Paolo Androtti watched the two women as they stood in front of the painting of the old man. He knew Francesca well but the other woman had fascinated him since he'd seen her come in to the gallery. She had a fragility and a gentle, natural beauty that excited him. He had to talk to her. He was about to head towards them when they moved away through the crowd. He would catch her later. He took a drink from a waitress and smiled a thank you. She looked back at him as she walked away. Paolo seemed unaware of the effect he had on women and it made him even more attractive.

Selma too was watching as the two women moved through the crowd and through a discreet hidden door in the display wall. It was between two canvases and Francesca had opened it with a fingertip touch on an invisible pad. Selma had heard their earlier conversation but now had lost their voices. It was probably a soundproofed room. With all the hack attacks on celebrities, many places had a safe area for private words. She went towards the door but the signal didn't improve. She'd have to wait until they came out. Dupard wouldn't be happy. This was an important meeting but there was nothing she could do. Perhaps Giorgio could find a way.

'Giorgio, I've hit a dead spot, you got any magic to work?' She spoke quietly.

'When the door's shut there's a seal that creates a sound vacuum. Nothing I can do,' said Giorgio. 'Want me to tell Dupard?'

'No, I'll do it.'

In Dupard's hotel room, a message pinged in from Selma about losing the audio. It didn't help his mood but wasn't a concern. But there was something that worried him. If Sara was to have any success in finding out anything of any use, she had to have something solid to go on, not just a possible direction from someone close to Rietti. Something that was a credible threat to whoever had done it being identified. But she knew nothing. At the moment she was as blind as he was. If Rietti's widow knew anything and was willing to open up, would Sara recognise its value and be able to act on it? And if she did, would she then be too vulnerable? His team were close by at all times, but what if they slipped up and she was hit or taken? He had to be able to control any situation. What could he manufacture to throw into the mix?

He clicked on the video link from the gallery. Selma was looking at a picture near the door, a young boy standing alone watching a woman walk away. Suddenly it came to him. The camera. Shit, why hadn't he thought of that before? Ben had a small camera and had been taking pictures at Paddington. The cheap child's throwaway camera had been returned to Sara only a month after he met her. It should have been returned earlier, but nobody had checked and Sara, in the mess she was in, hadn't asked.

After getting the camera back, she had regressed and had shut him out for days. When she had emerged, she wouldn't say where she had put the camera and refused to talk about it. After she'd gone, he'd tried to find it, but the clutter defeated him until he found it in a pile of old photographs in a box in the hallway under a heap of coats. The one place he hadn't looked. He'd had it couriered back to Canada, but there was nothing on the film that helped. What if there had been and she'd seen it, something innocent enough at first sight, but in the background, against the newspaper stand perhaps, a figure, out of focus but with enough there to find a small detail that would give her hope at finding who was responsible? It would be logical that she would jump at anything that might help her find the truth. It might just be enough to get things moving. Dupard picked up his mobile.

In the small office, Francesca held Sara's hand. They were sitting on a couch.

'I feel great pain too. I know I haven't lost a child. I cannot imagine what that must feel like, but my heart will never beat the same way again. I don't know why it happened or who could have done it. I knew little of Vittorio's business but he was an honest man. I was supposed to go to London with him but my daughter had invited me to Fashion Week in Rome and I went there. I feel very bad about that. What would have happened if I had been with him? Would it have made a difference?' She glanced at Sara and knew that she had punished herself in the same way. 'I understand the need to make sense of it, to get some sort of closure, to fill the emptiness with reason. But I also know that Vittorio wouldn't have wanted me to suffer. He will always be here with me but for the sake of sanity, my life has to move on.' She let go of Sara's hand. 'I'm sorry that I am not able to help you.'

Sara felt detached from Francesca and, for a moment, had to fight a sudden anger that she might be hiding something. But, in her heart, she knew that the woman was being honest and that really, in their own ways, they were both lost. The difference was that where Francesca had chosen not to look for a reason, Sara would carry on and turn over every stone of connection until she found something. She felt saddened that there was a new darkness where she had hoped to find light. 'It was good of you to talk to me.'

'What will you do now?'

Sara stood up. 'I have to carry on. But for now, I want to talk to Carlo about his work. He makes me feel as though I'm a child just beginning to draw life. It's difficult to understand but it feels as though I have always known him.'

Francesca smiled. 'He is a man who is loved and shares his strength and spirit with those he cares about. Listen to him. He gave me a reality when Vittorio was killed, not clean, not nice, wrapped up in gentle words, but a sense of what I had to do to live when all I wanted was to sleep and never wake.'

She put her arms around Sara, who, for a moment, resisted, then hugged her back.

'Take care.' Francesca Rietti kissed Sara on both cheeks as they stood outside the hidden door. 'I hope you find what you need. If you want to talk you can call me. Sometimes it helps to share with someone who understands.'

She gave Sara a small card with just a cell number on it.

Sara was moved. 'Thank you.' She watched Francesca walk away. Some women just had such natural style and elegance that they'd look good in a bin bag. Still, it would be a boring world if everyone in it was beautiful. A bit of character and life lived made people more interesting. Didn't it? It made her smile that she cared again.

She moved to one of the paintings, a spattered and monochrome abstract that exploded from the canvas.

'Not one of my top five of Carlo's works, I prefer the portraits. He did one of me that made me think I might have to kill him for the truth it told.' The man smiled as Sara turned. 'Forgive me. I should have asked Francesca to introduce me. I'm Paolo Androtti, an old friend of hers and Carlo's.'

Sara was thrown. Androtti was in his late thirties, olive-skinned, good-looking with a small scar above his right eye and deep brown eyes that were locked on hers, shutting out everyone else in the gallery.

He looked at the landscape.

'You like this painting?'

'Yes, it's wonderful.'

'Why?'

'Depth, light, freedom…'

Androtti laughed. His teeth were white but not perfect and his eyes crinkled with lines.

'Right… what do I know? I just collect what I like and I have four of Carlo's. How long have you been in Siena?'

'Just over a week.'

For an instant Sara wanted to run away at the invasion of her space but something kept her there. She looked around the room for Carlo and saw him being interviewed on camera by an intense looking woman with big hair and tight leather trousers.

'He won't be able to come to your rescue so, if I disturb you, I will go away. But that might just break my heart.' He looked at her for a long moment then smiled. 'I think you are a spirit that is in need of… depth, freedom and light. I want to make you laugh.'

Sara laughed. 'Fuck off.'

'It worked. Let me get you a drink?' He caught the eye of a beautiful young waitress as she passed them with a tray of champagne and took two glasses. 'Thank you.' The waitress looked at him, reddened, then smiled and moved off.

'Do you often have that effect?'

'Only if they can't see through my skin-deep charm. You are a painter?'

'What makes you say that?'

'Your hands are beautiful but they are working hands... And there is still a little paint under the nails.'

Sara looked down at her hands. 'I thought I'd scrubbed up well.'

'I studied philosophy and art at Cambridge,' he said.

'Oh.' She smiled. 'Clever and creative.'

'If you're here to steal the soul of Siena then you will have to find it and that's not an easy task. But if you let me expose my city to you, you'll have a chance. Some things you would have found as you explored but others only I know.' He saw Carlo approaching them. 'Carlo will vouch for me.'

Sara was excited. Bythis opportunity to perhaps find out more about Rietti from someone who knew the family, and the total focus he was giving her. She was enjoying it and the envious looks from other women. The thought of her vanity surprised and amused her.

Carlo gently put his arm around her. 'Sara, I'm sorry to have left you so long but at least you have had Paolo to amuse you. He is incorrigible but intelligent and knows a little about art.'

'Thank you, Carlo.' Androtti kissed Sara quickly on the cheek. 'I'll leave you to talk to the old man. Perhaps you would join me for a drink before you leave.'

Sara smiled at him. 'Perhaps.'

Androtti walked away. Carlo watched him go. 'Too attractive and too much money, but he has a good heart and will make you smile, if you let him. Now, tell me if Francesca was any help.'

Dupard watched the feed and listened to Carlo and Sara as they talked. First about Francesca then about his work. He had sent an info request on Paolo Androtti to Rome and was impatient for a response. It would be good to know who the man was and for a moment considered that if he felt he wasn't good for Sara then perhaps he would find a way of warning him off. That thought was a surprise to him and an unexpected moment of weakness. He couldn't allow that. Being guided by the memory of what he had shared with her got in the way, so he closed it off. Thinking of her as anything other than a necessary tool to catch a killer wasn't useful. He knew he would let it play out. His guys on the ground were good and could think for themselves. Any hint of real danger and they would move in fast and hard. He watched Carlo being persuaded into another TV interview.

Carlo apologised to Sara and invited her to have lunch with him at a restaurant hidden away in a street behind the Duomo and owned by his oldest friend, Marcello. He would meet her there at twelve tomorrow. It was called Il Capo. It would be easy for her to find. Everyone knew it.

As Carlo was led to another part of the gallery and Sara moved closer to a portrait of a young girl, Androtti found her again.

'There is a bar downstairs. We can have a drink away from the glitterati of Siena. You can tell me more about your work and what you know of my city. And if you are free tomorrow for me to show you her beauty.'

Sara smiled. One drink wouldn't hurt and Paolo was fun, even if she turned down his offer.

'One drink?'

'Whatever you want.'

'And tomorrow, I'm sorry, I have a date with Carlo.'

* * *

Sara sat on the small balcony outside her room overlooking the lights and sounds of the city. She felt a bit woozy after the drinks with just a few canapés to soak it up. She was sipping the hot chocolate Elena always insisted she had to help her sleep, dipping the thick and nutty homemade biscuits until they were soft. It was really sweet of her but not always wanted, although it did have a memory of childhood that was warm and safe. And tonight, it was the perfect way to end the excitement of talking to Francesca and seeing Carlo's incredible work. Perhaps meeting the gorgeous Paolo might have helped colour her spirits a little too.

She and Paolo had spent two hours in the small bar and one drink had turned into a shared bottle of Chianti that was produced by a friend of his in the hills between Siena and Florence. Perhaps mixing it with the champagne she had already drunk at the gallery wasn't as good an idea as it seemed at the time. He had wanted to take her to eat. She had been tempted but said no. He hadn't tried to push.

He had been charming, funny, and, more surprising to her ego, had really listened when she talked about her work as an artist, and had been knowledgeable and focused in his responses and perspectives. She had to temper her passion about painting and not go into a creative babble, although she was sure he would have taken the ride with her. She didn't mention her cover as a journalist nor the real reason she was there. Something stopped her. She'd been honest with Francesca but that was different. Paolo didn't need to know about that life, or her pretend journalism. Perhaps she didn't want to lie to him. He was easy to be with and she felt relaxed but wary at the fluttery feelings that crept up on her when his eyes held hers or his hand touched her arm. First Peter and now Paolo. It suddenly struck her and she laughed.

She did the actions. 'Two little dickie birds sitting on a wall, one named Peter, one named Paul. Fly away, Peter, fly away, Paul, come back, Peter, come back, Paul.'

A sudden memory, clear and detailed, of her dad singing that with her on a beach in Spain. They were sitting in shallow water, watching her mum bodysurfing in on the waves. She had almost reached them when she screamed and started flapping about. She'd been stung by a jellyfish and they'd had to go to the hospital because her leg had swollen up hugely. It took days for it to go down and her mum, who loved being in the sea, stayed on the beach and wouldn't let Sara go in either. She remembered being really cross with her mum.

First Peter and now Paolo. Were these the steps she had to take? Open her heart to chance so she could start really living again? She didn't feel disloyal to Peter. She had made no promises and they each had their separate lives. And she had only just met this man. Where the hell was her perspective? But she'd had a really good time with him.

He'd talked about Siena and his passion for it and its history. He brought to life the story of the Palio, explaining how the adored and insane horse race around the Piazza del Campo had grown out of the annual Carnival in the Middle Ages where boxing, jousting and, bull fighting had taken place. When the bullfighting had been banned, the races were organised, first on buffalos, then donkeys and finally in the mid-seventeenth century on horses, trained so their only life led to the Palio. It was a hugely important event that created fierce competition between the districts of the city. They were called contradas and named after animals, insects, or birds. Paolo's contrada was Leocorno, the Unicorn.

The Palio also fed the rivalry between Florence and Siena, which was as old as the cities themselves and centred on the eternal argument as to where the boundaries between the two should lie and which was the richer in history.

He explained the name Palio was the Italian for Banner and the winner still receives a silk banner adorned with the face of the Virgin Mary.

Sara had felt a growing attraction to Paolo. She felt at ease with him. When they left the bar he said that he would take her to the Palio. By now, the tickets were like hidden jewels but he knew where to find them. She didn't doubt him. He said she would see a change in the city from the next day as the Race took over its soul and spirit. When he left her at the guesthouse with a kiss on each cheek, she felt a tingling excitement.

* * *

While Dupard was waiting for Rome he had been
checking out Androtti. He had a house near Monticelli,
was hugely wealthy, and his parents had both died in a
helicopter crash near Nice five years ago. Androtti bred
horses, was an art collector, and seemed to be linked to
a stream of stylish and beautiful women, most of whom
had more celebrity than him. He was well liked and
moved in the high social whirl of Siena.

Dupard's mobile rang.

'Handing over to Marco. Lights have just gone out in
her room. I'll pick up at six,' Selma said.

'What did you think of Androtti?'

'Not my type but probably could have had his pick,'
she laughed. 'Of men or women.'

'Why Sara, then?' A note of suspicion.

'Different, unknown, a challenge, a Brit. She's got
something though, energy, vulnerability, strength. A
quiet beauty that only shines when she lights up. As she
did with Androtti.'

'OK.' He was impressed with Selma's clear analysis.
She had summed up Sara perfectly.

'Night. Boss.'

'Goodnight, Selma.'

* * *

Sara had woken needing the loo and thought she
wouldn't get back to sleep, but she did as soon as she
got back into bed and snuggled down. Her last

conscious thought was about Paolo Androtti and his promise to take her to the Palio.

Dupard was thinking about Androtti too as he cleaned his teeth. In the mirror his eyes looked tired and sore. He'd had too long on the screen. He hoped that Androtti had potential as someone who knew Francesca Rietti and realised suddenly that he felt a pang of annoyance about Sara and him having fun together. Then he pushed it away, rinsed his mouth, put out the light, and stood for a moment looking at the silhouette of his reflection. Perhaps this was how others saw him, through a glass darkly. He laughed.

Twenty kilometres outside Siena, Androtti was crouched on a bridge that looped across two railway tracks. A hundred and fifty metres ahead there was a sharp left turn that pulled the rails out of sight. The night sky was dark, almost black, just a few far-away hints of light seeping through the clouds. It was cold but he didn't feel it. At this point there was nothing but the game. He was ready now, his breathing slow, his mind focused, his muscles tensed for the right moment. In the distance he could hear the sound of the train. He pulled his goggles over his eyes, checked the straps on his boots, and waited. The locomotive would have to start to slow here as it approached the first of three bends but it would still be doing a reasonable speed, perhaps 40kmh. He had to judge it perfectly. There was no room for error. Even a slight miscalculation could finish him.

The large spotlight mounted on the front of the engine lit up the tracks through the shadowy curve of the bridge.

Then he hit the zone and there was only the space he was in. Sight, sense, and sound in acute focus. The roaring of the engine and the twenty freight trucks resonated, the first screech as the brakes started to catch and the taste and smell of metal on metal. His breath caught. Now, it had to be now. Underneath him the first truck passed through the bridge, then he jumped. For a moment he thought he would fall between the trucks but he landed dead centre on the third one and flung himself flat onto the roof. It had been a perfect jump and he felt the exhilaration pound through his being as he clung to the metal, his gloved hands gripping the handles on each side.

CHAPTER SEVENTEEN

Sara slept until eight. Woke with joy turning to sadness as the images of Ceri and Ben chasing her with a large crab slowly faded. The room was warm and coloured with light filtering through the thin blinds as the sun found its way through the cracks, and the sounds of normality of early day life slipped in at the edges of the open balcony door. Slowly she eased into the reality of the day but her memory of what had lived in her sleep was clear. In her dream, even though she could hear, see, and touch Ceri and Ben, she knew they were in a different life. She could hear Ben's bubbling laughter and Ceri's soft and musical voice. 'Love you, Mummy,' said Ben so clearly she turned to find him. But he wasn't there.

'And I love you too, sweetheart.'

It was strange but Ceri now seemed to be always in her dreams too. It had been like that since that first night with Peter when she saw him and Ben as the storm raged and she knew she was awake. Perhaps she had forgiven him for not keeping his promise of protection. It felt good and safe that they were together when she was in their world.

She stayed in bed for another hour, pushing her thoughts back to the skill and emotion she found in Carlo's work. He was a wonderful painter and she wanted to soak up his talent and use it to feed her own. Not that she had real doubts about her ability, more that her ego was lazy through lack of use, and needed stimulation. Would Carlo like her work? She would love his wisdom and try not to be defensive. She wondered what she would show him. She had loaded some images of her works onto her new phone before she had left Wales. Not the violent, raw and cathartic cries that tore out of her grief but some of her earlier pieces, or the two new ones she had done since meeting Peter, which were not bad but could be improved. They were still about loss but more bearable. It was as though her creative self had evolved with her new and hesitant sense of being.

Then her mind butterflied to Peter. Where was he? Was he still in the US? Would she tell him all that had happened? Without him she would not have made it this far. He had wanted to come to Siena. It would have been good to have him with her, but she knew that this was something she had to do on her own. His realistic assessment of what she would have to do to find some sense of peace and closure had been what she needed. It seemed now to her to have been almost structured through levels of reason. But that was his skill. It was what he taught. And he had broken through her psyche and let the sexual too give her release. She would always be in his debt for that physical escape alone. With a shock she realized that she was thinking of him in the past, as though he had served his purpose and she could now move on to others who would help her on to another stage.

Jesus, that was a shitty thought.

But she was overthinking it. When she saw him again it would be fine. But for now she had to find a way to get to know more about Rietti's life. Despite Francesca's negative response, she hoped that Paolo might be able to help. He obviously knew the family well.

She looked at the time. 'Oh, shit.' She would be late meeting Carlo. That was really nothing to do with getting up late and letting her mind roam. It had always been the same since she was a little girl. She was always late and even if she had plenty of time to get somewhere, she would find something to do to waste it. It used to drive her parents, friends, and Ceri to fits of frustration.

She went into the small bathroom and turned on the shower. In the mirror she looked tired. She got into the shower. She was looking forward to meeting him again. She thought about Siena and the Palio that he had talked about, and the invitation to join Paolo there. Perhaps she would stay for it. He did say he could get a ticket. She realised she was excited at the thought of seeing him again.

She got out of the shower.She pushed Paolo from her mind. She dressed quickly. She had to leave now. Now! She checked how she looked in the long mirror that leaned against the bathroom wall. She'd do. She wore the leather jacket, jeans, boots and a cashmere sweater that she had bought at the airport on an expensive whim. Not much of a fashion statement but good enough.

On her way through the streets to Il Capo she felt the buzz and murmurings as the Palio started to take hold of the city and those in it. It had been simmering in the background since she arrived but her mind, filled with other things, had stored it away until she was ready. Until yesterday she hadn't thought about it and didn't really notice it. However today it had moved up a gear and was impossible to ignore. Still over a week away, Elena had told her, but already everything in Siena revolved around it. The feasts in the contradas began in a few days and the first of the Race heats took place in a week.

The doorway to Il Capo was small and the sign almost hidden. You had to know it was there. Sara had been pointed to it by a tall clown who tried to give her a flower, swore undying love, and wiped a tear, miming a broken heart as she walked away. Inside it was larger than she thought it would be but still had only eight tables. There were six in the main room and two in separate arched alcoves. A small bar surrounded by bottle racks was next to a menu board with three handwritten dishes for each course. All the wall space was taken up with drawings and paintings. Sitting on a stool at the bar was Carlo, talking with a man of around the same age who smiled at her, his teeth white with a flash of gold in one corner. Carlo noticed, turned, and got up to greet her. He held her in his arms for a moment. She felt like a child.

'You have a little more peace today, Sara. I hope Paolo amused you. I did warn him that I would add demons to his portrait if he wasn't the perfect companion.'

Sara laughed. 'I liked him, he was fun. He told me about Siena and the Palio and then walked me back to my hotel.'

'Good. Did you sleep well?' Carlo asked.

'Yes, thank you.'

The other man came around the bar. He was very short with a barrel chest, a large belly, and no hair on his head but a mat on his arms and stubby fingers.

Carlo put his arm around the man's shoulders. 'This is my friend, Marcello, capo of Il Capo. We went through school together and when we were sixteen, I found my torture of art and he joined a circus on the high wire. One day he fell. He recovered, grew up, and opened the best restaurant in Siena, where he fed me and my beggar friends and let us drink all night for the odd scribbles to hang on his wall.' He pointed to the wall. 'Fifty years of our lives there. Few are left from the early days but Cello and I refuse to give in.' He pointed at an old photograph almost hidden in the corner. 'That is a young Cello winning the Palio. We celebrated for days and almost drank the bars of Siena dry.'

Marcello stretched up and kissed Sara on both cheeks.

'It was many years ago when I did not fear the end. But now you must eat. I will steal your heart with a taste of paradise. Carlo, please take your guest to your table and I will choose a wine for you.' He smiled at Sara. 'Don't believe all he says.'

Carlo led her towards one of the alcoves.

'Did he really join a circus?' said Sara as she sat down.

'Marcello is one of those people who has the strangest truths, in that he will have done all he says he has. He finds it impossible to embellish the truth even for a better story. It is as it is. I love him for it and would trust him beyond any other.'

The food was as Marcello had promised and she soon realized that they were on their second bottle of wine. She'd have to watch her drinking and not let it get out of hand. Marcello had told her of Carlo as a young artist and his passion for women both real and created. The only time they had fallen out was over a woman who Marcello adored. She had not felt the same way and had slept with Carlo on his twenty-fifth birthday. Marcello had almost challenged him to a duel but instead made him walk a high wire that he had put up between two buildings. He had walked it first then taunted Carlo until he had done it. Halfway across Carlo had fallen but Marcello had caught him. It was enough. They had got drunk and the woman had gone off with another friend who she married, and they were still together, old and fat and in their seventies. On the wall amongst his other lovers was her portrait, painted by Carlo. Sara was challenged to find her. She failed. Marcello showed it to her. The portrait of the woman had such a life and energy. Her dark eyes taunted and challenged and with her full lips, smile, and dark velvet skin she promised strength, passion, and the feeling that she would choose her path and companions. She wasn't beautiful but it was a face and a show of spirit that would break your heart. Sara felt a pang of regret that age would have taken away the promise of the painted youth. She understood why young men fought over her.

Carlo smiled. 'She might now have the mask of time but her soul is unchanged. Some things may be hidden but will never be lost. Remember that, Sara.'

Marcello talked about the circus and the thrill of danger. He missed that rush still.

After he left, called to a table in the now full restaurant, Carlo sat back in his chair. 'Now I will tell you about my friend Vittorio.'

Outside the restaurant, Selma sat in her car. This time it was an old and battered Fiat, a newer version of the first car she had owned, except that one had been yellow, not black. She'd bought it with a summer's work at a meat factory and she had loved it. This one looked its age but had a new engine built for the chase.

Selma had picked up Sara outside the guesthouse. She followed her on foot and when she had gone into Il Capo had arranged the car. The audio feed wasn't working inside the thick walls. Jesus, they could hear people in Space but the walls of old Siena had beaten their best. All she could do was wait. She couldn't follow Sara into the restaurant. It was too small and was now full. She had glanced through the door and seen Carlo at a table. She couldn't see Sara but she would be safe with him.

'They're taking a hell of a time.' Dupard's voice was impatient. 'I want to know what he's telling her.'

Across from where she was parked she saw Giorgio enter Il Capo. 'Giorgio's just gone in. He's going to see if there's a table free. There won't be. He'll try and get a pin near them,'

'Let me know when she comes out. You want me to try and feed through to you if Giorgio manages it?'

'I'll catch up later if there's nothing important.'

'I'll let you know if we're in.'

Giorgio walked past Carlo as he stood up. He bumped into him and put his hand on the table for support, then apologized to Carlo who smiled and said, 'Sorry, at my age, my sense of space is not so good.'

'My fault.'

Sara was looking at a photograph on Carlo's phone of a wild seascape and didn't notice.

Carlo headed for the toilets and Giorgio went to look at the wall of paintings then crossed to one of the waiters and asked if there was a table free soon. There wasn't. Giorgio went towards the door. Outside he touched his mouth and headed for a street leading towards the Duomo.

'Subtle?' said Selma.

'Seamless,' Giorgio laughed.

'Let's see if it works first.'

'It does.' Dupard sounded relieved.

* * *

'I met Vittorio over twenty years ago,' Carlo said. 'When he asked me to design a logo for his vineyard. It was at the Palio. I was with some friends from the winning contrada and he had been invited by one of them. His first wife had recently died in childbirth leaving him with two young daughters and he was not coping well. I had lost a love the same way many years before and we found a lot to talk about. I knew his family and his father and I had interests in common. I liked him straight away. He was easy to read, clever, witty, and knowledgeable about many things including art. It was a long night and, by the time we had parted and with the wine drunk, I had promised to design a logo that would be a masterpiece. I didn't, but he bought several of my paintings. Over time we became close friends. I knew little of his business affairs apart from the wine and horses. Francesca turned his life around. He adored her and she was a wonderful mother to his girls and the son they had later. They were happy and shared much of life except for his horses. Apart from riding them she had no interest, particularly not in the racing. Although she went with him all over the world, I don't think she ever saw a race. But he didn't push her. He was happy that she was with him.' Tears filled his eyes. 'I always knew him as an honest man and a true friend. That is all I can say about Vittorio.' He wiped his eyes.

Sara was beginning to sink. She didn't want to hear this validation of the man who had caused Ben and Ceri's death. Carlo held her gaze for a long moment then touched her gently.

'I know this is hard for you but you have to know the man I did. Do you want me to stop?'

Sara fought the tears, cross with herself for not being strong. She had wanted to know.

'Go on, please.'

'After the shock of his death and when Francesca was strong enough there was space for anger and confusion. It seemed such an incredible and unbelievable thing to happen. But I am not a child and know enough of the world to look at all possibilities. I have a colourful group of friends who found paths to those both inside and outside the law. Nothing came from it. He had no shadow in Siena.

Elsewhere, I don't know, but I believe that there was nothing in his life which could have given a reason for his murder. That, my sweet Sara, is all I can tell you.'

Dupard sighed. 'Fucking useless.'

Giorgio, in his earpiece, laughed. 'Couldn't have put it better, boss. But there's still Androtti. Anything interesting on him?'

'No, nothing yet, but they're digging deeper, into the widow too.'

* * *

Carlo and Marcello were arguing over the bill. Carlo wanted to pay.

'Why should you start now?' Marcello laughed. 'But if you want to impress Sara, let's play a game of chance. If you can pick up the chair with her on it in one hand then you can pay. If not, I will finish your meal with a Limoncello Amalfi that is truly the nectar of the gods.'

Carlo laughed loudly. 'He knows I won't try. It's a trick he has been doing for years and I think he wants to show you the young man he once was.'

Marcello smiled at Sara. 'May I?'

The others in the restaurant were watching.

Before Sara could refuse, Marcello bent down and in one hand gripped a back leg of the chair and slowly and without any strain lifted it gently until he was standing. Then, with a huge smile, he put it down again, just as gently. 'I will get the Limoncello.'

He went towards the bar nodding at the applause from the other tables.

'That was unbelievable.' Sara said.

'He's a bad loser so I let him win,' smiled Carlo.

Marcello joined them for the Limoncello but was soon gesticulating loudly in friendly argument with another of his diners.

Carlo put his hand on Sara's arm. 'If you want to continue with your quest I will be there if you need me but, in my heart, I know you will find nothing. It will be a torture for you to look for a reason. It will never be enough. It happened and is now in the past. But your loves will always be with you.' He smiled gently. 'I have grown fond of you in the short time since we met. You are strong and courageous and I want you to embrace the life you now have and let them live in your heart and work.' He paused, 'I want to suggest something. I have a studio on Elba. It is a beautiful place that embraces the world and those in it. I have to be in America soon. I'll be there three months, for a lecture tour and a retrospective at MOMA. I want you to use the studio on Elba whilst I'm there. There is another that you could have but I want you to feel the heart of this one. You are welcome to everything. Caria and Pietro have been looking after me there for years and they will do the same for you. They live in a small house in the grounds so you will have your own space. There is food, drink, and even a boat for you to use. Think about it, please. It is a place for healing.'

Carlo got up from the table. 'I have to go. I have a television show to do. I would much rather stay with you but I have given my word I will be a part of the selection panel for Young Artist of the Year.'

Sara hugged him. 'Thank you for the meal, I'll think about Elba.' She kissed his cheek. 'I shouldn't have had the Limoncello. It was delicious but I feel a bit pissed.'

Carlo chuckled. 'Good, now let's leave before Cello sees us and I will walk you back to your hotel.'

Sara saw Marcello glance over and break away from the couple he was talking to and head for them. 'Too late,' she whispered to Carlo.

* * *

Dupard read through the report on Androtti. Nothing shady. It made him less concerned for Sara, but frustrated that he might not be able to offer her anything that could be of help. But, who knew, there might be something that stimulated a connection that would go somewhere. Androtti probably had a large group of friends, perhaps some even in government in Siena, and it wasn't too much of a stretch to think that one of those might be involved in something that linked them to a world even darker than politics. And he and Rietti moved in the same social whirl. So he could lead them to someone else. He'd had one bit of positive news from Adolfo. His contacts would look at the picture and see if they could find a face they knew. It was a long stretch, particularly as Dupard didn't have a Paddington photograph yet. But he'd got the techs in Toronto to mock one up and it should be with him in a couple of hours. They were using CCTV from the platforms, mobile phone shots, and the footage that had inundated the police. They knew roughly from the position of one guy who was standing behind the Italian and had been covered in bits of brain that it was a black spot for the CCTV cameras. And everyone else had either been unaware or had only seen a shadow in amongst the crowds. Nobody had seen a face. You'd have thought that even in a crowd of unobservant people, one of them might have noticed someone with a gun. But just having the photo looked at would get word out that Sara was searching, and if it got to whoever had ordered the hit then she would become a target. Dupard's team were always close to her and would move fast if there was danger. There was a risk that they'd take her out from a distance, but he guessed that they'd want more from her. See what she knew, and if she was doing it alone or had others with her.

Selma's voice made him start.

'She's home. Braggio walked with her then left her at the door. She looked like she'd had a good lunch. I'll stay out here to see whether she goes out again. We're picking up the audio feed now. If she's in for the night, is it all right if I get relieved a bit early. I promised to take Silvia out for a meal. I missed her birthday last month and can't let her down again. She'd never forgive me.'

'Sure, I'll get someone there in an hour.'

How long had it been since he'd done anything like that with his son? He'd missed so much of Marcus growing up and now he'd soon become a father himself. Dupard wondered what it would be like to be a grandfather. He would have to visit and try to rescue their relationship before then. For a moment he considered ringing him to touch base but that moment passed. He put him out of his mind and went back to the reports.

* * *

Sara came out of the bathroom. She had been bursting for a pee and run straight in without seeing the room. So she was surprised to see flowers tied with a red and white silk thread on the bed. There were five pure white roses and a single deep red one. Attached to the silk was a small rolled scroll of vellum. That was a classy if over the top touch. Sara knew they were from Paolo Androtti. She opened the scroll. There was a phone number and the letter 'P'. For a moment she wasn't sure how she felt about it. Wasn't it a bit creepy to send someone you have just met flowers that obviously meant something? Or was it a lovely thing to do? She decided on the latter. She hadn't had flowers for a long time, and they were beautiful. Somehow, they looked like they'd been picked from a garden and not shop bought. It made her feel good about herself for a moment. Then a memory slipped in of Ceri giving her an orchid and a yellow rose when he asked her to marry him and she felt a wave of pain wash over her. She hadn't usually liked romantic gestures like that but somehow it was just right and she knew she wanted to marry Ceri. She loved him more than she ever thought she could love anyone. And then when Ben was born her love was shared. The love for Ceri hadn't changed but for Ben it was all-consuming, powerful, and shocked her to her core. She knew she would die for him.

But she hadn't died for him. He had died and she couldn't change his destiny to hers. She sat on the bed and the tears came. There was a knock at the door. Elena was there, holding a vase. At first she took the tears for joy at the flowers, then saw there was more depth there.

'What is it, Sara?'

'A sad memory.'

'The flowers?'

'Yes, they're beautiful but they reminded me of someone who died.'

'I am sure that gorgeous young man would not have wanted them to do that.'

'No.'

She handed Sara the vase. 'I brought this for them, and I wondered whether you would like to eat with us tonight. Julia is home for a couple of days and she would like to practice her English with you.'

This bit of normality helped Sara to recover.

'I'm sorry, but I've eaten too much today. I just had a huge lunch and probably too much to drink which always makes me emotional.'

'Perhaps you could talk with her at breakfast then.'

'Yes, of course. Thank you for the vase.'

Elena smiled and left, gently shutting the door. Sara arranged the flowers in the vase carefully and stood it on the small dressing table. She picked the vellum off the bed, looked at the number, then found her phone in the depths of her bag.

'Hello.'

'Paolo?'

'Yes. How was lunch with Carlo? Entertaining?'

'Yes, it was, but I think I had too much wine.'

'You do when you dine with Carlo. What did you think of Marcello?'

'He was fun and a little…' She searched for the right word.

'Crazy. Yes, he is. Did he do the chair thing?'

Sara laughed. She felt at ease. It was like talking to an old friend. 'He did. I was afraid he would collapse.'

'He's a bull.'

'Thank you for the flowers, they are lovely.'

'Not too much?'

'I wasn't sure. It felt a bit creepy at first but I enjoyed the thought behind them.'

He laughed. 'That's honest.'

'Sorry.'

'No, it's fine. I love honesty, even if it flips you now and again. Are you free for a trip around my Siena tomorrow?'

Sara hesitated for a moment. 'I'd like that.'

'I'll pick you up at eleven on my scooter. Wear something you will feel comfortable in. It will be fun but not luxury. Goodnight, Sara.'

'Goodnight, Paolo.'

Sara was excited about meeting him but it was shadowed with the memories the flowers had brought. She knew she could have a day out with a man without feeling guilty, but it still felt strange. It was as though it was happening to someone else, another Sara, one who was allowed to have fun. And as Peter had said, life, in all its passion and pain went on. You either rode with it or gave up. Thoughts came and went like feathers in the wind. Wasn't it time she found her own reason? But she had to have room to do that. These three men kept slipping in and out, sharing space and clouding her focus. Peter first, then Carlo, and only hours ago, Paolo. Carlo was safe and, she knew, would grow into a friend she could always trust. She was sure about that. Were these snap judgments going to be a part of her new life now?

Then the meanderings paused like a sharp breath before action. The ordered part of her understanding started to separate and scan. Peter was… what? Nothing came to her instantly. She had always relied on first thoughts. What did she have with him? Was it something to hold on to? A safety net? That wasn't fair to him. She should try and talk to him. Should she call him now? He might be out of the wilderness with his son… No, she had left enough messages. He would call when he could.

She had to stop trying to analyse her feelings about the time with Peter. It was something that had happened and helped. He had given her the courage to drag herself out of her grief and anger. She owed him for that. But with a shock, she realised that she didn't feel a need for him anymore. It was a balanced thing between them. Perhaps it was the moment in time for both of them when they found strength. Would she be able to love him? Where the fuck had that come from? Random. It didn't help that she now had a hangover. Although compared to the gut-wrenching ones she used to suffer, something she could easily handle. She got off the bed and stood on the balcony. See, that's what happened if you let go. She went back into the room, took some ibuprofen, found her sketchpad, and started to draw. It calmed her as Carlo's face slowly appeared.

* * *

Dupard needed a break from the screen to clear his head. The small café was a block from his hotel and filled with taxi drivers from the rank outside. The food was cheap but tasty and the coffee strong. He would have loved a glass of wine but he had a feeling it would be a long night. He wanted to get the composite of the Paddington photos ready to go by morning. They'd sent him three versions he could cut and paste to come up with something that worked for him. He then had to send it back for the guys to make it look original and then, once that was done, get it over to the reluctant Adolfo. He finished his coffee, paid up, and went out. Walking back to the hotel he wondered if he would ever get to enjoy cities like Siena for their beauty and culture, or whether they would always carry an image of this world he inhabited in his work.

He watched a young couple kiss passionately and felt a sudden sense of lost moments and innocence, as they held hands and ran to the other side of the road, dodging the traffic, laughing at the blaring horns. He felt old and weary. Perhaps he should look at his life again. His time in Wales with Sara had given him a glimpse of something that might be possible. But it would be in another life with people who had not coloured this one. He didn't feel bad about that. It was just what it would have to be. He forced his mind back on to what he needed to do and walked quickly towards the door of his hotel in the small back street.

CHAPTER EIGHTEEN

Sara slept right through the night and woke with a shadow of a dream about Ben and Ceri but she couldn't remember what happened in it. Still, she felt differently this morning. More positive. It was a beautiful day and she wasn't exhausted. She was looking forward to her adventure with Paolo. If nothing else, she hoped she would learn more about Siena and its art, history, and architecture. She had already decided it might be best to get to know Paolo a bit before asking him about Rietti. To enjoy today without the looming anticipation of framing the question in a way that wouldn't seem the reason for spending time with him. That wasn't true. She felt excited about seeing him and seemed to have put away the guilt for now.

She lay there and listened to the sounds from outside. It was noisy with everyday activities and the added bluster as the Palio preparations began in earnest.

Then Peter flashed into her mind again.

Just before she had gone to bed she had tried to call him. She hadn't intended to, just found herself doing it. He wasn't there and she hadn't left a message. She wouldn't do it again and this time would wait for him to call. Perhaps she wouldn't hear from him ever. He might have decided that a relationship with a damaged, mercurially emotional woman was not a pathway to a peaceful life. How would she feel about that today? Strangely she still felt as she had yesterday. It might be better for both of them in some ways if they could move on. She would miss the trust and wise words though.

As she was getting out of bed she saw the sketchpad on the floor and picked it up. The drawing of Carlo was really good. How long had she worked on it? It must have been hours. But it was worth it. She had found some of the truth in his eyes.

She yawned suddenly. What time had she gone to sleep? She looked at her watch. It was ten fifteen. She would have had seven hours even if it was three before she dropped off. Then came a moment of panic when she realized she was meeting Paolo at eleven and she didn't know what she was going to wear. Not that she had a great choice. There were the black jeans and a few tops.

Then she sprang up. What was she doing still sitting on the edge of the bed? Suddenly she remembered promising to have breakfast with Elena's daughter, Julia. She didn't have time. She hoped they wouldn't be upset. She'd try and see her later today. She ran into the bathroom.

* * *

Paolo was waiting outside the guesthouse, sitting on a bright red Lambretta 200; not that Sara knew what it was or really cared. He looked gorgeous. It was eleven thirty.

She smiled. 'I'm really sorry, I woke up late.'

Paolo got off the scooter and kissed her on both

cheeks. 'Today there is no such thing as time.' He passed her a helmet. 'You ridden on one of these before?'

'I had an off-road bike when I was a kid but I got fed up being soaked in mud and rain. I was quite good though.'

'Then this will be a wonderful experience. Being on a Lambretta is like nothing else.' He touched the scooter. 'She is my love.' He got on. Sara sat on the pillion seat. 'You need to put your arms around me but it is more a practicality than a pleasure for me. Although I am sure it will be that too. It's going to be a bit bumpy in parts but she loves the streets and hills and will be proud to carry you around them.'

'Why is it a she?'

'I'm a man. For you it could be 'he'.' He turned round and smiled. 'Fasten your helmet and hold on.'

He started the scooter and they moved off. Sara did up the strap and then quickly put her arms around him. It felt strange but really nice too.

For the next couple of hours, they rode through the narrow streets that criss-crossed the city, over bridges, climbing hills, and speeding through parks. With Paolo shouting out when they passed a wall fresco, a beautiful church, the home of a famous artist, or places where assassinations had taken place during the battles between contradas.

They stopped for 'the best ice cream in Siena'. Paolo charmed the girls serving while Sara waited outside with the scooter. She watched him. He had a childlike quality that was endearing and natural. The ice cream was delicious and probably the best she had ever tasted.

'I was six years old when my grandfather brought me to try the ice cream of his friend, Angelo. He told me that once I had tasted it, I would never enjoy another so much. He was right. Angelo would never give away the secret of his recipe. It had been in his family for a hundred years and he would die rather than reveal it. Even now with Alberto, his grandson, running the gelateria, despite many new flavours and soya and frozen yoghurts, it is still the bestselling ice cream.'

Sara finished the last of her ice cream. 'That was just unbelievable.'

He smiled. 'It will have spoiled you for life.' He got off the scooter. 'Now, you have to make a choice: we can have lunch or I can show you one of my hidden treasures.'

'No contest, the treasure.'

Paolo laughed. 'You want to drive?'

'What?'

'Risky, I know, but where's life without a bit of danger?'

Sara felt a spark of challenge. 'If I kill us it's your fault.'

'Sure.'

'And if I want to stop, you take over.'

'Yes.'

'You like taking risks?'

'I do.'

'Why?'

'It's a challenge to the gods.'

His easy laugh made her smile in agreement, although she felt a bit nervous at taking on the scooter.

Then he kissed her cheek, sat on the back, and she was ready.

She got on and he talked her through the gears and throttle. She started it up and let out the throttle slowly, then stopped. She felt Paolo's arms go around her waist and hold on gently. No pressure.

She turned to Paolo. 'Ready?'

'Of course.' He smiled. 'Go.'

She let out the throttle again slowly and they moved off. It didn't take long for her to find her balance, then it all came back. It was similar to the trail bike, heavier to steer but she could handle it. She started to have fun. Paolo gave her directions, cutting through narrow side streets when the traffic stopped or sliding past when there was just enough space. When they finally came to a stop in the Piazza del Campo she turned to Paolo. 'I loved that. You were right, she's a star, and she seemed to like me.'

Paolo laughed. 'Next time we go off road too.'

He climbed off, opened one of the carriers, and took out two pairs of rubber boots, one in blue, the smaller one in red. He handed the red ones to Sara. 'They are a size thirty-nine, a six in the UK. I thought they might fit.'

Sara took them. They were shiny and new-looking. 'They will, but why boots?'

Paolo smiled. 'You'll find out.'

Sara put the boots on, and Paolo put on the blue pair. He put their shoes into the carrier and locked it. He got on the scooter. 'I'll be back soon.' He drove off across the road and into a small alley at the side of a building.

Sara hadn't felt like this for a long, long time, light and free and easy. No weight of decision spinning in dark circles of the past. It was just being here now and letting go. She loved this feeling of excitement at not knowing what was going to happen next. She had been impulsive when she was younger. Ceri had loved and hated that. It shook his order and control but excited his edgier side. She had changed when she had Ben. Life had to be built around the focus he needed. But it was good to be back, even if it was only going to be for today. And she was having fun with Paolo.

He walked out of the alley. 'Angelo, my grandfather's friend, is ninety-four and still has his ice cream every day. He plays with wood and has a shed at the back of his apartment building. He will look after my precious until we return.'

'Where are we going?'

He took her hand. 'To show you a treasure.'

In a green Suzuki 750, Selma was watching from fifty metres away as Sara and Paolo walked hand in hand across the Piazza towards the Fonta Gaia. All around were the preparations for the Palio. They were marking up the crowd barriers and the dozens of stalls that would sit on the periphery.

'Marco, have you got them.'

'Yes. Giorgio?'

'In front.'

'Boss, is the audio good?'

'Good enough. She's not going to raise Rietti now. It's wrong. She's bright, she won't want him to think that's all she wants.' There was silence. 'Shit, the audio's gone again. I thought it worked even if the phone died.'

'Sometimes it goes down. We have to wait.' Selma was calm. It happened a lot in Siena. Even if the batteries on a phone were good, the buildings didn't help. Technology needed minimal architecture to be at its best.

'Don't lose her. Giorgio, Marco, I'll have your balls if you do.'

She heard 'I won't, boss,' from Giorgio. And 'Hang on…' from Marco.

'What is it?'

'I can't see them. They were heading towards tables outside a restaurant. I'll get a bit closer.'

Paolo and Sara reached the restaurant. Paolo spoke to one of the waiters who helped him move a table. Underneath there was a manhole cover that he pulled up with a metal lever.

'What are you doing?'

Paolo laughed. 'Down here is one of Siena's special secrets.'

'And we're going there?'

'Sure.'

'Are we allowed?'

Paolo laughed. 'Of course.' He showed her the lever. 'I have the key and permission from La Diana for a special visit. A friend of my father's is one of the chiefs there. And as there are no official tours because of the Palio, it is the only way you would be able to see it.'

'What's La Diana?'

'An association, almost as secret as the Bottini, that runs the waterways under the city.'

'What's the Bottini?

'A magical place that carries water to all of the fountains in Siena. A hidden world built more than eight hundred years ago.'

'Not a sewer then?'

'That wouldn't be a treasure.'

Sara laughed. 'True. Let's go.'

Paolo produced two torches on headbands and handed one to Sara.

'Aren't there any lights?'

'No, but these will be enough. Trust me.'

'OK.'

This was a day when she just went with the wind.

'You go first and I'll close the cover behind us. It's OK, the steps are safe.'

Sara climbed into the hole and disappeared, Paolo followed and the cover was pulled shut.

In the Piazza, Giorgio turned and walked away. 'They've gone down into the Bottini. The entrance was a manhole under a table in a restaurant. I heard someone say that it wasn't official. No way I could follow them.'

Dupard laughed. 'Shit. The Bottini feeds the fountains right?'

Selma joined in. 'Yes.'

'How big is it?'

'There are twenty-five kilometres of tunnels.'

'We'll have to wait until they come out.' Dupard was amused. 'Anyone been down there?'

'Once,' Selma answered 'but it was with my first real boyfriend. We were fourteen, and slipped away from the guide to discover each other. So I don't remember much about it.'

Marco laughed.

Dupard interrupted. 'Enough. Marco, Giorgio, any other way for them to get out?

'I'm on it now, boss.' Marco was already moving.

'Me too,' said Giorgio.

'Don't imagine they'll do the full route. So the nearest place will do. Selma, you wait there.'

Dupard wasn't concerned. It was only a part of her day with Paolo and they hadn't eaten yet. They'd be back soon.

* * *

'They were built between the twelfth and fifteenth centuries. To bring hill water to Siena to feed the fountains and, for those rich enough, a supply directly to their homes.' Paolo pointed to names written on rough squares of plaster: *Casa Giuseppe, Casa Ronaldo*. Each had a diagram of their location to the tunnel and the path of their water.

Sara loved the style of the barrel-shaped tunnels. It was as though time hadn't moved on down here. The light from the head torches they were using was white and uniform. She imagined the fiery torches of the early Sienese flickering around the walls. 'It's beautiful.'

Paolo turned towards her from the narrowing passage. 'The workers used a tool called an Archipendolo, a sort of plumb line, to measure the inclination so that the water would flow purely and freely. It was hard work and the men who spent most of their days down here were called the Guerchi, the blind.'

He checked his watch and walked back towards her. 'I think perhaps we can come back to the Bottini another time. I promised it would only be a short visit and Camillo in the café will report back. I don't want to lose the good will of my uncle.'

She was confused. 'Uncle? I thought it was your father's friend?'

'I thought it was too soon to introduce family favours.'

'And now it's OK?'

'We have shared the secret of the Bottini, so you should know the truth.' He laughed. 'I'm sorry. I promise from now on I will share family and friends too.'

Sara smiled. 'I'm glad to hear it but I have my secrets too.'

'Tell me one.'

'I don't know you well enough yet.'

'I can wait.' He smiled, turned and the shadows bounced around the walls.

Sara was a bit disappointed. She could have stayed there for hours just letting her eyes roam around the shapes and textures. It was good material for her to use to create abstract images when she was ready to explore that again. 'OK, but I'd love to come back soon.'

She followed Paolo along the tunnel and into the arched entrance to the stairs and the trapdoor.

'The fountains the Bottini fed were always guarded and the supply limited and those found there without permission would be punished. Fonte Gaiai is the site of the only person burned at the stake in Siena. She was found there at night and, although she probably had done nothing wrong, the fact that she might have done was enough. They burned her.'

'Horrible.'

'Yes, a harsher time.'

He pushed up the trapdoor.

In the street, Selma saw the trapdoor open and first Paolo then Sara come out.

'They're out, boss.'

'OK, Marco, Giorgio, get back here. If they're going on the scooter again, you've got a bit of time.' There was the sound of the trapdoor shutting. 'Audio's back.'

'Video feed is good too.'

* * *

Sara kissed Paolo on the cheek. 'Thank you, that was special.'

'One of many treasures. Are you ready to get back on my beauty?'

'Where are we going next?'

'For a light lunch. Later, if you are willing, I would like to take you to a very special restaurant so we need just enough to keep us going. Is that alright?'

Sara felt excited and at ease. The fun of being with Paolo stretched out enticingly and she wanted it to go on as long as it could. She was enjoying a moment where there were no shadows. There had been times when she thought that would never happen. 'Of course.'

They walked across the square and went down the alley towards Angelo's. Paolo took her hand again.

'With luck, Angelo might still have some ice cream hidden in his fridge.'

* * *

As the Lambretta came out of the alley, Giorgio, on his larger, newer Piaggio scooter, pulled in front and Selma followed. Marco, on a big Harley, waited then set off after them. They were covered whichever way the couple went.

Sara held tightly to Paolo as they changed direction taking a narrow street ahead then turning into another that proved to be a steep incline. 'I love Siena.' Paolo laughed. 'You cannot help it.'

They had to slow as a large bike pulled out in front of them from a side street and shot away, overtaking a scooter that was stopping in front of a small café.

'The Harley-Davidson is a wonderful machine," Paolo said. 'I had one when I was young. But it was not the love affair I have now with this angel.'

He kissed the handlebars of the Lambretta. Sara laughed.

Giorgio watched as they went past and out of sight. 'They're having fun.'

Selma laughed as she passed him. 'Boys and their toys.'

A guy pulled up on a Honda and Giorgio got on it as the driver got off and went to the Piaggio. Giorgio turned at the next street. 'Marco, where are you?'

'Heading up Lazza. Where are you?'

'Should pick you up in five minutes.'

Later, Sara and Paolo stopped for an antipasti snack at a small mobile café overlooking a beautiful park. It was four p.m. and still bright with sunshine.

He told her about his first trip to London when he was nine and wanted to meet the Queen.

'My father said she was too busy to meet me and took me to see the Changing of the Guard instead. I had to make do with a photo taken outside Buckingham Palace next to one of the soldiers.' He paused. 'I did meet Prince Charles though, at a charity awards ceremony at Cambridge where he…'

He noticed that Sara had stopped listening.

He reached out and touched her arm.

Sara had slipped into a painful past. For a moment she almost told him about Ben and Ceri and their last trip to London, but it was too much for now. She smiled at his concern.

'No, it just brought back a memory. It was a strange dream I used to have when I was little about a band of guardsmen with bearskins who played as they marched towards me but never seemed to get closer. They were all deaf. I don't know how I knew that, I just did. It was frightening and used to wake me up. I think the fact that they couldn't hear their music is what upset me. I played piano and violin and tried to block up my ears so that I couldn't hear the music I was playing. But it never seemed to work. The music was always in my head. I haven't thought of that for ages.' She laughed. 'Crazy Welsh woman.'

'It's why stories are shared, to spark off memories and make more stories.' He got up. 'Come on, we need to change vehicles for the next part of your day out.' He took her by the hand and pulled her up.

They rode ridden down another alley in between two townhouses on a quiet street and into a beautiful walled courtyard with two archways. They went through one and into a small garden overflowing with roses, chrysanthemums, and bougainvillea. Paolo pulled up outside a small house. A woman in her forties came out to meet them. She was slim and stylish.

'Paolo,' she smiled. 'You should have called.'

He kissed her on both cheeks. 'It has been a day of freedom without thought.' He turned to Sara. 'Forgive me, Sara, this is Sophia, she lets me have a room here when I have an early start.'

Sophia laughed. 'I am his *governante* here.' She searched for the word. 'Housekeeper in English.'

Paolo put his arm around her. 'Much more than that.'

'I'll get some coffee?' said Sophia.

'I'm sorry, we haven't time. Will you ask Bernardo to meet me at the front with the car.' He turned to Sara again, 'Bernardo is Sophia's husband and is responsible for both this beautiful garden and my car.'

Sophia smiled at Sara. She was relaxed and her beauty was gentle and subtle. 'It was nice to meet you.'

'And you.' Sara felt drawn to her. Perhaps next time they would talk. 'What next time? Why would they meet again?' She glanced at Paolo as if he might have read her thoughts but he just smiled at her.

'Did Barnardo get everything?' he asked Sophia.

'Yes, it's in the car.' Sophia smiled and went into the house, taking out a mobile, as they walked away. She didn't look back at them.

* * *

Selma watched as a tall man in an open-top blue Mini Cooper stopped by Paolo and Sara. He got out and Sara was introduced to him. She and Paolo got into the car and drove off. The tall man smiled as he watched the car disappear, then he went into the alleyway.

'Marco, they're on the move again in a blue Mini Cooper and heading your way.'

'I see them.'

Dupard watched the Mini Cooper from behind as it twisted and turned through the streets and onto a wider road. The car took a right at a sign to Monticelli. It was where Androtti lived. Perhaps he was taking her home. Bit much for a first date, but might be useful.

Dupard had managed to get his boss to authorise a drone and the pilot was linked into their audio. It made life a bit easier but was an expensive toy and its use had to be requested and validated each day. At least they were covered from the air and by the personal cameras his team used on their vehicles and bodies. For the next couple of days anyway.

The video feed changed and the car was picked up from the front. He zoomed in. Sara looked relaxed but excited, as she soaked in everything the Mini was passing. There was cello music playing. Dupard hadn't heard it before. It sounded like a contemporary piece.

'Where are we going?' Sara said quietly.

'Wait and see.'

There was warmth in Paolo's voice. She turned her head towards him and he glanced at her. It was a brief, held moment.

He turned his eyes back to the road. After a moment Sara did the same.

Dupard knew that closeness between them might bring trust. He hoped Sara would play her part and not let emotion distract her. He was pretty sure she was focused but he had to be ready to play a curve ball too.

He stretched. He was wading slowly through the pages of reports on the series of killings again and already he was going word blind. Despite the number of times he'd read them, he hoped that this time he might pick up on something he'd missed. He was looking through the London stuff and reading the statement of the young man who had been covered in bits of Rietti. It would be a constant nightmare for him.

He rubbed his eyes and thought about meeting Sara that first time. She was achingly raw but there was a shadow of spirit and passion that might have drawn them together if his truth had been more innocent…

'Fuck.'

He had to stop that happening. Those moments, usually when his energy was low, when he thought of her not as a means to an end, but as someone who needed compassion, only got in the way. He had to be focused on what must be done, coldly, clinically, and objectively. It was the only way.

He pushed it out of his mind and went back to the screen, scanning through the pages knowing that if there were something there he had to find it. The music in his headphones always helped him focus, but was soporific if he was tired. Like now! He needed coffee. The noise of the traffic increased, horns blared and a siren screeched in and out of his hearing.

'Selma, everything all right?

'Yes, just shit traffic and everyone's pissed with it. We're ten kilometres from Monticelli. Gio's taking over from Marco soon. He's got his kid's birthday party to get to by six. Twenty seven-year-olds and an ex-wife and her new man, lucky boy.' She laughed.

'Glad I'm way past all that," Dupard said. "Sounds like a nightmare. I'm going to have a break. I'll call when I'm back. Anything important, text me."

'Sure, boss. Do you want a bite to eat later?'

'Maybe.'

He took off the headphones.

* * *

Paolo stopped the car at the bottom of a steep, winding road that led up to what looked like a medieval building on the top of the wooded hill.

'Beautiful.' Sara smiled at Paolo. 'It's a monastery?'

'Yes. It was built in the thirteenth century for an Order of Benedictine nuns called the Poor Ladies. The abbess was famous, she was called Agnes of Monticelli and became a Saint. Her real name was Catarina, she was the daughter of a count whose cousin was one of the original disciples of Francis of Assisi. Catarina and her big sister, Clara, ran away from home to join Francis, who gave her the name Agnes. Later Clara was sent by him to found the Order of the Poor Ladies who soon became the Poor Clares. Agnes went with her, and so did her mother. Which must have been the final humiliation for the old count who had tried and failed to bring his daughters back. After a few years Clara sent Agnes to found an Order at Monticelli. Agnes built the monastery here in 1230. So it's a bit of an old heap. Want to have a look?'

'Another of your father's friends?'

'No, I live there.'

It took Sara a moment for that to sink in.

'Shit!'

He laughed, then checked the road behind and accelerated up the hill.

High above them, out of sight, the drone continued to feed sound and pictures back to Dupard.

* * *

Selma and Giorgio were waiting for instructions. They had held back far enough to avoid the risk of being seen but stayed close enough to see where the mini Cooper went.

Dupard's voice came through the car speaker.

'I'm back. Are they at the house? The feed's a bit busy to see detail but it should settle down.'

'We're still at the bottom of the hill. Be tricky to follow them up there now. I don't know what we'd find and what the sightlines are like. We could move up if they're still there when it gets dark.'

Selma looked up at the monastery. What a place to live! Too isolated for her, she was an urban fox, needed the city in her blood. Must be worth millions. With that sort of wealth he would be well protected. Riches had their downside though. She wondered how many 'staff' he had there and if they lived in. There would be at least a couple who did. They'd have to be careful when they went up to look, although the 'spy in the sky' was pretty good at picking up most tricks if the interference wasn't deliberate.

'Giorgio, you can get off now,' Dupard said. 'Selma, I'll join you in a couple of hours, once I've got some info on the house.'

'I can handle it.'

'No, I want a closer look at the place and I need Giorgio back here at six a.m. fresh and bright. I've got a trip to Rome first thing and I need him to liaise.'

'Give us a call when you're close and we'll meet you.'

Giorgio smiled at Selma. 'I'll tell Marco on my way back. Have fun!'

CHAPTER NINETEEN

The Mini drove through huge wooden gates that opened as it approached.

Paolo smiled. 'A message between car and gates is wonderful, but difficult when technology breaks down and you have to open them manually. They are solid teak and hard to manoeuvre.'

The gates closed silently behind them. They drove up a short avenue of trees and n through another leaf-covered gate that again opened to let them through. And in front of them, was where Paolo lived.

'Fuck! Sorry, it's... stunning.'

'It's home.' He laughed.

Paolo's 'heap' was a mishmash sprawl whose scars of time had been healed with a delicate and skilled conversion. The cloisters ran alongside a vast glass wall which wrapped itself around the building. There was a small chapel and outbuildings made of sandstone and travertine coloured with the outlines of faded frescos. It was surrounded by a walled garden and offered a grandstand view of the beautiful medieval town of Monticelli. Vines and olive trees cascaded down the hillsides.

'It took years to bring life again to St Agnes but now her breath is sweet and her heartbeat strong.'

'Are all your possessions female?' Shit, she thought, the words had just come out, fast and spiky.

He laughed. 'Forgive me. I will try to introduce you to the masculine too.'

An old man came out from the cloisters. Tall, elegant, and white-haired, dressed in dark trousers and a white shirt that were stylish and exactly right. He also wore red suede loafers. Paolo smiled at him.

'Just in time, proof that not all things in my life are feminine.'

He got out of the car and went around to open Sara's door. 'I am proud of my heap but not boastful. It is all down to family, luck, good advice, and a bit of instinct.'

The old man came towards them and took her hand in his. His face was gentle, his eyes twinkled, his large nose was aquiline, and his smile easy. Sara thought he looked like the sculptured heads she had seen of Julius Caesar.

'This is Roberto. He was my grandfather's dearest friend and now he lives here with me, beats me at chess, and stimulates my brain. He also has a magical way with my horses.'

Roberto smiled. 'He exaggerates, as always. My daughter and her husband look after everything here and allow me to help. Paolo lets me stay in the house with them.' He kissed Sara's hand. 'Good to meet you, Sara.' Sara glanced towards Paolo. Roberto smiled. 'Sometimes he is like a little boy when he is excited. He told me he met you at Carlo's show.'

Sara was a bit unbalanced by the old man's truth. God, he and Carlo would be a fair old tag team.

'Did he?' She realised her hand was still in Roberto's and gently pulled it away. 'It's nice to meet you, Roberto.'

Paolo grinned. 'Now that Roberto has destroyed my credibility, he can show you around. I will open some Franciacorta, a wonderful sparkling wine, and plan the menu for tonight. I hope you will be happy to dine at Paolo's. I told you it was a very special restaurant.'

'Are you cooking, or is Roberto's daughter?'

Roberto took her arm. 'Sonia and Tonio are on holiday, but the boy has spirit and style and learned to cook at one of his grandfather's restaurants in Florence. It will be simple but delicious.'

Sara needed time to take everything in. 'I'd like to use the bathroom.'

Paolo watched as Roberto led her into the house. 'Will you be eating with us?' she asked the old man.

'Not tonight. It would have been a delight but I am playing chess against an old friend in the town and I will stay the night there, if he is not too angry when I beat him for the third time this month.' He opened a small hidden door. 'The bathroom.'

She rejoined Roberto and as they went along the cloisters, Sara glanced back at Paolo. He was unloading bags of food from the boot of the Cooper.

She had never met anyone like him before and it had unbalanced her. She should focus on being in control but the urge to just let things happen was too strong. Why not, though? She was owed some good swings of fate.

Ahead of the couple, part of the glass wall slid open and she followed Roberto into a huge atrium filled with plants and sculptures. Above was a circular glass roof. There was a balcony and what looked like an upside-down tree made of blue steel hanging centrally from the dome to the level of the balcony. It was ugly but right for the space.

'Sara,' Roberto called.

'Sorry, too much to see.' She followed him.

* * *

Sara was standing on a terrace. Below her the tiered flower garden, rich with colours and scents, tumbled down to the olive trees which, deep below in the distance, ended at a late-sun-speckled Monticelli. She was sitting on the edge of a long wooden table that would easily seat twenty but was laid for two. There was a long deep sofa covered with cushions and rugs and a brick barbecue oven. It was beautiful and peaceful and she felt good. It had been a perfect day so far, taking her into wonderful worlds of surprise and sensation.

After Roberto had shown her around, she had told Paolo more about her painting and was embarrassed when she realised he had hardly spoken before he got up to finish making their food.

The house, if you could call it that, was fantastic; an abstract mix of old and new with rooms of all shapes and sizes. There was a calm and tranquil semi-circular library of floor-to-ceiling shelves, with deep armchairs, a glass table with books, papers, and bits of sculpture, and on the flat wall one of Carlo's wonderful abstracts; a room overlooking the terrace with huge stuffed sofas; a small three-row cinema with wide comfortable seats and a large screen. A glass-walled dining room led to the balcony and overlooked the roots of the upside-down tree sculpture.

Roberto had also taken her up small runs of steps leading into what were once the nuns' cells and were now a mix of rooms. One was cluttered with pictures of horse races, cups, and rosettes; a music room stood where several of the cells had been knocked through, complete with piano, small organ, and several guitars; there was a dressing room with riding colours, and one with an altar and prayer mat that Roberto said was a quiet room for any guests who wanted peace or to touch the spiritual.

The next floor housed a series of bedrooms and bathrooms and finally the tower room that had a huge bed, doors opening on to an outside balcony, a sliding glass roof, and a walk-in wardrobe. This was Paolo's.

Sara had thought her barn was too big, but this was in another dimension altogether. Yet the strangest thing was that, despite its size, it felt like a home, warm and welcoming. With a feeling of calm, as if whatever happened in the world outside, this would remain a place of sanctuary. Perhaps that was to do with those who first brought it life.

Paolo came onto the terrace with a large bowl of salad and bread. 'Another five minutes and we can eat. I am sorry I've left you on your own.'

Sara smiled. 'I'm happy just being here in this beautiful place.'

'Let's hope the food lives up to it.'

Paolo went back inside. Sara poured a glass of wine.

CHAPTER TWENTY

The light was fading as Dupard pulled up behind Selma's bike on a small hidden track just off the main road. He was driving an old Ford Fiesta that was blue, battered, and easily forgotten. Selma was sitting against a tree, an iPad on her legs. In one ear she had a small pod. She smiled as he approached her carrying a pizza box.

'I thought they'd got rid of that pile of junk. Does nothing for your style.'

'There was nothing else available. But it's invisible and speedy enough to keep up.'

'You want to put money on that, boss?'

He laughed. He was glad he had found Selma. She was tough, smart and efficient and he liked her irreverence and casual responses, as well as her skills. She could handle most situations thrown at her with an instinctive, often oblique, focus.

'Not you and the bike but I'll give Giorgio's scooter a run. Are you getting the feed from the sky spy?'

She showed him the iPad.

They watched Paolo and Sara eating at the table on the terrace, their faces shadowed in the flickering light from two huge candles in table-high stands.

'What are they talking about?'

'Nothing interesting. Painting, the view, horses, just chat. But I think it's going to end up in something a bit steamy. You want to listen?' Dupard rolled his eyes, and Selma laughed. 'Now, I mean, not to the mucky bits later.'

Dupard sat down next to her. 'No. Seen anyone else up there?'

'Only the old guy she met when she arrived. He left a couple of hours ago on foot and headed towards the town. I'm waiting for an ID to come through. No hot spots of anyone else in the house.' She looked at the pizza box. 'Is that for me?'

He put it next to her. She handed him the iPad and a spare ear pod from her jacket.

'Should still be hot, I picked it up from a van about ten kilometres back.'

Dupard slipped the pod into his ear. Selma dug into the pizza.

Her phone buzzed in her pocket. She pulled it out and handed it to Dupard. He read the text from Rome.

'The old guy is Professor Roberto Pietro d'Angelo. 80 years old. He lives at St Agnes with Paolo Androtti. He was a Vice-Chancellor and chair of Classical Languages at the University in Florence. His wife Micheline died ten years ago. Wrote travel books and, together with Carlo Braggio and Antonio Androtti – that's Paolo's grandfather – owned a couple of restaurants in Florence. He retired six years ago and now spends his time playing chess and helping with Paolo's horses. Nothing to concern us there.'

Selma spoke with a mouthful of pizza. 'Where does he keep the horses?'

'He has stables on the other side of Monticelli.' He handed the phone back to Selma. 'I want to try and get a bit closer after you finish that… and try not to talk with your mouth full, it spoils your style.'

'Hah!

*　*　*

'Paolo, that was fantastic. What did you call it?'

'Fagioli all'ucceletto. It's a traditional Sienese dish. Plain, simple, and passed down through families. Each one adds its own touch so no two will ever be the same and you will never forget the first time you ate it. I wanted it to be special for you.'

Suddenly he felt nervous. It was unusual for him, but he didn't want Sara to think that he was typical of Italian men. Of course, in some ways he was, but not in his attitudes towards women. Sara's gentle beauty, her openness, sense of fun and the inner fragility he sensed, had touched him and he wanted to make her feel safe with him. He picked up the bottle of wine and shared the last drops between the two glasses.

Sara touched his hand. 'It was, thank you. And the whole day has been too.'

He leaned towards her gently kissing her cheek, then her lips.

Suddenly Ben's eyelash butterfly kisses slipped into Sara's thoughts and then out again. It was only a moment, then it was gone, but it was too late.

Paolo moved away. 'I'm sorry.'

Sara shook her head and moved towards him pulling him up from his seat and holding him tightly against her, unable now to stop the tears. 'What is it, Sara?'

'Just hold me, please.'

Paolo wrapped his arms around her and led her to the sofa. Then held her, her face buried in his neck, his voice soothing. He knew she would find a way out of this moment on her own. Slowly she stopped crying and he gently smoothed the wet away from under her eyes. 'Do you want to tell me what hurts you?'

Sara looked at him and felt such a deep longing that she could hardly breathe. She moved towards him and then they were together, kissing, touching, uncontrolled. They pulled their clothes off and suddenly, sharply, crying out, she pulled him inside her.

* * *

Dupard and Selma were hidden amongst the olive trees near the wall on the terrace side of the house. The intruder systems found by the drone could easily be isolated and a fault introduced. The sensors were expensive, sophisticated, but nothing out of the ordinary for the wealthy. The trickier game was when there were some real players who needed serious protection and Androtti didn't seem to be one of those. Dupard' team was on standby, but by the look of what was going on between Paolo and Sara they were in for a quiet night. When Sara had started to cry, it had touched him but he shut it down quickly. Paolo had surprised him. He had been gentle and caring.

Selma chuckled. 'I told you. Lucky girl.'

Dupard was looking at her.

'What?' she asked.

He smiled. 'Nothing. I'm going to get back. I'll brief the team and send someone to take over from you.'

Selma checked the iPad. Paolo and Sara were wrapped around each other, their heads close together. 'When are you back from Rome?'

'Early evening," Dupard said. 'Keep me updated. You're in charge but treat them gently, they're not all as smart as you.'

He disappeared into the trees.

Selma watched for a moment and then turned back to the screen. Paolo and Sara were making love again. 'Oh, for God's sake, give me a break.'

Suddenly, she felt a longing to be home with Silvia and to share their life with someone other than her wonderful, uncomplaining mum. It had been four years since her husband, Patrick, a cop too, had been killed in a raid and she still missed his voice and touch. It had taken her two years to start dating again but they had all been disastrous and so she had given up. Now Silvia was trying to get her onto dating sites. So far she had resisted. She wanted what Sara had with Paolo. A brief affair might not do that.

Her phone vibrated in her pocket. It was Dupard.

'I called Milo. He's on his way, should be there in half an hour. Get home to Silvia, have breakfast together, and take her to school in the morning before you clock in.'

He hung up.

Selma smiled. Did he have a feed to her thoughts now? It wouldn't surprise her.

A loud cry echoed in her ear. Thank Christ for that! Perhaps they'd give it a rest now.

Sara looked at Paolo, his eyes closed, his face relaxed. He was beautiful. His legs were entwined with hers and his arms around her. She could feel his breath on her face slowly deepening as he slipped into sleep. The lovemaking had been all she hoped it would be and the sense of closeness was giving her peace and her whole body felt calm. For a moment she fought the sleep, then gave in to it, her head close to Paolo's, her breath a mirror of his.

Sometime in the night they had woken, gone to Paolo's bedroom, and made love again.

When Sara woke it was almost eleven o'clock and she was on her own. For a moment she didn't know where she was. Then it all came back and she laid her head on the pillows and looked up at the blue cloudless sky through the open roof. This was a glorious room and the bed was incredible, the biggest she'd ever slept in and probably the most comfortable. She wondered where Paolo was and then on the pillows next to her found the note he had left.

'Cara mia, when you wake, Roberto will take you to see the horses. I am testing out a young stallion for the Palio next year. If you want to go to Siena, he will take you there instead. But I long to see you. P.'

In the kitchen, she made toasted ciabatta and ate it with honey while waiting for her coffee to cool. It had taken her time to find things but it was fun searching. The kitchen was a bit big for her tastes but the mix of original and contemporary technology worked really well and the huge old butcher's block was comforting to sit at. It reminded her of her aunt's farm and the breakfasts with the family and farm workers, surrounded by dogs, cats and, sometimes, an orphaned lamb, as the huge Aga breathed warmth and security.

She had just started her coffee when Roberto came in.

He smiled at her. 'I am sorry I wasn't here to make you breakfast but I had to go into town to pick up a prescription I had forgotten to take with me last night. I thought you would find something if you were awake before I got back. I hope you slept well.'

'I did, thank you, Roberto. Paolo said you would take me to the stables. Can we do that on the way back to Siena.'

Roberto smiled. 'Of course. We can leave as soon as you're ready?'

Sara finished her coffee and took her mug and plate to the sink and washed them out. Roberto watched her, amused.

She smiled at him 'What?'

'It's good to see a guest who does not take things for granted.'

'Ten minutes.'

'Perfect.'

* * *

Morosito was Paolo's favourite horse, a beautiful dappled-grey, strong and fast with the heart of a hero. Paolo had trained him for two years and felt that by the time of the next Palio, he would be ready. Emilio Giatta, a three-time winner of the Palio, who Paolo had met when the young man had moved to Siena ten years before to work at the Androtti stables, had already promised to ride him, if it could be arranged. It had taken him five years to win his first Race but now he was sought after by all the contradas. However, he would ride for Leocorno if Morosito was ready.

Paolo loved being out on Morosito. He took him on a circular track that went around a field the same size as the Palio course and was covered with the same mixture of earth, volcanic stone and sand. He also rode him around the hills to build up his strength.

This was their second circuit and Paolo spoke quietly to the horse, pushing him to go faster. He rarely used the whip on these practice runs. They came around the last turn and as they sped past, Paolo saw Roberto and Sara reach the gate into the field. For a moment he lost concentration and Morosito, sensing the change, began to slow. Paolo slapped him on the rump and urged him on until they reached the measured end, then slowed and trotted round again to the gate.

Roberto rubbed the horse's nose and as Paolo jumped off he threw a blanket over Morosito's glistening back. 'There must be no distraction,' he said.

Paolo put his arm around Roberto. 'You are right.' He touched Sara's hand. 'Roberto is a master and has taught me to understand the horse, but seeing you surprised me and I forgot everything. I thought you would wait at the stables.'

Sara kissed him lightly. 'I wanted to see you ride.' She touched Morosito as Roberto led him back towards the stables. 'He's beautiful.'

'Then you'll have to come next year to see him run the Palio. In a few days you'll know what he'll have to do to win. But he is fearless and by then he will be impossible to beat.' He laughed and, as Roberto went out of sight, he put his arms around Sara. 'Do you mind if I kiss you?' Sara moved towards him and they kissed gently. 'It was hard to leave you this morning but I had no choice, I had an early business call then had to come here.' They kissed again, then Sara pulled away.

'I have to go back to the guesthouse.'

'Why? If there are no clothes that fit you at the house, I will buy whatever you want.' He kissed her nose.

Sara laughed. 'That doesn't work. I have my own things and I want some time on my own to work through what I'm feeling.'

Paolo was surprised by her honesty. 'In a good or bad way?'

'I'm just a bit unbalanced by last night. Yesterday was the best ever and staying over was a surprise but nothing I didn't want with all my heart.'

'Then you will stay again tonight?'

'No. I will take you to lunch tomorrow, if you're free, and then you can show me the secrets of the Palio.'

'It's a deal. I'll miss you but I will somehow manage. Now, before Siena, I want to take you to eat at a small café here. Is that alright with you?'

'Only if Roberto comes too.'

'Of course. It's his cousin's café so the food is better if he's there.'

She kissed him and he took her hand and walked back towards the stables.

The café in the village was small and filled with locals, but a table had been set in a small alcove for them at the back of the bottle-and-photograph-covered-room. Everybody knew Roberto and Paolo and greeted them with the warmth and irreverence of old friends, and they were all treated the same by Roberto's cousin, Andrea. Andrea was short, stocky, and looked fit. His face was lined and burned by the sun and his eyes sparkled with life. Sara liked him immediately. He had a little English but Roberto translated for him.

'How old do you think he is?' Roberto asked Sara, his arm around Andrea. 'It's all right, he knows I will ask you?'

'So probably older than he looks. Seventy?'

Roberto translated for Andrea who barked a laugh.

'He's ninety.' Andrea enjoyed Sara's surprise. 'He runs the café with his daughter and son-in-law who are in their sixties and works harder and longer than both of them.'

Andrea spoke to Roberto and then headed for the kitchen.

'He said that the food today is pasta with his magnificent tomato sauce.' He pointed to the menu board where there was only one dish chalked up. 'The dish is different every day. Nothing is repeated, even if it looks the same, the taste is different, sometimes more subtle, sometimes stronger, but always memorable.'

Sara had never tasted anything like it. The meals and flavours she had already been introduced to were wonderful… but this was special. They drank the local red wine, rich and fruity, and she began to feel it as

Andrea brought another bottle and sat down with them. Roberto talked about his parents, who had a small farm outside the village that was now worked by his cousin's grandson. He told her about Paolo's father and grandfather and how they had all met and their deep friendship. Paolo hardly spoke during the meal, listening to the old man tell stories he had heard many times before. When they left, Andrea made Sara promise to come back so he could introduce her to his family. They would want to meet someone Paolo cared so deeply about.

Paolo touched her arm. 'I'm sorry, Andrea has an old man's cheek, don't take any notice.'

Andrea winked at her. 'I know and care for this boy like my own heart. I see also that you feel the same way.'

Later as they drove back to Siena she fell asleep and didn't wake up until they reached the city centre. Outside the guesthouse, Paolo took her hand.

'I have something to say.'

For a moment Sara looked horrified. 'Was I snoring?'

Paolo laughed. 'No. Perhaps a little.'

'God! Sorry. What then?'

'Let me finish before you answer, please.'

Sara smiled at him. 'Okay.'

Paolo laughed. He hesitated.

Sara was intrigued now. 'Go on then.'

Paolo held her look for a moment. 'Would you consider staying at my home for the rest of your time here? You could have your own room. You'll save money and there is a space with lots of light that you could use as a studio to paint. We can get everything you need…'

Sara was surprised at the excitement she felt but she tried to hide it.

'Will you think about it?'

'Yes, Paolo.'

She kissed him and got out of the car saying she would meet him at Piazza del Campo by the fountain, the next day at one.

She watched him drive away and was surprised at the emptiness she felt.

For a moment a wave of sadness hit as thoughts of Ben and Ceri surrounded her but then, as she heard their laughter, it was gone and they had disappeared. It was as if they had said. 'Don't worry. It's fine by us, we don't mind, he's a nice guy.' She went into the guesthouse.

Parked along the street, Selma watched as Sara went through the door.

She had just taken over from Milo. Last night Silvia had been ill and Selma had been up most of the night, so Milo had stayed on until she was able to come. She felt guilty but he didn't give her a hard time, knowing she would do the same for him. He told her he'd fallen asleep and had woken in a panic, luckily just before Androtti left the house. He then followed Roberto and Sara to the stables and had waited through the long lunch in the café and followed them back to Siena. But he didn't want to risk being seen in the village so had had only a bar of chocolate and a bag of crisps, found in the car, to take the edge off his hunger. Luckily there was plenty of water. He'd gone home to eat and sleep before going to pick up Dupard at the airport.

Selma's thoughts strayed to Silvia, her regular bouts of sickness and particularly the migraine headaches she'd suffered since her dad had died. Selma wondered again if it might be better for her daughter if she had a normal job. That wasn't going to happen, though. She was good at this and the money, if not brilliant, was enough. She knew it was selfish but she was able to justify it by knowing that if she was happy in her working life then it would be better for the quality time spent with Silvia. The usual seesaw half-truths making it work for her. The thoughts stopped as she heard Sara make a call to her dad. The audio was good again and the sky spy had been stood down for now. There was the sound of the shower and then silence.

She was probably exhausted after a night of sex, the lucky cow.

Selma rang home to check on Silvia. Her mum told her she was sleeping and should be okay for school in the morning and that she would take her if Selma got held up.

'Thanks, Mum, love you.'

'Love you too.'

CHAPTER TWENTY-ONE

Sara was awake by six. Her sleep had been dreamless. Or perhaps it was just that nothing had stayed with her into conscious thought. It was a relief that she had not been rocked with images that blamed or battered. Those lasted into the daylight. Even as she had begun to find light with Peter, the pain and guilt had been constant and as real and necessary as a heartbeat.

But now this bright morning, for the first time, there was nothing of that, just a feeling of calm, and then as she thought of Paolo, a flutter of excitement and anticipation.

As she lay there watching the early sunlight slowly change the movement of shapes and shadows, listening to the sounds as Siena started its day, she knew the time she had spent with Paolo had changed her. It had not only made her see the shell she had wrapped herself in but had allowed it be opened. She couldn't wait to see him again.

Suddenly she felt a crack of panic. What about Ceri and Ben? What would they think? But then on the edges of her sight, she saw them smile, warm, loving, and content that she had, for whatever reason, found peace. They knew they were locked tight into her heart and would always be a part of every breath she took.

She looked around. The room that had warmed and welcomed her was now bathed in light from the open balcony doors. She would miss it.

She couldn't remember when she had made the decision, consciously or not, that she was going to stay with Paolo. She wasn't sure about the feelings that she had for him. It was too soon but they already seemed full and edged with what might, perhaps, grow into love. But she was going to take the chance. If she got hurt at least she had had this time to recharge her emotional world. But somehow she didn't think that would happen. There was something between her and Paulo that had surprised them both but it felt right. And, for now, that was enough. She had spent too much time locked in her grief. Now she had space to breathe freely again. The loss of her boys would always inhabit her spirit but would not hold it back anymore.

And then another thought pushed that out. Did she still want to find why Rietti had been killed? Was that the most important thing in her life? What good would it do? It wouldn't change anything. Ben and Ceri would still be in their other world. Talking it through with Peter before she left for Siena, she'd thought that she would kill the one who had murdered her boys but, in reality, she knew she wouldn't be able to do it. But would finding the reason for the killing that had taken her from a place of love and safety to a dark and dangerous swamp be enough to heal the wound? No, it wouldn't. It might destroy her again. Before meeting Paolo she hadn't cared; now she did. She decided she would just let whatever fate had in store for her take its course and when the time was right, talk to Paolo about it. She would have to share with him at some point. If she and Paolo had a chance, she would have to open up the book of her life. Until then she would not make a final decision.

At breakfast she told Elena that she was leaving because a friend had come to Siena for the Palio, was renting a house, and had asked her to stay. It was a last-minute trip and she would be there the next day. She offered to pay for the week but Elena wouldn't take it. She had enjoyed having Sara there and with the Palio, the room would be let as soon as she told the tourist office. Her only disappointment was that Sara hadn't had time to talk with Julia before she went back to college. But perhaps she could take Sara's cell number and ring her to see if she was still here the next time she came back, which would be after the Palio.

As Sara ate, Elena sat with her and told stories of the Race. Her face animated and joyful at the memories of the first time she had been taken there and the many times since. She wouldn't go this year with Julia away but she would join in the celebrations if her contrada won or destroyed a rival. It was only four days away and all of Siena bled into the preparation, secrecy, intrigue, and prayer. Only four days until dreams were realized or shattered, fortunes lost or won, and bitter rivalry oozed into the sweet need for revenge that might come next year.

Sara was entranced. It was the most animated Elena had been since she met her. She glanced at her watch. It was twelve o'clock. Only an hour to get ready to meet Paolo.

'Elena, I'm sorry but I have to go, I'm meeting my friend in an hour. Thank you for telling me about the Palio. I can't wait to see it.'

'I'm sorry if I talk too much. Sometimes I get carried away, there are not many who haven't heard my stories.

Go, you mustn't keep your young man waiting. In Siena there are always temptations.'

Sara laughed and hurried to her room.

* * *

As she looked around the crowded Piazza del Campo she thought it would be impossible to find Paolo, but she made her way towards the fountain through the shouting and passionate crowds. A hand touched her back and she went to slap it away.

'It's alright, it's me.'

'Thought I'd never find you in all this.'

'I'm sorry. It's the assignment of the horses. But I have a place where we can watch.'

He put his arm around her and led her through the crowds to where Roberto stood near the judges.

Roberto kissed her. 'Sara, you look lovely. What do you think of this madness?'

As Sara went to speak, there was a roar as the next assignment of horse and jockey was announced.

'Do you want to stay and watch or shall we go and eat? I have somewhere outside the city I would like to take you. Roberto will stay to the very end.'

'Will I miss anything?'

'Just more of the same and, of course, we will have the Palio.'

Sara kissed him. 'Another adventure?'

Paolo smiled. 'I have one planned for later.'

'What?'

'You'll have to wait.' He leaned towards Roberto.

'Are you staying in Siena tonight?'

Roberto smiled. 'Of course.' He turned towards Sara. 'Enjoy your day.'

Sara smiled. 'I will, thank you.'

Paolo led her away through the mass of excitement and anticipation. For a moment Roberto watched them, then turned as another horse was led through and the Judges prepared for the next assignment.

Selma had been standing behind Sara. As they turned and moved away she pushed herself deeper into the crowd.

'Gio, they're heading towards the car.'

'OK.'

'I'll get back to the bike. You've got that, boss?'

Dupard spoke quietly. 'Yes, don't lose them. Stick with Gio.'

Selma moved through the crowds to the edge of the square. She saw Gio in the green Alfa.

'Where are they?'

'Just gone down the alley to the old guy who owns the ice cream place. Androtti left the Cooper there.'

'I might join you when they stop. I need to get away from the screen and it's too busy to walk the streets.' Dupard sounded tired.

'Are you alright?' Selma caught Gio's eye and smiled.

Dupard sighed. 'Sure, just going through all the report stuff again. There's got to be a link.'

Selma saw the blue Mini Cooper come out of the alleyway and slip into the traffic moving away from the Square. Gio pushed in too and followed several cars behind. She started the ten-year-old Ducati. It had been her Patrick's and still held his spirit. The body was worn but it had a brand new 750cc engine and a top speed of a hundred and fifty. She'd never take it up anywhere near there. Its heart was big but the body would fall apart. Still, it was great the times she used it for work. No one took any notice.

She guided the bike across the slow-moving traffic and accelerated up a side street.

* * *

Dupard had spent the last six hours going through the reports of the deaths in Canada, France, Spain, and the UK. The only connection between those who had been killed was that there was no connection. There was a tenuous link between the designer and the opera singer. They had both worked at La Scala, Milan, but on different productions, years apart. It was the designer's only foray outside of fashion and hadn't been a great success, with biting scorn from both the traditional and the contemporary factions about a set and costumes anchored in the world of the catwalk. Dupard had seen the designs and quite liked them, but the reviews had been toxic and the three million dollars they cost a waste that became a weapon for the negative attitudes towards elitist opera. Surely not enough for someone to follow him to France and kill him, though.

But Rietti had been different. Why? Could his killer, despite throwing out that theory before, really be a copycat? It didn't feel like it. It was always the same MO. The killer had appeared and disappeared like a shadow in the sunlight, always in pulsing crowds in public places. High risk, but it had all the quality of a professional hit. And it was over before anyone had really seen what was happening.

He yawned and stood up, stretching. His back ached and he felt that he needed to do some exercise. He'd go into the park across from his hotel and hope that the crowds would still be watching the assignments at the Piazza. He would come back to the entry and exit control lists for travel, extending the time span by up to a month either way.

'Boss.' It was Selma. 'They've come to her guesthouse. He's still in the car and she's gone inside. Oh, hang on, she's coming out with a suitcase and backpack.'

'What?'

Where the hell was she going? Not back to the UK, surely. She could be going to stay with Androtti. He felt a flash of annoyance at Sara. Why? It wasn't because she would be safer in the guesthouse. He still knew where she was and, if there were something strong between them, then the Italian would be a line of protection. It might even be useful if she asked for his help. But somehow, he didn't think Sara would tell him the real reason for her being in Siena. And if she was happy then he should be pleased for her. Was he feeling this because of what they had shared as he slowly guided her to seek revenge? That was no reason, it was he who had used her.

He again pushed those thoughts away and, as always, whatever his personal feelings, he assessed all in terms of the job. If he felt it was moving in a way that could be a problem then he would have to decide what to do. It was simple. There was too much at stake for her to spoil it now. He could have Androtti warned off but he was rich enough not to take notice. He would do a bit of delving into his business interests. Perhaps there was something he could use as a lever.

Dupard would just wait. If she had fallen for the Italian and he were suddenly to drop her it would make her all the more vulnerable. But that was for later. He locked the Mac in his safe and went out of the room. He needed ten minutes away from it.

* * *

Paolo smiled across at Sara as they turned onto the road to Montalcino.

'What?'

'Beautiful.'

Sara laughed. 'Where are we going?'

'Pienze. '

'One of your treasures?'

'It is. It was originally called Corsignano but was rebuilt and renamed by Pope Pius II, in the fifteenth century, as his retreat from Rome. Pius's parents had come from Siena to the village and he had been born there. It was built around the Duomo and three Palazzos, for Pius, his bishops, and a Comunale. The Duomo has five altar paintings from the Sienese School. They have great beauty. I'll allow you time to share with them and then take you to a wonderful restaurant that, if not there in Pius' time, is certainly blessed by his spirit. After that we will go to my house to prepare for tonight's adventure.'

'Wonderful, but I'm paying for the meal.'

Paolo smiled. 'Sure.'

Sara smiled, leaned over, and kissed his neck. 'What is it?'

'What?'

'The adventure.'

'You think a kiss will buy that. No, you have to wait. But I promise it will be something you have never experienced before.'

In the Pienze Duomo, entranced by Mateo di Giovanni's painting, Sara didn't see Paolo watching her. He looked at his phone.

'Can you see how he has been inspired? Composition and figures from di Pietro, colour and texture of the cloth from Vecchietta, and St Catherine is a direct steal from di Bartolo.'

Sara laughed. 'Just what Wikipedia says.'

'Not impressed then?' He put his phone away.

'No.'

She went over and kissed him.

He touched her face. 'Are you ready to eat or do you want more time with the Madonna?'

'No thanks, I'm starving.'

'Me too.'

Selma, now dressed in a shirt and jeans with large sunglasses on her head, watched as Paolo and Sara turned into one of the little streets off the square. She always had a couple of changes on these sorts of jobs. People remembered clothes more than faces, particularly if you were a youngish woman.

'Gio, have you got audio?'

'No, I think she left her phone in the car. It's switched off.'

Paolo and Sara approached a small restaurant.

'They're going to eat. We'll pick them up after.'

Selma watched as they sat at a table outside and Paolo leaned over and kissed Sara. Jesus, it was a long time since there'd been a bit of romance in her life. Still, she had Silvia and couldn't imagine what it would be like to lose her, like Sara had done. The thought made her go cold. How could she keep her daughter safe? She couldn't watch her all the time. Silvia was sensible but only a child. They were a good team and even their fights didn't seem to last long. One day she would have to let her go into the world and fight her own battles, but until then she would do all she could to protect her. It would be nice though to be in a relationship again that was full of respect, warmth, passion, the simple joy of sharing and not being afraid to laugh or cry at silly things. It was how it had been with Patrick. But it wouldn't be the same. No one could be like him.

She started to think about him then pushed it away. Sometimes, small trickles in her mind became waterfalls and unless she stopped them she could drown in the dark memories. Then she heard Paolo and Sara laugh and it broke the clouds. She was being pathetic. It made her angry.

'Fuck it!' she said, louder than she thought.

'What?'

She'd forgotten that she was still linked to Gio and Dupard. 'Nothing, except deciding to go for taste over calories.'

'Bit of a strong reaction,' said Gio.

Dupard laughed. 'Glad to hear it.'

Dupard had decided not to join them. He had an international conference call rescheduled for six. Selma was disappointed. He'd promised to eat with her later. He was good company, if a bit work-centric.

Selma turned away. Balls to all of them: she could see a gelateria across the street; she'd have the salted caramel, maybe even a large one. And next day off she'd take Silvia out shopping.

* * *

It was nearly nine p.m. After finishing his pizza, Dupard had checked with those who were watching Paolo and Sara, but the audio link with Sara's mobile was still down. Her phone was in the Cooper and the battery must be out. He couldn't remember the last time he had been free of his, perhaps a few times when he first met Sara and had deliberately cut himself off. The drone was having problems too. Sometimes it picked up sound but the walls were mostly too thick.

He realised that he had promised to eat with Selma and it had completely gone out of his mind. Then he remembered that she had asked if she would see him later and he had said no, he would meet her in the morning before she went out to Androtti's. He sent her a text apologising. He would have liked an evening with

219

Selma. They got on well and it was good to relax, except that they were never far from the job.

He started thinking about Sara and Androtti. He was pleased that Sara seemed happy, but he was still concerned that if she got too close to Paolo, she might stop looking for answers.

He thought of Sara as two different people. One, the woman he had a relationship with, the pleasure he felt at the memories of their time together and some regret at the way he had led her from grief and pain to anger and revenge; the other, a woman who could lead him to a killer.

Perhaps it was time she moved on and part of him felt that, if something didn't happen soon, he would have to pull the team out and start again. Rietti was clean. There was nothing linking him to any of the networks of organised crime or even individuals, although he must have had relationships with people who had darker sides without Rietti knowing. From what he had learned about the man he certainly wasn't a pushover but everything about him, including Dupard's instinct, told him Rietti had been an honest man. It might be time to up the stakes and put Sara sharply into the frame. Perhaps he could set up something to threaten her, and then she might talk to Paolo and perhaps persuade him to help. He would have connections in Siena that Dupard couldn't reach.

He rubbed the sides of his forehead where he felt the beginnings of a headache. He was tired, his eyes hurt from too much screen and his thoughts started to get fuzzy. Perhaps she had already told Paolo why she had come to Siena and he had convinced her that there was nothing there. He had known Rietti too and mixed in the same social world.

There was a ping as a new mail came in from Toronto. He read it slowly.

It flagged up something that didn't seem important but was an interesting fact found after trawling through the miasma of statements and reports from the different countries.

Around the time of each death, there'd been a large social event that had drawn the rich and famous. Something that was an annual part of the international calendar that was where you needed to be seen if you were to keep your celebrity status. A sporting tournament, or a festival of some sort. For Rietti it had been Cheltenham and the yearling sales.

All those who had died had regularly attended these events.

It was a simple fact that had been missed in the hundreds of statements that had been taken. It was understandable, the professional world of these people more important than the pleasures they bought with their money and influence. It was only one facet of their lives. It should have been noted but it hadn't been.

He replied to the mail asking his team to send details of only those travellers who had been in all of the cities where the killings took place. They should look at a week either side of the killings. Perhaps they'd find a name he could link to someone with the right criminal profile.

This had been one of the most difficult cases of his years with IIF. Apart from one guy who had been flagged up by the Paliano family and passed on to him by Adolfo, there hadn't had a sniff of anything. Dupard had the guy checked out and found that he was indeed a hired killer but was serving a twenty-year stretch at a maximum security prison near Rome. Within a week he had been found dead in his cell. Adolfo thought it was the Palianos who had lost him in the system but needed payback for a hit he had done on one of their close family members. Dupard was more pissed at the lead coming to nothing than Adolfo being used to find the guy. The only good thing to come out of it was that now Adolfo still owed him big time.

He yawned again, stood up, stretched, and decided to go for a walk, lose himself in the excitement of the Palio. The crowds might help to focus his mind. For a moment he wondered whether it was too late to call Selma. No, she had Silvia and he wouldn't want to visit her home. It was a line he never crossed. The guys who worked for him had the right to privacy. It was enough that they were on call and he could always reach them. It was different for him. He had to hold everything together. It was what he was good at though, and the need for something more personal and satisfying was rare.

However, every now and then, he felt that it was not enough to be on his own. But then, who would want to share his life? Although he always managed to qualify what he did with the positive result of helping to make the world a better place, most normal people would feel that the extreme means needed could in no way justify the successful ends.

Perhaps he should call it a day, go back to the university, or write a novel in his cabin by the lake. Still that decision was for another day. For now he just needed some distraction, and the buzz of the Palio would do it. He had wondered whether the Race was part of the international calendar and been told that it was more for local passions and rivalries than the celebrity circuit. But he would check if any of the high rollers were passing through the border checks. Of course, if someone from Siena or the rest of Italy was involved then nothing would show anyway.

* * *

Sara and Paolo were making their way down a steep staircase that led from the monastery to the bottom of the hill.

She had been thrown off balance when, an hour earlier, Paolo explained what they were going to do, but slowly, gently, he had persuaded her to trust him. He had done it many times before and wouldn't attempt it unless everything was as close to perfect as it could be. There was always the element of real danger but without that thrill there was no point in doing it. He told her that when he was at Cambridge he had joined Night Climbers. They were a group of students who scaled the walls and clock towers of the colleges and occasionally jumped off high bridges at night. It was addictive, and balanced his careful academic path with thrills and danger. This wasn't about the wealth and privilege of his life but something that was just him and whatever challenge was set. His strength and skill were all that would help him succeed. They were all equal and whatever happened was down to each of them, alone and without any advantage life had given them. He was hooked. But now, like tonight, he only jumped trains or climbed an occasional sheer rock face. Which might be a step too far for Sara though.

Sara held back as she tried to process the craziness of it. She had never done anything reckless like this, but then that hadn't stopped the worst thing from happening. She hadn't kept her family safe. She felt herself sinking into guilt and anger but tried to contain it. Paolo felt a shadow slipping over her.

'It's all right, Sara, if it worries you, we won't do it.'

Then Sara's mind suddenly cleared. If the worst did happen she would be with her boys and if it didn't then she could use this test to move on. And if it meant being with Paolo then she would go for it. She would challenge fate and for once would win, either way. She kissed him.

'No. I want to, Paolo. I can't promise not to be scared though.'

He laughed. 'And I promise you that the thrill will be worth it.'

He had found black boots, jeans, a jumper, and a zip up jacket for her. He seemed to have a supply of women's clothes for every occasion. But she didn't care why or whose they might be and as she blacked her face and put on the balaclava, she felt excitement rising and realised she couldn't wait for it to all begin. Paolo packed the head protector caps, goggles, and thick slipover padding to cover ankles, knees, elbows, and neck, into a black backpack. They were ready to go.

They had come into an open space around the steps that led down to the bottom of the hill. Paolo opened a door which led into a small overgrown lane. A motorbike and two trail bikes sat there. He gave Sara a helmet, pushed the motorbike outside, then closed and locked the door using his phone. When it was shut it blended perfectly into the hillside. The motorbike was black and became one with the darkness. Paolo started it. Sara got on the back and folded herself into him as he moved off. The engine sound was not as loud as she thought it would be, but it was deep and powerful. She realised that they hadn't spoken for a while. Paolo had smiled and kissed her. Perhaps this was part of the game.

As they exited the lane a comet tail disappeared amongst the stars.

Gio and Marco were unaware that their quarry had left the house. The drone had picked up a motorbike a while ago but that had been way below them, and since that monent nothing had moved. They settled down for the night. Gio taking the first four-hour shift.

* * *

There was a thin crescent moon as Paolo and Sara stood on an ancient bridge sitting over a gentle narrow curve with a single track. Paolo talked her through the jump. He had strapped one arm around her so that when he moved she had to keep pressed against him and not hold back. If she resisted, it could be dangerous for them both, as the timing was crucial and also she could pull his shoulder out. She promised she would go with him. He showed her how to soften her knees just before they jumped. He would take her weight and use his other arm to hold them both on the roof. As soon as she hit the train she had to relax her body and flatten herself against it. She wouldn't fall off. The train would hardly be moving as it came around the bend under the bridge so there was little risk of missing it.

'You have to trust me totally.'

She smiled at him. 'I do.'

They heard the train and saw the light on the front of the engine snake through the trees at the side of the track. Sara felt her breath catch as the train got nearer. She was so tightly pressed against Paolo that they looked like a large black bird ready to swoop. The train as it approached the bridge had slowed and the freight trucks passed underneath. Paolo waited until there were only two more trucks left then with a whispered, 'Now'.

He stepped off. Sara closed her eyes momentarily, snapped them open again, then let herself drop. They hit the roof perfectly together and flattened themselves against it as the train started to pick up speed. Paolo was glowing, his hand gripping the small climb rail on the side.

'Are you all right?'

Sara could hardly speak, her heart pounding.

'I think so.'

She had never felt like she did when she came off the bridge; terrified and excited and scared her heart might stop. In fact she thought it had, for a moment, as an image of her boys came into her head. And then it was over and she'd hit the roof hard. The pads and gloves took most of the impact but she knew she'd have bruises too.

'What happens now?' She moved her head as close to Paolo as she could.

'Three kilometres further on there is a small station. The train will stop there for twenty minutes. The driver and guard always have a drink with the signalman. It hasn't changed in ten years. Where we are will be in the darkest part of the platform. We'll get off there. Someone will pick us up and take us to the bike. He's the father of an old friend and was a great jumper in his time. He lives near the station.'

When the train had stopped, Paolo released the straps around Sara and his arm, stretched it and then helped Sara stand. Her legs shook and he held her as the strength came back.

'Ready?'

'Yes.' She hugged him briefly. 'Thank you, that was amazing.'

Paolo climbed down the ladder on the side of the truck and then dropped the last metre to the platform. Sara followed him.

A shadowy figure appeared briefly and Paolo took Sara's hand and led her towards where it had been. They climbed over a wall and found a tall man, running to fat, with a large smile, standing by an old Fiat Campagnola. He limped towards them.

'Paolo, you are getting past it. Emilio drives his train like an old man.'

Paolo replied in English. 'It's my friend's first jump! I didn't want to frighten her off.' Sara punched him. 'Sara, this is Luigi. He used to teach English and was a local wrestling champion so I can't be rude about him to you.

His son, Bernardo, and I were at school together. He was a clever scholarship boy and I was rich, arrogant, and believed he was below me, but he was tough, like his dad, and one day, he'd had enough and we fought. He easily beat me but didn't ridicule me. It was over quickly and he helped me up and reset my nose, his dad taught him how to do it, just in case one of those of those little snobs at the posh school managed to get a punch in first. I hadn't had that experience before and we became good friends. He lives in New York now so I keep an eye on the old man for him.'

Luigi smiled and took Sara's hand and kissed it.

'Sadly this boy lives in a make-believe world. You're much too good for him.' He looked her up and down. 'No damage done?'

Sara smiled and shook her head. 'I'm sure that I'll hurt tomorrow. It was fun though.' She glanced at Paolo. 'Do you jump onto faster ones, then?'

'Sometimes.'

Luigi moved around the Fiat. 'Come on, Emilio will be on his way again soon and I don't want him to see me. He thinks I owe him money for cheating at cards.' He laughed. 'Which I did.' Paolo opened the door for Sara then got in next to her.

They bounced through woodland on a narrow track between the trees.

'Luigi taught me to jump,' said Paolo. 'He was fearless and holds many records but chanced his luck one too many times. He could have been killed but managed to grab on to a tree which saved his life. His leg took the full force and he was lucky they managed to save it, but no more train tumbling.'

Luigi smiled. 'It was a long time ago. It shouldn't have happened. I lost concentration trying to impress a woman watching from the bridge.' He lit a cigarette and winked at Sara. 'I think one time will be enough for you.'

Sara bounced as they hit a bump. 'Maybe.'

Luigi dropped them off at the bike and then drove off. 'What now?'

Paolo smiled. Sara moved and kissed him. She had controlled her excitement and arousal at the danger but now that Luigi had gone she gave in. Paolo didn't stand a chance, but he pulled away.

'We have too many clothes on.'

Quickly, comically, they undressed, then silhouettes in the pale moonlight they touched, kissed, and made love on their discarded clothes.

'I love you,' said Paolo, gently kissing her lips.

Sara hesitated. 'I love you too, Paolo.' She started to cry and he held her tightly.

'What is it?'

'Too much excitement.'

When they got back to Paolo's it was two a.m. They went straight to bed, Paolo leading her up an unlit staircase to his room. Sara was exhausted as much by the emotion released as the train jump and went to sleep wrapped in Paolo's arms.

He watched her face, gently touching it. He was in love with her. It had happened so quickly it surprised him. She was astonishing and adventurous and he could see a future with her that fulfilled them both. As he drifted to sleep, he realised that he was content for the first time in many years. Soon perhaps he could start a new life with Sara.

CHAPTER TWENTY-TWO

Paolo woke early, just as the darkness eased and the first light touched the sky. Sara, turned away from him, was still in a deep sleep. Gently he got out of bed, dressed, and left the room.

In the kitchen, he turned on the coffee machine and then went outside.

Gio saw him come out and watched as he went towards the chapel, took the key from a ledge above a water barrel, unlocked the door, and went in. Perhaps he was getting some spiritual guidance for the day. If you were super rich you could probably buy a little quality time with God.

Gio finished the last of the coffee. He looked at his watch. He had another hour before Marco, who was snoring gently in the sleeping bag, took over for the last bit of the shift. Then it was Selma's turn. He had two days off. Perhaps he could persuade Maria and the kids to come to the Palio. She hated the crush and always worried about Teresa and Aldo getting lost or trampled. Maybe she'd let him go on his own, he could use his old police pass to get a good spot to watch. Some of the guys from his old team were moonlighting on security and they'd help him. Particularly Pietro, who owed him after he'd put in a good word for him to make sergeant and take over his old job.

He checked the computer for the drone and then remembered they didn't have it today. Even Dupard couldn't justify unlimited time and the money it cost. He wondered how long they'd keep up the surveillance. The extra cash was good, but it was getting boring watching people with limitless amounts of it have a good time.

Then he saw Paolo come out, lock the door, and put the key back. Gio checked his watch: ten minutes since he'd gone in. He wrote it down.

Paolo went to get coffee then changed his mind, switched off the machine, and went back to bed, snuggling up to Sara and kissing her neck. Sara slowly came round, turned towards him, and they gently kissed.

'Hello,' Sara smiled as he pressed against her. 'Just what I was thinking.' She rolled over on top of him.

* * *

It was nearly eight when Selma arrived. It had been a frustrating morning. The bike wouldn't start so she had to take her car, she had been late dropping Silvia off, and Toni had phoned as she was waiting for him, saying he had been throwing up all night and could she find someone to cover. Luckily, Marco had agreed to a double shift. She hadn't been able to get hold of Dupard either. His phone was off and she wouldn't use the room line.

Gio smiled and waved as he disappeared into the foliage. 'Have fun, see you on Friday.'

Marco passed her a coffee and brought her up to date.

* * *

Sara and Paolo didn't wake again until eleven but were ready to leave by eleven thirty. She was excited at the thought of the Palio and Paolo seemed to be too. But he was less relaxed than she had ever seen him. She put her arms around him.

'You look like a little boy waiting for his birthday.'

'It's always the same ever since my grandfather first took me to see my dad ride,' Paolo laughed. 'We need to go, it will be difficult with the traffic but I have a plan.'

Sara kissed him. 'I'm sure you do.'

Marco waited until they passed and followed. He almost missed them because they were in a dark green Jeep that came around the house. Jesus, how many vehicles did this guy own? He tried to reason with himself that huge riches brought their own troubles but, somehow, he couldn't see the downside.

'Angelo, they're on their way. Dark green jeep.'

'Got it.'

'Be careful, keep well ahead. Luca is the other side of Monticelli. He'll pick up from me.'

Selma had been about to leave when Dupard sent her a text: 'Wait for me there.'

Dupard was driving fast. The road was pretty clear compared to the pile up of traffic heading the other way towards the Palio. 'Luca, where are you?'`

'We've just turned off the main road, a couple of kilometres outside of Monticelli. Looks like we're going across country.'

'Don't lose them.'

'I think I know which way they're going. I can cut round and pick them up from the other side.'

'Good. Marco, keep me in the loop. I'm heading for the house to have a look round while it's clear.'

Dupard was tired, he had caught a few hours' sleep but it had been fitful and eventually he'd given up and gone back to the files. He checked his phone but it was dead. He searched and finally found the charger and plugged it in.

On the list of passengers in and out of Siena he'd found Paolo Androtti. It was a surprise, and one he wouldn't have been interested in if Paolo and Sara hadn't got together. He checked the times and dates again. Androtti had flown into Toronto a week prior to the killing and then returned to Siena on the day after. Details about London were a bit more tricky to find, as he had arrived a couple of weeks before the death on a scheduled flight and left a week later on a specialist horse transport plane with a young colt he had bought at the sales in Newmarket. He had flown to Madrid, arriving the morning of that killing and leaving two days later. There was no record of him being in Paris. Dupard asked for a detailed passenger check on trains from Paris to Siena.

It might have no significance, but he felt the charge he always did when his gut instinct was troubled and excited by circumstance and strange coincidence. Of course Androtti was part of the international wealthy set and had travelled for years to the same destinations with many of the same people being there each time. Nobody had been killed then or, at least, none that he'd heard about. He would check out all those who had travelled from Siena but Paolo Androtti was the only one having an affair with the wife of one of the victims, even though that particular victim was just an accident of fate. It was a long shot. If Androtti was the killer and had found out about Sara's search, and wanted to hurt her, he would surely have done so by now. But it was enough of a coincidence to look into him in a bit more depth. So, with Androtti and Sara on the way to the Palio, watched by the team, it was an ideal opportunity to look around the monastery.

He checked his phone. There was a message from Selma and a sharp note from his boss about the money it cost to hire drones and keep a team running. And the warning that if nothing happened soon, she was going to pull him out. Dupard ignored that one and sent another text to Selma to wait for him at Androtti's. He didn't feel that Sara was in danger but he still didn't want her in the way of anything that might kick off when he picked him up. And if Androtti had nothing to hide, he'd be fine.

For a moment his mind took him to another place.

Would Sara understand what he had done to her, and why?

Intellectually she would, but realising the emotional explosion of betrayal might be too much for her. Shit! He couldn't think like that, it would distort what he had to do. Shocked at the realisation that it mattered, he pushed it out of his mind, sped dangerously past a couple of very pissed off swerving drivers, and felt a cold calm slip over him. It was a state that always conditioned his thoughts into that one aspect of the chase that he loved, the psychological twist and turn that took him into the opponent's mind and played with it until one of them made that simple mistake that lost or won the game. An all-consuming mind game of morals, mental agility and might that almost always crossed the legal and moral Rubicons of right and wrong. Did the end always justify the means? An academic question he had argued with his students, but in the reality of the world in which he lived now, there was only one answer. Doubt and compassion had no place in the decision.

On the road in the Jeep, Paolo was telling Sara about the thrills of winning and the pain and anger of losing this Race of races. His passion for the Palio was palpable and, on this day, it was all about coming first. Second didn't cut it. One jockey who'd lost had almost been beaten to death. It was twelve months after he had been applauded and enriched for bringing the trophy home to the contrada for a fifth time when those who had given him their hearts over the winning years attacked him. Paolo looked at her and smiled. 'I think that is enough for now, or you will know too much before you feel it for yourself.'

Sara kissed him. 'I can't wait.' In front of them a motorbike pulled out of a lane and sped off. 'Will we...'

'What?' Paolo glanced at her.

She laughed. 'I was going to ask if we'd get somewhere where we could see everything, but we will, won't we?'

'Of course.' He turned off the road into a field and stopped. 'I will tell you the plan.'

Luca looked back, slowed, and waited on a long stretch of lane where he was out of sight and could move off again without being seen. He could only be a few minutes ahead of them. But they didn't come.

'Marco, I think they've stopped.' He laughed. 'Probably for a quickie before the Palio. Are you close enough to check?' He gave him a map reference.

'Let me have a look. The one time we need the fucking drone we don't have it.'

Sara and Paolo were making love on a rug on the grass in front of the Jeep. Sara turned her head at the sound of an engine.

'No one will disturb us.' Paolo smiled as the noise of the car grew fainter. 'See, I told you.'

They kissed deeply. Paolo pulled away and looked at her.

'I love you.'

Sara felt the tears. 'I love you too. I never thought it would happen again, that I could meet someone who filled my heart.' She touched his face. 'I want to tell you something.'

'What is it?'

'Tonight, after the Palio.'

'Perhaps I will share some secrets with you too.'

Marco almost missed the back of the jeep as he passed the gate.

'Luca, I've got them. They're in a field. There's a track I can double back on and get behind them again. Let me know when you pick them up.'

'Will do.'

* * *

Dupard brought Selma up to date on what he'd discovered about Androtti. She was cynical. 'Why?'

'Why not? Let's look at the house. With luck I can get in with Gio's set of magic keys. He left them in the car. Did you know he had them?'

'Yes. What about cameras?'

'We managed to block them before the drone went. Don't think he'll check in now, and if he does head back we can pick him up.'

'What do you want me to do?'

'Look around outside. Stables, storerooms, chapel. Have you got contact with Gio and the team? My feed's dropped out.'

'Mine too, must be a shit signal today. Working through the radio but that's on charge back at the car. Want me to get it?'

'No, leave it.'

Selma found nothing out of the ordinary and there was no one around. She was about to try the chapel when a very pissed off Dupard came over.

'Can't get in anywhere? Should have realised it would be tight, lots of alarms too. You found anything?'

'No, just the chapel to try. Gio told me there's a key above the water barrel.'

The key was well-used and the lock slipped easily. The chapel was tiny inside and very simple, with a beautifully carved altar and an image of the Madonna in the window made predominantly of heavenly blue stained glass. The light shining through touched the crucifix on the opposite wall and the effect was stunning, as the Christ figure seemed to glow. There were three lines of wooden benches, each big enough for four people, and in the corner there was a confessional, which seemed out of proportion to the size of the chapel. On one wall there was a large painting of one of the saints.

Selma was taken by the stillness and beauty of it. It was a perfect retreat for thought and prayer.

Dupard was walking close to the walls looking for another door. There wasn't anything. He went into one side of the confessional and then the other. She saw his torch shining under the curtain.

'Selma.'

She went over. Dupard was running his fingers around the edges of a large flagstone, which he'd found under some straw matting.

'This moved when I stood on it. Is there something to lever it up with?'

'There was a pick in one of the storerooms.'

She went quickly. Dupard sat back on the priest's seat. Of course, it might just be loose.

Selma came back and together they managed to pull up the stone. Underneath, a quarter metre down, there was another flag with a raised crown of sharp pointed thorns on it. Dupard was about to touch it when Selma stopped him. She'd found a small soft prayer cushion and laid it over the crown.

'Must be a reason for the thorns.'

She was trying to see if it moved, when there was a click and the whole stone slid in on itself on a hinge.

They could see steps going into the darkness. Dupard shone the torch down. After a few metres the space seemed to widen.

'Check with Marco and Luca where Sara and Androtti are and make sure we're still alone here. Be careful.'

'Sure. Wait for me before you go down.'

'I will.'

While he waited, he checked out the layout plan of the old house, on his phone. It showed the chapel but nothing underneath. Perhaps it was a secret escape route for the monks.

He heard Selma's footsteps. She pushed the curtain and came in.

'All clear. Sara and Androtti have reached Siena. They've just parked up. Do you want to pull him in?'

'No, just make sure we know where they are. Get Marco to organise a couple more sets of eyes.'

Selma sent a text to Marco.

Dupard glanced at her. 'Right, let's go down. Bring the cushion, we might need it again.'

It was a tight squeeze through the hole until it opened out. They moved down the steep steps until they came to a level where there was what looked like a trompe l'oeil wooden door that matched the wall so perfectly they almost missed it. Another small, raised crown of thorns carved in the wall had given it away. It was almost too simple. Selma used the cushion again. The door slid into a recess in the wall. Dupard shone his torch in.

CHAPTER TWENTY-THREE

Marco watched as Paolo and Sara got out of the Jeep, opened the back door, pulled down a ramp and wheeled out a scooter. There were crowds of people moving down the hill towards the city centre.

'Fuck.' Marco watched Paolo lock the Jeep, then he and Sara got on the scooter and moved slowly away, weaving through the traffic. 'Luca, have you got them?'

'Yes, behind them now. Tania's on a moped, she's got a sight on them too.'

'They must be heading for Campo. We'll go there now. Sara's phone is still out so no audio and I've lost the boss and Selma now too.'

Luca had to stop as an ambulance, siren blaring, pulled out in front of him. By the time he had managed to get around it, they'd disappeared.

There were two ways they could have gone. 'Marco, I've lost them? Tania?'

'No visual, but I know which way they were going. I'm after them now.'

Paolo and Sara pulled into a tiny alleyway, turned into a garage and stopped. Paolo shut the door behind them, put the helmets into the carrier, grabbed Sara's hand, and led her through a door at the back of the garage. They came out near the church of San Giovanni del Staffa and joined the singing, excited crowd as it followed a magnificent white horse, led by drummers, dignitaries, a priest and acolytes, into the church.

Tania glanced into the gated alleyway as she passed the entrance but saw nothing.

Marco tried to get both Dupard and Selma on their phones but there was only the answer phone. He left a brief message. Jesus, he was in deep shit now.

'Have we got any eyes on them?'

The reply from all was negative. They'd just have to search the crowds around the Palio and the churches. They were a striking couple and Androtti would have a prime spot. Shit, shit, he hated days like this and hated Gio for having missed this fuckup and left him to carry it.

* * *

Dupard stood in the doorway looking around a small room. He shone the torch on the wall to the side of the door and found a pad. He pressed it and subtle lighting along the walls came on. He moved into the room so Selma could get in. The floor was stone and there was a deep leather armchair and a screen which stretched across one wall.

'This where he watches porn?' She laughed at Dupard as he glared at her. 'It's a bit odd though. Why would you come here? He lives on his own. Unless he's into the dark stuff.' She touched the screen and nothing happened. She tried again, tapping the keyboard Dead. Dupard was looking at the wall. There was a slight gap between the stones. He shone the torch in. There was something metal there. He tried to reach it with a finger but it was too far away. He took out Gio's keys. One of them was long with a hammer point. He slid it in and tried to move the metal. 'Damn.' He'd got it stuck. He tried to free it. Suddenly there was a soft click and the wall moved. Dupard, and Selma behind him, stood back as the opening grew. Another room.

Dupard opened the door, reached inside, felt for the small pad and pressed it. He expected the same sort of subdued feel as in the first room, so was blinded by the harsh and brilliant wash of light. It took him a couple of moments to focus on what was in front of him. 'Sweet Jesus.'

'What is it?' She came to a quick stop. 'Fuck. It is him.'

Stunned, they both looked at the large photo of a smiling Rietti and, next to it, a blown up newspaper shot of Ben and Ceri. It was grainy and blurred but definitely them. Below that were the articles that had accompanied reports of the deaths at Paddington station. But the surnames of Ceri and Ben weren't there. Slowly Dupard looked around the rest of the room. There were photos and newspaper cuttings of all the victims with dates and times. There was also a montage of a beautiful woman in her forties, her face and head shot from all angles. It took Dupard a minute to find her name in his memory. Juliette Sanquist. She was an American film star, a two-time Oscar winner. She had been the lead in *Angelique*, one of his favourite films.

'No!' Selma cried.

He turned to her. 'What?'

'Juliette Sanquist is guest of honour at the Palio.'

Shards of guilt sliced into him. He had allowed Sara to go with Androtti. Should he have seen something? He was responsible. He tried to order his thoughts but his sense of reason was spinning. And he was taking too long.

'Boss, for fuck's sake, we've got to go, I haven't got a signal down here.' Selma had her phone out and rushed out of the room.

As suddenly as he had lost it Dupard regained his balance. He ran after Selma.

* * *

San Giovanni della Staffa, oratory of the contrada of Leocorno, is a thirteenth-century church, rebuilt in the sixteen hundreds. The nave ceiling and the walls are frescoed with depictions of events in the life of John the Baptist, to whom the church was dedicated.

Sara had checked out San Giovanni on Wikipedia after Paolo had told her about his family and their connection to the church and contrada.

Today it was beating with the collective heart of the community. Sara, sitting with Paolo in their reserved seats in the back row, was fascinated by the sense of theatre. The church was bursting with people. The seats nearest the altar were filled with politicians, contrada officials, celebrities, priests, acolytes. At the very front, in a place of honour between the Mayor and an important-looking man with a sash and brooch of office, was a woman in her early forties, blonde, stylish, and beautiful, clearly entranced by the spectacle in front of her.

Straining against the barriers, the people and their passions threatened to explode into the central nave. Sara felt herself drawn into the intense and solemn mass of excitement and anticipation as the priest gave a short blessing. She tried to concentrate on the tableau but there were too many faces filled with emotions that distracted her. The calm look of the jockey and the ceremonial words spoken with a grave face. The young and old, holding back, waiting for the moment of release, to scream out their support. The myriad masks of smiles, tears, and prayers, all around her.

Sara glanced at Paolo. He was focused, still, affected by the reverence of the moment and perhaps, she thought, by memories of his father and grandfather, in their time, standing where the jockey was now, in his white, orange, and blue, to the left of the white horse draped in the same colours. She touched his hand but he didn't react. She moved it away. Let him have this private moment.

He was looking at the woman. It wasn't his family that Paolo was thinking about.

It was Vittorio Rietti.

Killing him had been the ultimate test.

The others had required skill but although he knew them all. They were not close to him and he was able to distance himself. Vittorio was different. He was a good friend. Paolo had had no reason to take his life. That was the perfect part. The ultimate control of head and heart. The danger that he might be caught. Not at the scene, he was too practised for that, but later during the investigation into the death. Yet he was not suspected.

London was the perfect place as they were both going to the yearling sales at the Cheltenham Meeting. He only thought of Rietti now as a lost friend. The killing was locked away and untouchable and he had no regrets.

And now, Sanquist was to be the last. He had planned it before Vittorio, when the film star was to have received an award at the Terra di Siena International Film Festival. But she had cancelled due to illness.

Then he found she was to be guest of honour here today. It would be the perfect kill in the heat and passion of the Palio. Then it would all be at an end. Sara would fulfil his life.

As the priest finished the blessing with a cry of 'Go and return victorious!' Paolo quickly slipped back into the present and translated for Sara. A huge cheer rose like a single voice then erupted into crescendo as the horse defecated in a great heap. Paolo laughed and leaned in towards her. 'If the horse shits, it is supposed to be good luck for the Race.'

They watched as the procession moved along the nave. Juliette Sanquist passed them as they waited to move. She was tightly surrounded by people and was talking animatedly to the Mayor in Italian. She turned her head slightly as her name was called by an adoring fan, gave a quick smile and then looked back towards the Mayor.

Sara didn't see the coldness in Paolo's eyes.

She kissed his cheek. 'Thank you.'

He turned, softness and love there now. 'There is more to come.'

* * *

Selma had never seen Dupard this angry.

'What, fucking what? They've lost them. How did they manage that? The fucking morons.'

He was about to get into his car when Selma dragged him to hers.

'Let me drive. I'm faster than you and I know short cuts. I called Gio, he's at the Palio to watch. He's going to link up with Marco and the others. There's CCTV all over the place and the TV networks are everywhere. Marco's sent photos of them to the control centre so they're searching now. We'll find them. But… you need to talk to Liechi.'

'Oh, shit, that'll be the icing.'

CHAPTER TWENTY-FOUR

Silvio Liechi was fifty. Head of the Organised Crime and Homicide unit in Siena. He was a hard-faced, thick-bodied man with wild curly grey hair and black pinpoint eyes. He was an expert tactician, as good at political manipulation as he was at the 'on the ground' policing. Tough, fair, but demanding, expecting his teams to be up to anything they might come up against and give their all.

Like any city, Siena had its share of horrors, but during his time in charge the percentages had moved in his favour. Liechi was respected and given freedom by his bosses but knew that any sudden shitpile could throw that all out. What he was hearing now was the mother of all shitpiles and he was angry. White-hot angry.

'Who the fuck do you think you are? You've been operating in my city for a month without a fucking word and now you're telling me that there's a fucking psychopath on the loose among sixty thousand people at the biggest event of the year and he's going to kill a fucking American film star, who just happens to be the guest of the Government of Siena! I don't fucking believe it.'

Dupard broke in, his voice flat, cold and hard. 'Shut up and listen. There'll be time to beat the crap out of me later. '

247

Liechi covered the phone and went to the door. 'Mario, Calvi, get your arses in here now.'

He picked up another phone. 'Get Archio Cavelli, yes, the fucking Mayor's assistant, and Piero Patroni.'

He slammed the phone down as Mario and Calvi rushed into the room.

Selma swung right in front of two cars and shot up a narrow lane, the old car bouncing on the uneven ground. Dupard was pressed into his seat, his phone tight against his ear. His words were measured.

'I've got heavy backup on this, way above you and me, and I need us on the ground now. We're getting close. Give me a place to meet. And get the American woman out of there.'

Liechi had calmed into action, his voice matching Dupard.

'We've got security around her and the Mayor. I can't pull her out completely. No one will get near. I've put more people on the cameras and there are two drones arriving in five minutes. I've put the feed through to you. You can link to the rest of your team. I'll let you know where I am. And I will pull your fucking head off after this is over.'

Dupard shut his eyes. They went through a couple of narrow tunnels and pulled onto a busy road. Selma cut across the traffic and screeched into a small, cobbled, street, slicing past a black Transit van and unbalancing a cyclist who ran into a recycling bin and fell off. She glanced in the mirror and saw the cyclist get up. He didn't seem hurt, but, even if he had been, she wouldn't have stopped, there were enough people and medical teams around. She drove fast, changing direction as she could into alleys and lanes. She knew the centre of the city and its many ways of getting to the same place, particularly the Campo. Finally they got to a small square that was packed with moving people and cars. Selma leapt out.

'We can get there in a couple of minutes.'

Dupard followed her. 'Call Gio, I'll get Marco... Marco, where are you? We've got two drones now. I'm sharing the feed, link up with the others. Any sign yet? I've brought in Liechi.' His phone beeped as another call came in.

'It's Liechi, keep me in the loop, Marco.' He switched to the other call and listened. 'We'll be there in five minutes.' He caught up with Selma. 'He's in the Clock Tower.'

'Not on the top?'

Dupard laughed. 'Courtyard.'

Selma led the way, moving quickly, pushing through the tight groups heading towards the Piazza. There were police at the end of the narrow street leading into the Campo, filtering people through. She showed her card. The officer watched them head towards the tower and spoke into his headset.

'Tell Il Capo, they've just come through.'

By this time, Sara and Paolo had followed the horse out of San Giovanni into the small square. The noise was deafening but the passion and belief of Leocorno drew everyone into its swirling heart. Ahead the processions moved forward towards the town centre and Campo. The drums drove the heartbeats of battle as the people sang and sent prayers to John the Baptist to give their heroes the strength to win again this year. Paolo put his arms around Sara and allowed the sea of shapes and faces to eddy around them. When they had space, he led her down a small street near the entrance to the church.

'Let's get a drink. There's a small bar here that my father owned and left to the man who looked after his horses for thirty years. It's called Ricardo's, after my father. I drink there on the day of the Race and always alone. But now I want you to be a part of a life that I have never shared. Daniele opens the bar just for me. It is a ritual. After the Race he will open to everyone else.'

Sara kissed him 'Thank you, but don't we need to get to our place soon?'

Paolo laughed 'There are two hours before it starts and we will not miss a single moment of it. Trust me, I have planned it well.'

'Of course you have.' She pulled him into the darkness of a small gateway and kissed him. For a moment he resisted, then gave in. The kiss was long, their bodies tight against each other. Finally Paolo pulled away. 'Daniele will think I've forgotten him.'

'That's all right, isn't it?' Sara put her hand on his arm.

'No!' He put his hand on hers. 'He will blame you and say you're no good for me. Family is important and he has known me since I was a child. He was a rider too. He and my father fought many times in the Palio. My father was ten years younger and, in the end, stronger, and Daniele retired. He taught me to ride like a warrior.'

Sara took his hand and pulled him into the stream of bodies rushing past. 'I can't wait to meet him.' She looked around. 'Which way?'

He pointed to a small alley opposite them. 'Down there.'

Ricardo's was small, dark, and smelled of old leather. It was a celebration of the Palio. Around the rough, stone walls were a mass of photographs, paintings, and posters interspersed with a vibrant variety of silk jackets, dried and stretched bullock-penis whips, plus certificates and trophies. Behind the bar two paintings stood side by side. One was of a younger Daniele and the other, Ricardo, an older version of Paolo, both proud and serious in their silks.

Daniele fitted the bar. He was small, dark, old, and leathery. As they came in he hugged Paolo then took Sara's hands, looked arm's length at her, kissed her on both cheeks, and gave a huge smile.

To Paolo he said, 'Sara, I think, is your equal, you must cherish her.' He turned back to Sara, 'And you must cherish him too.'

Paolo laughed as Daniele went behind the bar and poured drinks. 'I told you what he was like, but it could have gone the other way if we had been late. Now, as far as he is concerned, you are now part of the family. He knows I wouldn't have brought you here if you weren't in my heart.'

'Do I get a say in this?' Sara smiled.

Paolo started to protest.

'I don't mind, I think he's a sweetie.'

'Now, that is something I have never heard said about Daniele before.'

He put his arm around her and they moved to the bar where Daniele had laid out anti pasta, olives, bread, and three glasses from a special, once a year, Chianti Classico. He held up his glass. 'Bernardo Fratelli and his horse Spirito, Let them bring honour and victory to Leocorno.' They touched glasses and drank. Daniel swallowed, looked at the wine lovingly then held up his glass again. 'Possa la grande fortunal cadere sui nostra rivali.'

Paolo translated, 'May great misfortune fall on our rivals.'

Sara was surprised. 'That's not very sporting.'

Daniele looked hard at her. 'The Palio is not a sport, it is a battle for life itself.'

Paolo put his arm around Sara. 'Fairness doesn't come into it. You will see and be drawn into the passion too.'

She laughed and clinked Daniele's glass.

She looked at the two men as they talked. With a warm feeling she realised that she felt comfortable with Siena and its people, at least those she had met through Paolo. She was in love with this beautiful and charismatic man and would happily stay here with him. She had nothing to go back home for and she could paint here where the light was beautiful and, just as important, keep her independence, her sense of who she was apart from a life with him. She knew instinctively he would give her the space she needed to grow and progress as an artist. She shouldn't hesitate and allow in the darkness of doubt. Life was too short. That singular fact was now etched into the contours of her being. Each day should be as good as she could make it. If it made her happy then she should do it. She would learn Italian and perhaps, if they were lucky, she would have a baby...

Shit, where did that thought come from? An image of Ben took her breath away and made her head swirl. Guilt, deep and blood red, seeped into her soul. Jesus, how could she think of another child when Ben was still in her heart? Where he would always be, as though, safe inside her body, he would never leave her.

The confusion made her hold on to the bar.

'What is it? Do you feel unwell?'

She looked into Paolo's eyes and felt calmer. Ben slowly disappeared. She smiled. 'Sorry, just need something to eat and probably too much excitement.' She touched his face. 'I'm fine.'

* * *

Less than a quarter of a kilometre away, Liechi and Dupard were in a mobile command vehicle behind the Torre del Magnia.

When Dupard and Selma met him in the courtyard he was cold and direct. 'Any sightings from your team?'

'No,' Dupard snapped back.

For a moment Liechi looked like he might blow but he remained calm. 'We've set up a Mobile Unit and got CCTV and drones feeding into it. It's like looking for a single turd in a pile of shit, but we might get lucky. Come with me.'

Dupard resisted the urge to slap him down. It was his city, even though Dupard outranked him. He knew he didn't have a leg to stand on and there was no time for being petty. They had to find Androtti and Sara.

Liechi had taken them through the tower to the Mobile Command Centre, squashed into a small space behind it.

Inside, it was calm, quiet, cool and concentrated. There were banks of screens for CCTV and drone feeds. The images from the drones were clear and focussed. The CCTV from around the Piazza, less sharp but still better than most, zoomed in and out on faces. Liechi turned to Dupard. 'I've got eyes at the top of the tower and on the roofs around the Square. There are thirty bodies moving through the Campo. We could get lucky.'

Dupard spoke quietly. 'Can we stop the Race?'

Liechi looked at him as though he was out of his mind. 'No, we fucking can't.'

Dupard felt helpless as he stared at the screen, willing Sara to appear. Selma leaned in to him. 'I'm going out, boss, this is insane, I need to do something active.'

Dupard nodded.

She left quickly. Dupard went back to the screens and the kaleidoscope of faces.

At the same time, Selma realised that it was hopeless. The Race was an hour away and the Piazza looked to be at its crowd capacity. It was a moving sea of colour and humanity with a life of its own and if it started to accelerate in panic, it would be impossible to stop and there would be carnage. The opportunities for disaster, with this number of people, were terrifying. On the positive side, the roars already echoing around the buildings would lose any noise the teams might make. But using a gun with the chance of missing and hitting an innocent was no option. They would have to get close enough without Androtti being aware of them if they were going to take him without collateral damage. She checked with Marco on the other side of the Piazza.

Marco was positive as ever. 'There's not a fucking chance of finding them so we might as well give up now.'

Selma almost agreed with him but pulled herself back. Where was her head? She was tired, but when wasn't she strung out? She focused again on the people around her. 'They're here somewhere. Keep focused.'

For a brief second, she thought she saw them, but after a struggle to get near, realised the woman was shorter and darker than Sara and the only similarities between the man with her and Androtti was that they were about the same age, male, and Italian.

As she pushed her way through, she talked with Gio, checking where he'd placed the rest of Dupard's team. They were around the track and at the doors of all the buildings that had balconies overlooking the Piazza. There was already tight security there but their guys knew what Sara and Paolo looked like, what they were wearing, and how they moved and spoke.

Androtti was bright, and wouldn't make it easy. If he followed the favoured MO he would be in and out if he closed on Juliette Sanquist. Why wouldn't they just pull her out now? The risk would be over. What possible reason could there be for putting her life in danger? Selma wondered if he would kill Sara too. She almost recoiled at the thought that slipped into her mind. Sara had served her purpose and they had found him. Was what happened to her immaterial? The reality was that this was the job they had to do. She hadn't made the decision to put Sara out there

She was pulled back by Gio, his voice sharp and insistent.

'Selma, are you OK, you went dead?'

'Yes, Gio, I'm fine, just got caught up in the noise. What is it?'

Gio was stressed. 'I'm getting grief from the guy leading the security where the Mayor will be to watch the Race. Ask Dupard to get Liechi to give him a slap.'

Selma chuckled. 'The boss is in line for a heavy one of those already. Sorry, I meant to ask before. Did you sort it with Maria and the kids?'

'No, life will be hell for months.'

'Jesus, I'm sorry.'

The Carabinieri were lining up at the start of the Race. They began a slow canter around the track, the cheers and shouts of the crowds increasing as they finished the first lap and started to speed up, their ceremonial swords flashing in the sunlight, as they reached full gallop.

* * *

Daniele came with them to the door of the bar. Sara kissed him. 'Aren't you coming with us?'

Paolo put his arm around Daniele. 'He doesn't watch. It is too painful, even at his great age, to follow and not take part.'

Daniele smiled. 'I stay here and pray that we will win and then live it through those who come to the bar. Their excitement is enough for me.'

As they walked away, Daniele closed the door. Paolo stopped. 'He won his last Race but a friend of his was killed. It was Daniele's fault. He can't forgive himself. It is partly why he and I spend the Race in the bar. But this time I will enjoy it with you.'

'I'm sorry, he's a lovely man.' She looked back at the bar. 'Can we go and see him afterwards?'

For a moment Paolo hesitated. 'Of course.'

'We don't have to.'

Paolo smiled. 'I was just thinking that we had better get to where we will watch it. We don't have much time.' There was a huge roar. 'From the sounds of it, the Carabinieri have just finished. There is one last hidden secret on the way to share with you.'

They went down a couple of alleys and came to the back of the buildings fronting the Campo. There was a narrow space at the side of one of them. Paolo pulled her in after him. In front of them a wall and to the side steps went below street level. 'Down here.'

They followed a long stone passage until they came to an opening in the wall. It was narrow but they managed to squeeze through it. Paolo smiled at her.

'It was easier when I was a child. I used to sneak out at night and pretend I was on a secret mission to save a princess.'

Sara was surprised. 'You lived here?'

'My family owned three of the houses in the Campo, all connected by secret passages for the owners in the past to escape if they felt threatened. Riches didn't buy you many friends you could trust then. Now, this is the Contessa Caravelli's house. It's where we once lived and has a great view of the Palio. We're friends, she won't mind us joining her select guests, even as unexpected ones.' He took Sara's hand. 'Come on.'

They ran up some steps and came out into a large utility area, at the end of which was another set of steps.

At the top they went through a door into a small open chapel. A group of people were moving towards the balcony. Paolo stopped and kissed her. 'I love you, Sara.'

'I love you too.'

He put his arm around her and they walked through the chapel. The noise from outside was intense, and the excitement in the room rising as the jockeys jostled for position and to do deals with those who had no hope of winning to create mischief with the other riders.

* * *

Liechi pocketed his phone.

'They've moved Sanquist and the Mayor to the Contessa Caravelli's. Her balcony has the best view of the Race. Apparently that was always the plan but on a need-to-know basis. The fucking morons have only decided to tell us now to keep any possible hack on the communications to a minimum.' He turned to the drone guys. 'Get them to focus in on the entrances and the balcony. We've got eyes on the front. No sign of Androtti outside or in the house. There are about thirty people already there. The Mayor will arrive in five minutes. They'll go in through the gate at the rear of the house. We've got that covered too.'

Dupard watched as the pictures streamed in from the drones. There were police blocking the large arched entrance to the Contessa's house. No one would get in there. They had all seen and taken in detail of the photos of the couple.

On the screen the Mayor and Sanquist, surrounded by security, reached the gate to the back of the house.

The street on either side was completely blocked off. Dupard spoke quietly, telling Selma what was happening.

'Yes, I know, boss, we'd already picked up on that. Gio and I will head there now. The other guys are still roaming.'

Liechi watched as the mayor and Juliette Sanquist came onto the balcony. 'Let's get over there. I think we might have avoided a disaster but I would rather be on the ground than waiting here.'

Dupard was checking out the CCTV feeds. He caught up with Liechi as he left the van. The two men had nothing to say to each other.

Carlo Braggio saw Sara and Paolo as they came out from the chapel and waved to them. He had a great position at the corner of the balcony. In the centre with the Contessa was Juliette Sanquist. All eyes were focussed on the track in the crowded and pulsating Piazza.

The moments before the start, the tension and excitement were palpable. It was an explosive cacophony of anticipation, hope, and passion. There was rigorous jostling for position amongst the jockeys, and last attempts made to unsettle the other riders. Here, at this time, there were no friends, only grudging allies tempted by money or favour and the reality of their standing amongst the elite. But they were all gladiators and once the race started, life or death of dreams and fame or failure, all rested on the outcome of the next three minutes of determination, skill, luck, and speed. It would make or break, deify or despise, enrich or impoverish, change lives and create gods.

Paolo and Sara were squashed alongside Carlo. His eyes twinkled.

'Sara, a delight to see you. I heard you and Paolo were spending time together and you both look as though it is good. My only surprise is that Paolo is here. I know the Contessa always hopes he will come but he prefers to spend these magic minutes in Ricardo's. So I am happy that you have moved him enough to change tradition. You will love the wonder that is the Palio. No words can ever give it enough meaning so you must not miss anything.'

Sara leaned forward to see what was happening and for a moment was clear of the others as she looked down into the multitudes surrounding the track. The jockeys were at last lined up and in position behind the starting rope.

Selma, looking up at the balcony, saw Sara appear. She started to run. 'Boss, she's on the balcony.'

Dupard, struggling to get through the mass blocking his way to the house, started to push harder, shouting to Liechi as he tried to keep up. 'Androtti's on the balcony.'

'Fuck.' Liechi put his head down and powered a pathway, shouting instructions that couldn't be heard as the roar of emotion rose and exploded. A loud bang signalled the start of the race and the noise became unbelievable, deafening, shattering any chance of communication. They reached the doorway. One man tried to stop Liechi but he was butted out of the way. Dupard was close behind him. A woman officer went for her gun but, recognising Liechi, stopped.

Selma and Gio got there just after them and were held back as their cards were checked. Then they were let through and followed Dupard.

On the balcony all sense of style and sanity disappeared, as the social elite hurled their prayers and encouragement at the two riders in front who were starting their second lap. They were lengths ahead, neck and neck and both were ready to kill to win for the glory of their contradas – the white, blue, and orange of Leocorno and the yellow and deep blue of Tartuca.

Only Paolo wasn't watching, his eyes ice cold, locked on Juliette Sanquist, her classic beauty in profile toward him. She was deeply excited by the race, immersed in the spectacle of what was happening on the track. Paolo went deep into himself, his mind already at its reach towards the inevitable conclusion. This was the ultimate challenge to the gods. It was his time, his moment, his fate and his destiny. Slowly he twisted the watch face on his wrist and a small sharp needle slipped out. Just a passing, hardly felt touch of the needle was enough to release the poison, and then he would be back with Sara, and people around Sanquist would think that the heat and excitement had brought on an attack which had killed her. Only later would they know the truth. Always, in this heartbeat, the sense of calm was absolute. There was nothing else, just this moment, this action, this time, life and death. He moved slowly towards the centre of the balcony.

Sara felt him leave but was drawn by the cheers as the Leocorno horse crossed the finishing line and she pushed forwards to see.

Paolo reached Sanquist. Liechi and Dupard hit the balcony. No one heard them or realised they were there. Dupard saw Sara. He moved towards her as Liechi dived towards Paolo, pushing between him and Sanquist.

Sara couldn't believe what she was seeing. Peter Brodsky, the man she had left in Wales, who she believed was in the United States, pushed past Carlo and wrapped his arms around her. Desperately, she looked towards Paolo. Liechi's gun was against his head. Juliette Sanquist was being bundled off the balcony. Sara's eyes locked on Paolo's in disbelief and shock. Slowly he lifted his hand towards his mouth and blew her a kiss, then pressed his watch against his neck. Sara, screaming, fought with Dupard to break free, but he was too strong. She watched Paolo's eyes mist as the poison took almost instant effect and he was dead before Liechi caught his falling body.

Sara's heart exploded in a scream of anguish.

* * *

Few on the balcony were now unaware of what had happened. As Androtti's body was taken away by Liechi's men, the Contessa, seemingly more angry at the intrusion and disorder than shocked at the unbelievable death of a family friend, held all her guests together by gently moving them into the chapel where they had taken Juliette Sanquist. The Contessa, from aristocratic stock that had faced many moments in their time which would have broken other families would allow no slip of control. Amongst her other guests, as well as the Mayor, were a Professor of Medicine, a young cardinal, dressed in civilian clothes, who was an advisor to the Pope on youth affairs, and two vigorous Sienese politicians who represented Tuscany in the Italian

Parliament. A coterie best placed to help ease any traumatic shock in the rich and powerful, and which would not allow Liechi and Dupard to find a way out of their ineptitude and failure to prevent the attack from happening. They would make sure it wasn't an easy ride for either of them.

Carlo took Sara from Dupard, who tried to hold on to her. 'She'll be safer with me.'

Liechi tried to stop him. 'I need to talk to her.'

Sara was out on her feet, her face set in shock, her mind shut down.

'She needs to find sanctuary from this madness' Carlo insisted. 'I will take her to my house and will let you know when you can see her.'

Liechi's anger was bubbling. 'I decide when I see her. And if you obstruct me, I will arrest you both. Your celebrity will not help you, Signor Braggio.'

Carlo smiled. 'If that is what you want, go ahead.'

'You arrogant bastard.'

Liechi moved towards him but Dupard pushed between them.

'Let her go. You'll know where she is. There's enough for us to do before the political shit storm starts and she'll be best away from all that.'

Liechi, realising the truth in that, reluctantly stood aside.

Carlo led Sara away.

Liechi and Dupard were eft alone on the balcony.

The noise from the Piazza was unbelievable. Celebrations and shredded dreams created a storm of sounds that seeped into the buildings and roared into the skies. But on the balcony there was a quiet and coldness.

Liechi looked at Dupard for a moment then, without warning, hit him in the stomach. Dupard doubled over. It took him a moment to get his breath.

'Feel better?'

'No, I want to strangle you.' Liechi walked away. Dupard looked up to see Selma. 'Suppose he didn't feel words did it for him, boss.' Despite the pain and embarrassment, Dupard smiled. 'I guess not.'

'They're taking the body through to next door,' Selma said. 'All these houses seem to have connecting passages. I managed to keep them back until Braggio and Sara had gone. He had his own way out and his place is a couple of streets back from the Square. Gio's there already and will stay until I take over and try to talk to her. Braggio said he would allow it as long as he stayed with her, but that he would decide when she was ready.'

Dupard nodded, straightened up, and walked slowly off the balcony. Selma looked down at the crowds and then followed him.

CHAPTER TWENTY-FIVE

Carlo and Sara were squeezed into a tiny red Tazzari electric car. It was parked in the small courtyard at the back of the Contessa's house.

It had taken Carlo a while to be persuaded to buy one but once he had given in, he had fallen in love with it. He was a big man and looked comical in it but he loved its easy movement through traffic and the small space he needed for parking. He had strapped Sara in and slowly driven through the gates and into the blocked-off street. They had to wait for the police to phone Liechi and get his permission to let them through the barriers. Then they slowly moved into a crowded lane, edging through until they reached the entrance to the lower level of Carlo's large house. He parked and helped Sara out of the car. She hadn't spoken or shown any emotion since he had taken her from the balcony. Everything had shut down to counter the impact of what had happened. She was in a deep state of shock, able to move with help but not think or feel.

Carlo hadn't said anything to Sara either. There would be time for words when she had soothed and replenished both her mind and body. He had made a call to a doctor, Angelique Cantona, before starting the car, asking her to come to his house as soon as she was able to get away.

Dr Cantona, who had been watching the race from another balcony, had moved quickly and, let in by Francella, Carlo's studio assistant, was waiting as the lift came up from the parking dock below the house.

Carlo smiled and spoke quietly. 'Thank you, Angel, for leaving your family and the celebrations. You are wonderful. I wouldn't have disturbed you but there was nobody else with the skill needed that I could trust. Francella, would you take Sara for a moment.'

Francella allowed Sara to lean against her. Carlo moved close to Angelique.

'This young woman is in deep shock. She has seen her lover kill himself but there is more for her to know when she is strong enough. I will tell you everything once we have her in bed and you have given her something to help ease her to sleep.'

Angelique Cantona was thirty-five and Carlo's god-daughter. She had arrived in Siena a week before from a month's stint working with an NGO in Syria. The day of the Palio was sacrosanct for her and her family, and could not be missed. Carlo was the only person who would be allowed to break this tradition and also dare to call her Angel. If anyone else had tried it, she would have ripped off their heads, which Carlo knew was entirely within her capabilities.

Angelique didn't waste time with unnecessary words. She and Carlo had a special relationship and she loved to share space with him and would often spend time in his studio watching him work when she needed to recharge her batteries. Apart from her husband, Carlo was the only one with whom she would share the horror and helplessness she felt when working with the deaths and tragedies of innocents dragged into other people's wars. All this was why he wanted her here. If anyone was able to help Sara through the first shockwaves of her new reality, it was Angel.

They took Sara to a small bedroom on the second floor and Carlo left as Angel put Sara to bed and gave her a sedative to knock her out. She watched as she slipped into unconsciousness. Sara's face had relaxed. She looked young and fit with no sign of what was going on inside her head. Angel checked her pulse and thought about the moment Sara would try to understand what had happened and how she might help her. Physical damage was always more straightforward because of its visibility but psychological trauma had truths you had to find, break down and then carefully restructure so they would hold the reality of what had caused it. She picked up her large soft leather Hermes bag off the floor, searched around in it, and took out what looked like a man's watch, a small circular pad with straps. She fastened it around Sara's ankle. Then from the back of it she detached the tiny camera, looked around and, standing on a chair, positioned it high on the wall facing the bed.

It was technology that she had helped develop, a monitor run from an app on her phone. It would not only allow her to see Sara but would detect any rises and falls in heart rate, respiration and the changes in neurological patterns when inertia evolved into a more conscious state, perhaps, still not awake, but closer to the surface. It was a prototype, still being tested, but she had used it for months now and so far it hadn't let her down.

Angel pulled her iPhone from her pocket and checked that the app was working and the camera was in the right place. It was all good.

* * *

Braggio was in his studio on the top floor of the house. A huge open space that filled the depth and width of the building. Floor-to-ceiling windows surrounded three sides that were edged with a balcony filled with a forest of plants and flowers. There was a wonderful view across Siena and into the hills. At sunset the beauty of this natural canvas often moved those who saw it for the first time. In one corner of the studio there were chairs and low tables but the rest of the vast space was filled with a painter's world of organised clutter and mess. There were large canvases stacked up against the only solid wall and others hanging from the ceiling or on easels, and a multitude of paints, brushes, knives, scalpels, tools, and rolls of canvas. Braggio had other studios and houses but this one was special as was the heaven that was his 'escape' on the isle of Elba. This house was where he had lived with his first wife, Anita, and where she had written her first novel. The marriage hadn't lasted but they had parted as friends. She was still his severest critic and he was the first person to read and comment on her completed manuscripts. Three other wives had followed, but he was now alone and apart from the frustrations of increasing age, his work, close friends, and an occasional lover in her fifties made him contented with his life.

However, Sara had touched something in him. Her vulnerability and pain had made him want to help balance her world. Perhaps, if he could manage that, it might even soften the need for the desperate answer of why her husband and son had been killed. Maybe that would lessen the drive for a revenge that would never bring peace. He had thought that perhaps with Paolo, who he had known since he was born, she would have a chance to find happiness. The shock of what happened on the balcony to Paolo was something that he had shut out for now. There would be time to understand and process that later. Now it was all about Sara. It was a powerful strength in Carlo that he was able to close his own feelings down when he needed to find a strong focus to help someone he cared about. His visits to the little church in Florence to recharge his artistic and spiritual heartbeat fuelled his compassion and sometimes led him to see a clear and practical path to ways in which he could help rebalance some of the acts of fate that damaged or shattered lives. It was a way he could pay back the benefits that had been given to him in life. Of course, he wouldn't always be able to make things right but he believed that you should do whatever you can, even if it seemed small and was only a part of the answer.

* * *

Selma had taken over from Gio. He had told her about Angelique Cantona coming here and what he had found out about her in the short time since her arrival. He had taken a photograph and the guy in Rome who had picked it up knew of her and they were able to rush some info back to him. The list of her talents, achievements, and her altruism was impressive but the important thing, for now, was that she was a doctor, and probably an expert in trauma too. For a moment her presence had given Selma a stab of panic. Had something physical happened to Sara as well? Had her heart given out? It wouldn't be too much of a stretch with the shock of what she had gone through. Another death, attributable to them, would really send the shit flying.

She tried to contact Dupard but his phone was off. She didn't leave a message. She'd wanted to ask his permission to talk to Braggio and Cantona and give them a heads up on what had happened, as well as see the state of Sara. She didn't think either of them would go to the media. There was going to be a maelstrom of blame and accusation when it did get out, even without the official response to Dupard's under-the-radar operation.

She suddenly realised the reason for her concern. Jesus, what a self-centred bitch she was. It was all about avoiding blame. She pushed out the panic of the thoughts that swooped on what it would mean for her to be stained with it and forced her mind to think about what was real now and about what she could do for Sara.

Her heart had gone out to the woman when she saw her spirit almost visibly crumble as Braggio led her away. She felt revulsion for what they had allowed to happen. What were the chances of her meeting and falling in love with the man who had destroyed her life? Chaos theory didn't even come close.

Selma made a decision that might well be the last of her career in a job she loved. But, even if it did, what the fuck, she still had Silvia, and was young enough to do something else. Her her mind was spinning. She needed to focus. More important than all of that personal and ego stuff, was the understanding of what it was to lose someone you loved who was the heartbeat of your life. Like Sara, she knew. It had touched her too. She had raged against it with all her fury. How could she have let herself be blind to it? She should have not gone along with Dupard. So what if he had been pissed off with her? There were others who would have slotted in, without the baggage she carried. He would have replaced her. He had no loyalty except to the job he was doing. She felt disgust. She had to accept that she was as responsible as Dupard for what had been allowed to happen.

She breathed deeply for a few moments to find calm, then rang the video phone on the side of the large door. Nothing happened. She pushed again and kept it ringing. It finally lit up.

'Yes?'

'I need to speak to Signor Braggio. My name is Selma Massochi, I'm a police officer.' She hesitated. 'I want to talk to him about Paolo Androtti.'

Braggio and Angel stared at Selma in shock and disbelief as she finished giving them chapter and verse.

Braggio was barely audible. 'Paolo killed Sara's son and husband, and Vittorio?'

'Yes, and three others that we know about, but there could be more.'

Selma found it hard to meet his eyes. She glanced at Angelique, saw the coldness and disgust, and looked away.

Braggio got up and walked to the windows. 'This is like a nightmare. Unbelievable. Impossible. I have known him all his life. His father was my friend. How could he have done something so terrible? He...' He stopped as if his words had been snatched away. There were tears in his eyes.

Angel spoke quietly. 'You said she recognised your boss Dupard. How did she know him? She didn't know you were watching her.'

If Selma went this next step she was finished, but they had to know to be able to really understand the shock for Sara.

'Dupard is head of a Department at the International Investigation Force. He was given a white card by a government-level international group set up to investigate the killings. He went to Wales to get to know Sara. She thought he was a university lecturer looking for his roots. That wasn't a total lie. His great-grandfather emigrated to Canada and Dupard was, in another life, a tutor at McGill University in Montreal.'

Angel looked hard at her. 'Jesus Christ, the bastard set her up! Did he have an affair with her too?'

Selma couldn't stop now. 'I don't know. All he told me was that he did what was necessary. Sara decided to come here to find if there was a reason for Rietti's death. If there was, then it might lead her to the killer. We were watching all the time and, of course, we checked Androtti out, as we did Signora Rietti and you, Signor Braggio, There was nothing there to cause concern. It was only this morning that Dupard received information that suggested something needed looking into. And that led to us discovering what was in the chapel.'

She paused, uncomfortable with the dark accusing waves coming at her, but forced herself to look directly at Braggio.

'I don't believe that Sara was in any danger. It looked like he was in love with her and she wasn't a celebrity. Juliette Sanquist was his target.'

Selma felt drained and exhausted. There was nothing more she could say.

'Have you told us everything?' Braggio turned from the window. His voice was hoarse and flat.

'Yes.'

'Then I think you had better leave.'

Selma stood up, took a card out of her pocket, and put on the table. 'I will do anything I can to help.'

'That won't be necessary. We'll look after her now.'

As Braggio took her out, Angel checked Sara on her phone. Everything was okay. But when she came round, her world would be shattered again when she was told about Androtti.

Braggio came back into the studio. Any weakness in him had gone.

'I will not waste time on fucking with those idiots. I want to put all my energy into pulling Sara through this. My beautiful girl, will you help?'

Angel came over to him and touched his face. 'Of course.' For a moment she held him then he moved away.

'I have to make some calls. It's time to pull in favours from those in power.' He took out his phone. 'When she has the strength, I will take her to Elba.'

CHAPTER TWENTY-SIX

Dupard was locked into a meeting with the Mayor, Liechi, and the Police Chief. Androtti's body had been fast-tracked to autopsy and was due to go under the knife in two hours. The medic who'd examined the small wound on his neck thought that the needle could have been filled with some sort of poison, possibly a refined form of cyanide, which would have an instant effect, but until they had samples tested they wouldn't know. They had managed to lock down all media and even the escape of mobile phone footage had been avoided because of the profile of the few people on the balcony who had witnessed what had happened. And, anyway, with the Palio nearing climax, any phones using cameras would have been pointed towards the race. Most of the Contessa's guests were still at the house being interviewed. They were not an easy group to manipulate, particularly as it was one of their own who was dead. Many of them were in shock, not just about Sanquist, but that Androtti, a popular and influential member of their elite, had taken his own life. He'd had everything.

For once the insanity of the Palio had helped the police contain everything but it wouldn't last. Something would get out, money would change hands, photos of the dead Androtti would get on the web, and the story would slowly seep out. Liechi wouldn't have minded, but the political pull of those who ran the city needed time to protect their own. It was an unpalatable fact of Sienese life. It would overshadow even the desperate and tragic lives and battles around the globe of those who had little voice and less importance for the rich of the world.

The mayor's phone rang and, seeing the caller, he went out of the small office to answer it.

Liechi had been silent while the Chief laid into Dupard. Already this expected shitstorm had been taken to levels beyond his reach and a high-table protest was ricocheting around the IIF and the heads of governmental departments that had jointly allowed Dupard's investigation to be green-lit. Finding a calm space in his mind, Dupard had shut out the Chief's shredding of his abilities, personality, and heritage. He knew that he would be out of friends in power and would have to find a way to accept the repercussions, both in law enforcement and probably academia too.

The Mayor came back into the room. He was thoroughly pissed off.

'That was the Minister. Apparently Signor Braggio has been pulling favours and Signora Jenkins will stay with him. We will only be allowed access when Dr Cantona allows it. I've come up against her before and she is not an easy ride, but she's brilliant and the woman couldn't be in better hands. Braggio then plans to take her to his estate on Elba until she is well. At the moment there is nothing that I can do, but I have a few threats and a touch of blackmail that I use if necessary. Which leads me to you, Dupard. As of now, you are suspended from the IIF and, until you leave Italy, within my jurisdiction. So, if you fuck me about, I will make your life even more of a nightmare than it is already. Now… Braggio wants to see you. I said you would be there. I want to know everything that is said and unsaid. Try and talk to Signora Jenkins. Androtti is dead and she has, as far as I know, committed no crime, so she is free to go. Obviously I would like as much information as possible. I don't want anything to bite my arse. Is that understood?'

Dupard didn't react, just held the Mayor's raging eyes for a few moments, showing him nothing of the anger he felt at being treated like a disruptive child. But after what happened, ego was the last thing that should surface.

'Of course, but I don't think she would want to see me, or that Braggio would allow it.'

The Mayor pushed his face inches away from Dupard's. His breath was rancid and unpleasant. 'Just do it. This isn't a choice.'

Dupard headed for the door.

* * *

'You can't see her.'

Carlo was facing Dupard in the large marbled hallway of his house.

'I know.'

Carlo moved closer to him. He spoke quietly.

'I want you to leave her alone. I'll take care of her until she's able to be on her own. She has the strength to get through this but you must give me your word you won't pursue her. Strangely, despite all that you have

276

done, perhaps because of all that you have done, I believe that if you give me your word, you will keep it. There's no need for you to see her again. When she is well enough she can give her statement to the police here in Siena. You've achieved what you set out to do and your crimes have been solved. For Vittorio, I'm glad you've found his killer. For me, I find it hard to take in Paolo's part. But then this is not about me. This is about Sara. I don't want to discuss what happened with you. I've said all that I wanted and I believe there is nothing that you can say to me that I want to hear.' He paused. And now you can leave.'

Dupard was taken by the simple directness of Braggio. The old man had a tangible power and charisma and it was easy to believe that he would succeed in supporting Sara as she fought her way back. He felt pleased that she had someone like him on her side. But he realized that she would never understand how he could have manipulated her. He wouldn't be able to tell her what was hidden inside him. In the short time they were together, there had been love, but that was smothered and displaced by his determination to find the killer. It had got him to the right place. But he also knew what it had taken out of him and that his passion and energy for all of this was running out. He always knew that it would come and that this was as good a time as any for him to find another world to inhabit. Somewhere straightforward and quietly, perhaps boringly, satisfying peaceful. He had had enough of the noise.

He came back to the moment. 'I won't insult Sara by asking her to forgive me. Or you, to listen to the reasons for my choices.'

He held out his hand. Carlo ignored it.

'I'll go back to Canada tonight and that will be an end for me but I can't promise what will happen here. Though I think you probably have that covered. Liechi is going to escort me to the airport so there is no chance of me talking to anyone in Siena about the case. He was unable to deny it with you but then you have some powerful friends, Signor Braggio.'

He smiled and left.

As the door shut, the painter sighed deeply, the containment of his anger, had taken all his energy. Twenty years ago it wouldn't have done but now he accepted that it was what he had to live with at his age. And it pissed him off enormously.

Braggio's words had stung Dupard and for a moment, the remorse was there. But the reality was that he couldn't allow it to grow and fester. He had done what he had done. There was no way that could change. If there had been another way he would have followed it. It was extreme to turn Sara like that but necessary, and, although the way it had played out surprised him, the bottom line was that he had found the killer of six people. It didn't bother him that Androtti wouldn't stand trial. It would remove the grandstanding, save hundreds of thousands of euros, and probably be more acceptable as the political furore died down.

However, all that would not affect the decision of his bosses at the IIF. There was a game of international blame here too and the Italians were too pissed for him not to be collateral damage. He would leave with a large payment for his continuing loyalty and silence. He might go back full-time at McGill. If not, there were many invitations from all over the world to lecture on his particular skills and there would always be a call for his talents in the private world if he wanted to take them up. But, for now, he must complete his debrief.

Gio was outside the house with the car.

'How did it go? Didn't take long. Thought you might have called for help. The old guy looks like he can handle himself.'

'I'm sure he could but he was in control. Everything was on his terms. Where's Selma?'

'Gone home.'

'Good.' Dupard smiled at Gio. 'You might as well get off too.'

'If you're sure, boss.'

'I'm not in charge any more. The team's been disbanded.'

He got into the car. The memory of the Palio still echoed through the streets. There would be days yet of celebration and commiseration. The Palio would come round again and the whole maelstrom would explode in the way it has always done. The tragedy of Paolo Androtti would reverberate for a while then only those close to him would feel the continual pain of shock and betrayal. Whatever had happened wouldn't change the way of the world too much.

Gio interrupted his meandering. 'Where to?'

'Mayor's office. I have a meeting with the deputy minister of Home Affairs. I don't think that'll be much fun. You're welcome to stand in for me as a last nod to loyalty.'

Gio started the car. 'The privilege of a lowly position is that I don't have to face the high-level bullshit. Not that I don't feel for you. I'm just glad it's not me.'

Dupard laughed as Gio drove slowly to the end of the lane and turned into a busy street.

By 9.30 p.m. Selma was tucked up in her bed with Silvia. Usually that never happened unless Silvia was ill, but tonight she wanted to hold and protect her. Selfish, but her daughter loved it, which made it all right. Her mother was staying at a friend's outside of Siena. She hated being there during the Palio.

Silvia had dropped asleep halfway through *Pippi Longstocking*, which they were reading in English together to practise the language.

Selma gently moved her daughter to the other side of the bed and went to clean her teeth. Looking in the mirror she saw that the last weeks had left their mark. She had shadows under her eyes and was convinced that the lines around them were multiplying by the day. Lack of sleep and stress would have helped with that. Certainly these last days had seen their moments, but most of it was what you were used to in the daily drag on your resources. Only now and again did something shake her ability to cope with the life. What Dupard had done to Sara was cruel and lacked any compassion. Selma was complicit in it too. It wasn't enough that she was just following orders, the usual get out of jail card. She had a choice. It was too late for Sara, but now she had made a decision. She was going to think of Silvia and move away to something good and clean. She just didn't know which direction she would take yet.

She suddenly felt exhausted. She got into bed, cuddled up to Silvia, and after a few minutes, hugging her close and breathing with her, fell asleep.

* * *

Liechi drove Dupard to the airport and silently escorted him to the plane with two airport police, then stood at the bottom of the steps until he disappeared. Dupard didn't look back but smiled at the cabin crew and took his seat in business class. He had been booked in economy but wanted to sleep so had paid the extra himself.

It had been a difficult meeting with the Deputy Minister. A lot of Italian excitement and shouting. The gist of the diatribe was that he wouldn't be welcome again in Italy and he was lucky that he wasn't being charged with obstruction, perpetuating a crime, which was a new one on Dupard, and being an accessory to attempted murder. If there hadn't been a high-level interjection by the Canadian Government he would have been locked up for the next ten years. It was always good to get constructive and focused criticism, and halfway through he had switched off and let the Minister's histrionics and death glares from the Mayor and Liechi wash over him.

In the car Liechi had said that he was a complete asshole and made rubbish of all that made what he did worthwhile. The point was to get rid of the sludge of society, not ooze into it. And that was that. He hadn't said anymore, had just driven like a fucking madman, screaming at any traffic that didn't move out of his way.

It was only after his first drink on the plane, that Dupard could ease the locked muscles from the ride. On the long flight home he would slowly sift through the job and keep only the positives. Although he was sorry for Sara, he wouldn't let it affect his life. It was a job. It was over. He was moving on and the less baggage he took with him the better his future would be.

CHAPTER TWENTY-SEVEN

Sara could see Ben and Ceri racing each other along the sand towards her. They were at full speed, their arms and legs pumping. Ben was a miniature Ceri, his arms, legs, the way he held his head to one side as his breath pushed out his cheeks. And they were both laughing so much. They were hysterical, had tears in their eyes and the uncontrollable waves of ululating sound washed over Sara like a tsunami, rolling and bouncing as it came at her again and again. She was drowning in it. Then distorted through the mist of water she saw Ben and Ceri slowly move away, running backwards. They began to fade and as the water around was sucked away and swallowed by the sea, they disappeared. Then she was up to her waist in another wash of water and Paolo was riding a huge wave towards her. He was getting closer and closer and she started to run but her feet wouldn't move. In a sudden rush he was there, arms around her, holding her tight, and they were dry in the sunshine. Naked, pressed together, they kissed deeply. It took all the breath out of her. Then she saw Ben watching her from the top of a cliff. He was smiling at her and she could feel a warm wind as he blew her a kiss that landed on her neck with a sharp sting. She felt the blood and saw Paolo slowly pushing a needle into her. Suddenly, with a scream of rage, Ceri landed on top of Paolo and they rolled over and over into the sea and disappeared. 'No, wait for me,' she screamed and ran into a huge balloon of Ben that became her. She got bigger and bigger and her skin tighter and tighter until she saw the needle fly through the air and then she exploded.

Angel, holding Sara's hand, watched as she came back to consciousness. Her eyes flickered under the tightly closed lids then calmed until there was no movement and the lines of concern smoothed out. Slowly her eyes opened and tried to find focus. Angel smiled at her.

'Hello, Sara.'

Sara glanced towards her, frowned, then looked away, her gaze flicked around the room and back to Angel. Her eyes were flat and still and for a moment Angel just held her look so Sara could feel there was no threat from her. 'My name is Angelique. I'm a doctor. I gave you something to help you sleep. It will take a moment for your head to clear.' She picked up a glass of water and gently lifted Sara's head, pouring a few drops into her mouth. 'You are in Carlo's house. Carlo Braggio. He's a painter like you. You know him.'

Sara found it hard to speak or understand what this woman sitting on the bed had said to her. She had never seen her before. There was something familiar about the name she had said. Carlo. She felt the woman's hand on hers. It was soft but there was strength there too. She realised that she was holding the hand. It was warm and safe. Like her mum's had been when she sat with her when she was ill. In an instant she could hear her mum's voice as she tried to give her a mixture of honey, vinegar, and brown sugar to ease her throat. 'Try and have a sip, sweetie, promise it'll help. It'll make your throat feel better.' Her voice was so full of love and tenderness that it helped soothe the pain.

Then she realised that her mum wasn't there and she wasn't in her bed at home. She looked around the room. It was completely strange to her. There was a glow of light from a lamp near the bed. She could see colours, soft pastel shades. Slowly her eyes adjusted. She tried to sit up. The woman helped her. Where was she? She tried to speak but no sound came out. She waited and tried again. The woman didn't seem to mind as she struggled to force the words out. When they came, they were hoarse. But slowly, after more gulps of water from the glass held by the woman, her throat eased. Her voice was weak, quiet, emotionless, but audible.

'I don't know where I am.'

Angelique smiled. 'This is Carlo's house. He brought you here. You have been asleep. I wanted you to rest so I gave you a strong sedative.'

Sara looked at her, trying to make sense of what she had said.

This was a tricky moment for Angel. Sara's mind was still closed to what had happened. Sometimes that was temporary and sometimes it never went away. There was no particularly good time to manage the reactions of someone who had suffered deep shock. But when they came, that was when you needed strength and reason.

Angel had learned that there was never a set way to handle horror. Each time was unique even if the blood and damage was the same film played over and over again. One thing she knew was that her instinct, and a clear understanding of the cause of the trauma, allowed her to assess and react and find a way through in whatever diverse way it took.

There were other skills required.

The physical damage needed the ability to think quickly, do whatever was needed to normalise and remove the immediate danger, work with the tools you have, forget the rules of hygiene that would close operating rooms in the sane world, and just get on with it. But with a massively shocked and damaged mind, calmness, a neutral voice, patience, tenacity, physical strength, an understanding of how to rebalance confusion, anger and guilt, and the ability to listen for long hours once the silence is broken, are the only ways to edge slowly forward.

In Sara's eyes she saw the change begin. It was not instant but a slow burning light that moved through confusion to sharp memory. Angel waited for what was happening inside Sara's head to become whole. They were both still, only their minds moving. Sara's sifting and seeing and Angel's ready to react.

There was no sound as Sara saw Paolo moving towards the American film star and a man throwing himself through the crowd towards them. Then Peter Brodsky was pushing her into a corner and holding her so she couldn't move. Carlo was reaching towards her and over Peter's shoulder she saw the man holding a gun to Paolo's head. Paolo looked towards her, smiled, and touched his neck and then his eyes clouded and he just crumpled. The roar of the crowd exploded, people around her shouting. She was screaming and Carlo was snatching her from Peter and pulling her away off the balcony…

'Is Paolo dead?' Sara turned towards Angel.

'Yes.'

'Peter Brodsky?'

'He was there.'

'Why?'

'He was looking for Paolo.'

'Did he know I was there?'

'Yes.'

Angel was in control but this was not what she had thought would happen. There was distance in Sara's questions. Not disbelief, denial, or desperation, just a space for the words to fill. Angel had seen this before. She had to be ready for anything. But she knew she had to answer as directly as Sara questioned her. There had to be honesty for the trust to grow, no matter how hard it was. There was no choice. Not now that it had started. She was prepared for an explosion and had a fast-acting sedative in a pen ready to use. But for now, she had to let it play out.

Sara felt as though she was watching herself and this woman as they talked. She felt she was split into two parts, one that was spinning, out of control, trying to make sense of the reality she had found. And the other, calmly searching out the questions, knowing that for her, now, it was only truth she had to face. She didn't know what would happen when the spinning woman took over, as she would, but she couldn't go there yet. She had to know the facts for her to find safety again. Once the picture was there the spinning woman could understand.

'Peter is not the man I thought I knew.'

'No.'

'Who is he?'

'He runs the serious crime section of an international investigation force.'

'He's not an academic?'

'He was.'

The calm woman was running thoughts that bounced around the meanings of the words. Lateral puzzles needed reason to unbox. She was clever, the calm woman. She had the courage and discipline to make the choices the spinning woman would not be able to choose. She had no fear. She dealt only in facts not emotions. The spinning woman had the edge there.

'He came to Wales because of Ceri and Ben?'

'Yes, and Vittorio Rietti.'

'He wanted to find who killed them?'

'Yes.'

'And I was part of that?'

'Yes.'

The calm woman almost stopped. She knew this was the moment that could break them if the spinning woman took control. But she had almost enough to solve the puzzle. Use the clues to agitate the mind to calculate the answer before it came out as an awful truth. To try, in the end, to save the spirit of the two of them that formed the whole of her, she had to allow a wound to open. Without that she wouldn't have a chance to heal. Even with it, the odds were against her keeping sanity.

'Paolo?'

This was more difficult for Angel to answer. Part of him, a real part, was the man that Sara had fallen in love with, but there was another side to him too. She knew Paolo, but for now she had to close that down. To tell the truth in full or in part was the decision she had to make. In reality it had to be all.

'He killed people.'

This was it. The calm woman couldn't hold back the final, fearful moment. In her calm and clear mind, she already knew that, but she had to hear it to make it real.

'Ceri and Ben?'

'Yes.'

The spinning woman howled into the calm woman as the nonsense of it all broke the spell.

A split second before it happened Angel took the pen and pressed it against Sara's arm. She was able to hold her as she struggled and slowly laid her down as the drug took over.

* * *

Carlo and Angel were sitting on the balcony. It was late afternoon and the sky was beginning to transform into a beautiful sunset. Carlo touched her arm. 'How soon do you think we can go to Elba?'

Angel poured some coffee for them, dipped a biscuit in hers, slowly ate it with a look of pure pleasure, then put the last crisp bit into the coffee again until it got to the right sogginess.

Carlo watched her, smiling. 'You've done that with those almond biscotti since you were little.'

Angel moaned happily. 'I know, and they still taste as good as they did then. I try to keep them for myself but

Mario and the kids know all my hiding places. They don't have the understanding that you have to let the taste dissolve before you can get the full effect. And you have to have only one at a time otherwise the magic will go.'

She laughed, tucked her legs under her and thought for a moment, gently biting her lip. And to Carlo she was twelve years old again, doing her homework. Some things never went away. She felt his look, realized what she was doing, and stopped.

'I want to see how she is when she wakes up again. Sara's mind must have time to process what I told her without her actively blocking it out.'

'OK, that makes sense.' For a moment a large red and yellow butterfly distracted Carlo as it landed on a flower then he looked back to Angel. 'Is it possible she'll be able find any sort of normality again?'

'Depends on what you mean by normality. Are any of us normal? It's a blanket state that doesn't allow for each of us to be different. Dupard probably did a good job in finding a way through the nightmare she was living. He gave Sara a reason to recover. Revenge was a prime factor and, perhaps even more pertinent to her, finding out why it had happened to her family. He built a trust that she could balance on and then guided her into the belief that she had made her own decisions. It was her choice to come to Siena. But he planted the seed and fed it. Then his plan became confused. He wouldn't have been able to imagine that she would meet the man responsible or that Sara would fall in love. And that it would lead her away from revenge and distance her from helping him to find the killer. Although surprisingly, it did. It must have been tumultuous when he found the cellar and realized that he had succeeded but also put Sara in greater danger.

'As for Sara, even supposing she was able to think clearly, it's a really tricky one for her to resolve. There are direct positives as well as the obvious negatives.'

Angel checked her phone and saw that Sara was beginning to move as her sleep lightened. She was slowly coming to the surface. She stood up.

'The reality for her is that she has found the answer and she has had her revenge, but what led her to that was another betrayal of her trust. Falling in love with Paolo gave her the freedom to move on and not want the answers that led her to Siena. I think, from all that we've been told, that Paolo probably loved her too and wanted a life with her but he had one more demon to lay first. Although how he thought they might live happily ever after if he succeeded in killing his last target is beyond reason.'

She thought for a moment.

'If Sara's mind is able to deal with Dupard's betrayal, and Paolo's, by seeing the positive effect despite the horror, then, no matter how long it takes, she has a chance. A glimmer of hope and the will to carry on can become a journey with a new life at the end of it. If she can find that, then she will be able to explore something to balance what has happened to her. Something that lets her find a way to make a difference outside of the world she has known.'

Carlo was briefly confused. Then a smile lit up his eyes and he pulled himself out of the deep armchair, stretched his back, went across and hugged her tightly.

'You, my little Angel, have a plan.'

Angel kissed him lightly. 'Might have. Now, I need to go to Sara.'

'When can I talk to her?

'I'll come and get you if I think she's up to it. She is strong and I think she has a will to survive. How long it takes for her progress depends on how quickly she can find her way. We might have to wait a long while before we see any real movement. She has to want to move on. I think she will. But, as you know, I'm an eternal optimist and always up for a challenge.'

Sara was awake when Angel stepped into the room.

She had come round a few minutes before. When she opened her eyes she expected to see Ben there, but he must have been in the last shadow of her sleeping self. He had said he would always be with her and would look after her. He and his dad would never be far away. Ceri had then touched her cheek. 'Whenever it's too hard for you to get through, just remember that we are all one now, you, me, and Ben.' Slowly the memory soothed her, the stomach jumps that had started eased, and she was able to face the reality of being awake.

Angel sat on the bed.

'Hi, Sara,' she smiled, 'sorry I drugged you… again. I wanted to stop you before you really took in what I had told you.'

'Why?'

'Because your mind left alone, without emotional reactions, is sometimes able to deal with shock and bad things in an objective way.'

'I talked to Ben and Ceri.'

'What did they say?'

'I'm not on my own.'

'Did you believe them?'

'Yes.'

'Good.'

'Are you sure?'

'Yes.'

Angel decided to test how far she could go. 'Do you want to talk about Peter?'

Sara hesitated. A momentary panic flipped her stomach, then she felt a touch on her head. She knew her boys were there as they had promised.

'Yes, but can I ask you something first?'

'Of course,' Angel took her hand.

'How long have I been here?'

'Four days.'

Sara looked up.

'Carlo brought you here. He will do anything to keep the crap away from you. You'll be safe with him.' She paused and smiled. 'When I was little he would meet me from school and I would do my homework in his studio. My mum was an architect and my father a scientist so they were never on a normal clock. Carlo wasn't either, but for me he made sure he was always there when they weren't. He called me because you told him about Ben and Ceri and the reasons you were in Siena, and he trusts me because I'm his goddaughter. I'm also a doctor and have worked in war zones and have my own theories about helping ease trauma. He knew I would probably be able to help you. He also felt responsibility because you had trusted him and he had made it possible for you to meet Paolo.' She stopped and laughed. 'That's a few more truths than the normal doctor/patient chat requires but it helps build a trust between us if there's no 'it's just my job' bullshit hanging in there. It's personal too, for as long as you want it.'

'Shit!'

'Yes, heard that, and other less complimentary reactions too, but fuck them. I do things the only way I can. Is that good with you?'

Sara nodded. 'Yes.'

'Good. Now, back to Carlo. He's very fond of you. He also has many friends, some very powerful, so, nobody will bother you until you decide you are ready.'

Sara's eyes filled with tears.

Angel waited.

'I'm glad you're here.'

'So am I.'

'I can't work out why it doesn't hurt yet.'

'It will, but I'll be here and we'll get through.'

'Are you sure?'

Angel laughed. 'No, but I'm not going to tell you that.'

She handed Sara a tissue and she blew her nose.

Angel took the tissue and threw it into the bin in the corner of the room.

'Another one of the skills that makes me perfect for this job.'

Sara pulled herself up then reached for Angel's hand.

'Do you mind?'

Angel shook her head. Sara frowned.

'I feel distant. But I remember the pain after Ben and Ceri died. It was never-ending. There was nothing I could do to stop it. Even trying to kill myself was beyond me.' She smiled. 'It was because I didn't know how to do it. How sad is that?'

'Pretty sad.'

'But I do know that without Peter I wouldn't have come out the other side. Is that a good place to start?'

'I think it just might be. First though, how are you feeling? Any nausea, headaches, cloudy eyes, pains anywhere?'

'A bit spaced out still but perhaps that's a good place to be for now.'

* * *

Later that day, Sara had a little to eat. And Angel allowed Carlo a brief visit when he brought the food he had prepared for her.

For the most part Sara was able to talk about what had happened. It wasn't always calm but when it became too much, Angel would just hold her and wait for it to pass. She just listened, allowing the spaces and pauses to sit comfortably and safely until words came again.

She was amazed that Sara was able to let it out. Sometimes the time frame got mixed up and Paolo and her trips around Siena included Ben and Ceri too. It was disjointed and jerky, with moments when it flowed quickly to make sure it all came out. But there was a lot to build on and Angel felt positive about where they could go from here.

Angel had decided she was going to stay at Carlo's until they left for Elba. She felt a responsibility for Sara and the way she had been abused. If her husband agreed, she would rearrange her life so she could be here with her patient. She had conferences, a short lecture tour, and research grant applications to finalise, but nothing that couldn't wait. The most important thing was her bi-weekly clinics and she would still be able to do those. Everything else she could have covered.

So, as Sara slept, she went briefly home for a touch of family life, then came back and slept in the room next to Sara's.

CHAPTER TWENTY-SEVEN

Five days days after Paolo Androtti killed himself, Roberto d'Angelo called Carlo and asked if they could meet. Carlo had known him a long time and they had become good but not constant friends who met first through their wives, both successful novelists. He knew that Roberto would want to talk about Paolo and understood the pain he would be going through. He would listen and try to hold in his emotions.

They met at a small bar near Carlo's house. Roberto looked drawn, exhausted, and his eyes were full of despair. His natural style and elegance was still there but jaded with the fragility of the years that had overtaken him in the last days. Carlo, sitting at a table outside, got up and hugged him and when a waiter came out ordered coffee and brandy for them both. Then, until the drinks came, the two men let the silence settle between them. Both understood that this moment of calm would allow space for the difficult words to come. Sometimes the wisdom of age lets patience temper the agitation of wasting time.

Roberto took a large swallow as soon as the brandy arrived.

'I don't know how to start this but I will begin with the regret that Sara has suffered from what Paolo did. I had a great fondness for her and there is one truth between the two of them. Paolo loved her and would never have hurt her. I had never seen him as complete as when he was with her.'

Carlo felt a flush of anger and started to rise.

'No, Carlo, you and I are too old to fight, so please let me finish.'

Carlo held his look for a moment then sat down.

'Of course.'

Roberto breathed heavily and the words came slow and quiet. 'I had no idea there was this darkness in his heart. No thoughts or suspicions that his spirit was so damaged. I've tried to see if, over all the years he was like a grandson to me, there was a hint of what he carried. Any signs that, perhaps, the damage he suffered when his mother and father were killed would ignite this flame of evil. But there was nothing.' He clasped his fingers and touched the knuckles to his mouth.

A large overweight man approaching the bar slowed as he saw Carlo, smiled and waved. Carlo gave the guy a look and a slight shake of the head. The man nodded, gave a 'call me' finger and thumb phone and carried on past the table.

Roberto, unaware of the man, looked up, his eyes distant. 'I knew that he had little to prove to anyone and could do anything in the world that he desired. He was kind and approachable and gave generously to people and projects he felt could grow with his support.' He paused, feeling for the words. 'But I knew that he countered the balance of having everything by playing out games of extreme risk and danger, to test fate.'

A young couple at a table inside the bar laughed loudly. Roberto glanced towards them and then back at Carlo. He closed his eyes briefly and took a breath.

'This morning I remembered something that happened when he was ten years old. He was staying with us at our villa in Sicily. I think his parents and grandparents were on holiday again. Sometimes it felt like they had no time for him in their busy lives, and there was a sadness in Paolo that I saw but I never mentioned. Perhaps it would have made a difference.' He shook his head. 'Sorry, let me get back to the story. One night, when we were all in bed, I heard a noise coming from the garden. It was like a bird or small animal was trapped. As I went out the sound stopped and I saw Paolo stamping on a little bird. It was obviously dead. I wasn't sure if he was still asleep but I gently stopped him and carried him back to bed.' Tears were streaming down Roberto's face. 'I didn't tell anyone about it. I thought he had been having a nightmare.'

He took out a handkerchief and wiped his eyes. 'Perhaps, if I had alerted his father about that too, then this disease might have been discovered and he would have been helped. Maybe his parents' death was the trigger to wake the demon…'

There was a long pause as Roberto found control. He suddenly stood.

'I am sorry, Carlo, I hope you will forgive me.'

Carlo stood too, gently took his hand and held it for a moment, then let it go.

'Roberto, you are guilty only of loving,'

Roberto stood straight. 'Thank you, old friend.' He walked away slowly.

Carlo watched until he turned a corner and was out of sight. He sat down again. Slowly the anger left him and a deep sadness returned.

* * *

At the end of the first week, Angel drove Sara to the restaurant where Carlo had first taken her and they had shared a bottle of Rioja. Sara laughed for the first time since it happened, at Angel's stories of a younger Carlo and Marcello and their coaching attempts to get her into the school lacrosse team.

Then five days later, Carlo took Sara and Angelique to Elba.

Angel would stay for a while, and then Carlo, and Caria and Pietro, the couple who ran the five-hundred-acre estate for him, would give her the care she needed. There were other estate workers there too but with many from the same long-employed families, they were all trusted and loyal to the great man. Angel would be at the end of a phone or Skype and would come if needed. She had already decided to bring the family to Elba in the next school holiday, ten weeks away. It would be good for Sara that there was a finite time to see Angel again even if all went well with her recovery.

Carlo was well known on Elba. His privacy was respected and most islanders were proud that this modern Master had made his home there. There was a small gallery he had backed in Portofarraio and he often previewed new work there. He had huge celebrity but few knew when he came and went unless he allowed it to be made public. He flew into Elba Airport then travelled by helicopter to his estate.

Carlo was a careful man and knew that Sara would be on a media hit list, so he had arranged a new passport in her maiden name of Roberts. She didn't know about it yet. That could wait until she was ready to move on. Carlo had said she could stay on the island as long as she wanted. There was a small house so she would have privacy, and near it a large studio overlooking the sea that was hers to use if she wanted to paint. His own studio was attached to the main house.

It was a beautiful day when they left Siena, driven to the private airfield where Carlo kept his small plane. Sara was slowly recovering. Angel knew this was a fragile thing but she was strong and if anyone could get through it, she would.

EPILOGUE

A year later

Sara, Saddiq, and Marjia often walked to the beach before breakfast.

The children were eight-year-old twins from Aleppo whose entire family had been killed when a bomb dropped by a Russian plane hit their house. Angel had found them in the street hospital she was working in. They had both been playing out of the house and Saddiq had bad wounds to his legs and Marjia a head injury that was life threatening. Angel and the team had managed to get them stable and they made a slow recovery. She arranged for them to be treated in Italy and when they were well enough she had brought them to Elba. Carlo had paid for everything. Once they were well he would begin the long and difficult journey to adopt them.

Sara had been on Elba for three months when they arrived by boat and in that time had grown stronger, felt more positive, and had even started to paint again. Her creative soul was stretching and preparing for a gentle release. It was not every day, and sometimes weeks would go by before she picked up a brush. But slowly she was finding her balance. Each day she walked through orchards, woods, and olive trees. She sat for hours on the beach, the sun and the sea filling her with warmth and joy at their power and beauty. It built her strength and let her concentrate on the simple, innocent, and good things. It helped her too when the dark washed over her. As her spirit had broken when her boys had died so the nature that surrounded her and the subtle care from Carlo and Angel's positive though sometimes strange guidance, slowly began to give shape to it again. Ben and Ceri were always with her and she talked to them and felt their love and knew that as long as they were there, she was safe. She also began to realize that there would be a time for them to let her run and, though they would always be in reach, they would have to distance themselves for her to grow. It was a frightening thought.

Caria and Pietro, the husband and wife who ran the estate, had welcomed her as part of their family too. They had a son and daughter who both worked for Carlo and were in their early twenties. They gave Sara space but were always there willing to spend time with her. Carlo had stayed for the first six weeks, delaying a trip to the US, saying that if they wanted him, they would have to wait for him to finish a painting for a renovated church in Genoa. But it was really to give Sara time. She knew this and loved him for it. His wisdom and patience and sense of fun were good for Sara. He told her she was now his family, his daughter, and wherever she went when she left Elba, it would always be her home.

It took the twins a while to trust Sara but when they did she began to teach them English. They were very bright and had learned a little of the language at school so they soaked it up. She played with them too and gave them swimming lessons. Marjia was a natural but it took Saddiq more time as he was less ready for things than his sister and scared that he would drown. But slowly they managed to get him up to his chest in the water and he learned to float. She sketched them as they played and then painted them, giving them the finished canvas to hang in their room in the main house. Carlo had been away, but when he returned and saw the painting of the twins, he knew that Sara was on the mend. She had found the joy of childhood in them both and caught a look between them that showed not only a shadow of their sadness but their depth of spirit, love, and determination.

Then one day Marjia asked Sara if she could tell her about their family. The three of them talked for hours, sitting by a little rock pool on the beach. The twins cried and said they missed them. Sara said that was OK because they were always with them. She told the twins about Ben and Ceri. Once they had started they talked every day about the happy times as well the sad and difficult parts of their other lives. She knew that sharing this personal pain was a big step and the responsibility for all three was something that would give them all a will to try and only look forward. Together they were stronger.

There was no plan for any of them, apart from finding new pathways and challenges and to use what they had survived as a foundation to build their new lives.

THE END